THE LAST GUNFIGHTER
AMBUSH
VALLEY

THE LAST GUNFIGHTER
AMBUSH
VALLEY

William W. Johnstone
with J. A. Johnstone

PINNACLE BOOKS
Kensington Publishing Corp.
www.kensingtonbooks.com

PINNACLE BOOKS are published by

Kensington Publishing Corp.
850 Third Avenue
New York, NY 10022

PUBLISHER'S NOTE
Following the death of William W. Johnstone, the Johnstone family is working with a carefully selected writer to organize and complete Mr. Johnstone's outlines and many unfinished manuscripts to create additional novels in all of his series like The Last Gunfighter, Mountain Man, and Eagles, among others. This novel was inspired by Mr. Johnstone's superb storytelling.

All Kensington titles, imprints, and distributed lines are available at special quantity discounts for bulk purchases for sales promotions, premiums, fund-raising, educational, or institutional use. Special book excerpts or customized printings can also be created to fit specific needs. For details, write or phone the office of the Kensington special sales manager: Kensington Publishing Corp., 850 Third Avenue, New York, NY 10022, attn: Special Sales Department; phone 1-800-221-2647.

ISBN-13: 978-0-7860-1836-9
ISBN-10: 0-7860-1836-4

First printing: March 2008

10 9 8 7 6 5 4 3 2 1

Printed in the United States of America

Chapter 1

Peace and quiet . . . There was nothing like it.

Frank Morgan thought about that as a bullet chewed splinters from the doorjamb next to his head. Several of the tiny slivers of wood stung his face as he ducked into Leo Benjamin's general store.

"Marshal, what is it?" Leo cried from behind the counter. The emporium's customers, a couple of men and several women, all crouched in the aisles and looked around wildly, not quite sure what to do. All hell was breaking loose in the main street of Buckskin, Nevada, the silver-mining town where Frank Morgan had been the marshal for about six months.

Peace had reigned for most of that time, ever since the labor unrest that had shut down the mines for a while and the raid by a gang of notorious outlaws. That sure wasn't the case today. Frank had been ambling along the boardwalk in front of the store when several men came boiling out of the office of the Lucky Lizard Mining Company down the street. They had bandannas pulled up over their faces to serve as crude masks. That by itself would have been enough to alert Frank to the fact that something was wrong, but then the varmints had started shooting, too.

Their bullets sprayed around the street as the bandits fired at anything that moved, including Frank. He had dived into Leo's store to avoid the hail of lead.

Frank knew that the merchant kept a loaded Winchester under the counter. He turned and said, "Leo! Toss me your rifle! Everybody stay down!"

Leo complied with the order. He reached under the counter, brought out the Winchester, and pitched it with both hands toward Frank. The marshal grabbed it and wheeled back to the doorway. He went through the door in a low dive that landed him prone on the boardwalk. A bullet sizzled above his head and shattered one of the store's front windows. Frank worked the rifle's loading lever as he brought the weapon to his shoulder. He drew a bead on one of the riders charging down the street and fired.

The .44-40 slug punched into the outlaw's chest and swept him backward out of the saddle. One of his feet caught in the stirrup, though, so he was dragged along the street by the still-galloping horse.

Even before the man he'd just ventilated hit the ground, Frank had worked the Winchester's lever again and shifted his aim. He fired a second shot. This time the bullet struck one of the bandits in the right shoulder and twisted him halfway around in the saddle, but he managed to stay on his horse.

There were four outlaws in all, Frank saw now. The other two had taken notice of him and directed their fire where he lay on the boardwalk. He rolled swiftly to his right as bullets smacked into the planks where he had been a heartbeat earlier. Pushing off with his feet, he lunged off the boardwalk and landed behind one of the water troughs that were spaced at intervals along the street. He thrust the Winchester's barrel over the top of the trough as the outlaws thundered past. He began firing as fast as he could work the rifle's lever, coming up on his knees as he did so.

The bandits had their backs to Frank now, but that didn't particularly bother him. They had started the ball, and the way they were still slinging lead around, they were a danger to the town. *His* town. He had been here long enough now to put down some roots, something that the man known throughout the West as The Drifter had thought would never happen again.

Anybody who threatened the people of Buckskin would damn well get what was coming to them, at least as long as Frank Morgan was the marshal.

The deadly volley from Frank's Winchester tore through the fleeing outlaws. They plunged from their saddles and thudded to the dirt of the street. The man he had wounded in the shoulder was in the lead. He made it all the way to the edge of town before loss of blood made him pass out. He toppled off his horse, too.

All four of the hombres were down now. Frank leaped to his feet and ran to each of them in turn, keeping the Winchester ready to fire again if he needed to.

There was no need. Three of the men were dead and the fourth, the one with the bullet-shattered shoulder, was out cold.

Frank's deputy, the lean, buckskin-clad former prospector called Catamount Jack, came running along the street with his big old cap-and-ball pistol clutched in a gnarled hand. "Frank!" he called. "You all right?"

Frank waved Catamount Jack over to him. "I'm fine. Keep an eye on this one," he ordered with a nod toward the wounded outlaw. "The others are done for, but he's still alive."

"Does somebody need to fetch Doc Garland?" Jack's voice hardened as he added, "Or do we just let the son of a bitch bleed to death and save the trouble of a hangin'?"

"We're not letting anybody bleed to death." A crowd was starting to gather now that the shooting was over. Frank said to one of the men, "Run get Dr. Garland to tend to that fella." After the townie had hurried off toward the medico's office, Frank turned to one of the other men and told him, "Might as well let Claude Langley know his services'll be needed for the other three."

Catamount Jack snorted. "Never seen an undertaker yet who didn't come a-runnin' any time there was a shootin'."

Frank made no reply to that. He was worried about what might have happened inside the Lucky Lizard office. Those masked varmints had run out of there like they'd been up to no good. Thomas "Tip" Woodford, the owner of the mine and the mayor of Buckskin, might have been in the office when the outlaws came storming in. So, too, Diana Woodford, Tip's beautiful blond daughter, might have been there.

Diana had taken a romantic interest in Frank when he first came to the settlement, despite the fact that he considered her to be about twenty years too young for him. He had been successful in deflecting her attention to Garrett Claiborne, the mining engineer who worked as the superintendent of the Crown Royal Mine, but Frank still considered Diana a good friend and was concerned about her and her father as he hurried toward the office.

Tip emerged from the building before Frank got there. The beefy, florid-faced former prospector who had hit it rich with the Lucky Lizard had a hand pressed to his head. Blood seeped between his fingers. He was a little unsteady, and Diana was right beside him with an arm around him, helping to support him. Frank felt a surge of relief when he saw that Diana seemed to be unharmed.

"What happened, Tip?" he asked as he came up to Woodfood and Diana.

Tip didn't answer the question. Instead, he asked, "Did you get 'em? Did you get the thievin' bastards, Frank?"

"I got 'em," Frank confirmed with a nod. "Are you shot?"

Tip shook his bleeding head and winced because the movement caused obvious pain. "Naw, one of 'em walloped me with his gun when I didn't move fast enough to suit him."

"I thought they were going to kill him," Diana said in a voice that was drawn tight by strain and worry. "Are they all dead, Marshal?" She sounded like she hoped they were. Diana had a bit of a bloodthirsty streak in her that came out every so often, Frank thought.

"Three are, and the other one's hit bad," he replied. "Let me have a look at your head, Tip."

Woodford moved his bloody hand away from his head. Frank saw the gash that had been opened up in Tip's graying, rust-colored hair. The injury was messy but not too serious, Frank judged. Head wounds always bled a lot.

"We'd better go find Dr. Garland," Frank said. "You're liable to need a few stitches."

"I'm all right," Tip insisted.

"No, you're not," Diana said in a tone that brooked no argument. "Come on, Pa."

Frank fell in step beside them as they started down the street. "What did those polecats want?" he asked.

"The payroll for the Lucky Lizard came in on this

mornin's stage," Tip explained. "They knew about it somehow and figured to grab it before I could take it out to the mine and pay off the boys."

"Did they get it?"

"Yeah. Didn't have no choice but to hand it over. They might'a hurt Diana if I hadn't."

She said, "I told you, Pa, I wasn't scared."

"Well, I was scared enough for both of us, I reckon."

Frank doubted that. Tip Woodford was a salty old-timer. If Diana hadn't been there when the outlaws burst in, likely he would have told them to go to hell. But no amount of money was worth his daughter's safety to Tip.

Frank understood that feeling. He had a son of his own, although he didn't see Conrad very often, and in his heart of hearts he was convinced that he had a daughter, too, although Mercy Moncure, his first love back in Weatherford, Texas, had never confirmed—or denied, for that matter—that her daughter Victoria was his.

As they walked along the street, Frank's eyes found the horses that the outlaws had been riding. All four animals had come to a stop at the edge of town and were milling around there now, unsure of what they were supposed to do. Frank saw a canvas bag with its handle looped around the saddle horn on one of the horses. That would be Tip's payroll, he thought.

Somebody at the bank in Virginia City could have told the outlaws that the money was arriving in Buckskin this morning. Or someone connected with the stage line could be guilty of that, Frank supposed. There had to someone else involved somewhere, he knew, because the bandits had known the payroll was in Tip's office.

He would get to the bottom of that later, he told himself. Right now he just wanted to see that Tip got the necessary medical attention.

As Frank, Tip, and Diana came up, Dr. William Garland straightened from where he had been kneeling beside the wounded outlaw. Garland was a young, slightly built man with brown hair who usually had an intense expression on his slender face. Today was no different. He asked, "What happened to you, Mayor?"

"One of those varmints pistol-whipped me," Tip said. He moved his bloodstained hand away from the wound. "How bad is it, Doc?"

Garland studied the gash for a moment, then said, "I need to stitch it up, but you should be fine. You probably have a slight concussion, too, so you'll have to take it easy for a few days. Miss Woodford, why don't you help your father over to my office, and I'll be there in a few minutes."

Diana nodded. "All right, Doctor."

"I can't take it easy," Tip complained as Diana steered him toward the doctor's office. "I got a mine to run!"

"I'm perfectly capable of taking care of things for a few days," she told him. "In fact, if I'd been in charge of things, I would have had an armed guard waiting when that payroll was delivered, and it would have been guarded until all the men had received their wages."

Tip grumbled, but Frank hoped he would pay attention to what Diana was saying. Frank had been planning to suggest the same thing himself.

He nodded toward the wounded outlaw, who was still unconscious, and asked the doctor, "What about him?"

"I think he'll live," Garland said, "but he'll never have full use of his right arm again."

"Since that looks to be his gun arm, I reckon that's probably a good thing."

"I'll get some men to carry him down to my office. I can't do anything with him here in the street."

Frank nodded. "All right, Doc. And thanks. Take good care of the mayor."

"Of course."

Claude Langley, the goateed, genteel little Southerner who served as Buckskin's undertaker, had shown up with his wagon. A couple of Langley's helpers were loading the corpses of the other outlaws into the back of the vehicle. Satisfied that that was under control, Frank told Catamount Jack to follow him and headed toward the horses that the owlhoots had been riding.

The animals had been spooked by all the gunfire and the smell of blood, so they shied away as Frank and Jack approached. Despite all the long years of drifting he had done, Frank hadn't forgotten his days as a cowboy back in Texas. He spoke to the horses in a quiet, soothing tone, and within a few minutes they settled down enough so that he and Jack could take hold of their reins. Each lawman led two of the horses to Amos Hillman's livery stable.

The lanky, overall-clad liveryman had a black patch over his left eye. He asked, "What do you want me to do with these nags, Marshal?"

Frank took the canvas bag containing the Lucky Lizard payroll off the saddle where it was hung. He opened it for a second to make sure the money was there. It was. He told Hillman, "Just take care of them for now, Amos. I imagine you'll wind up selling them to take care of the burial expenses for three of their owners, as well as to pay your feed bill. The man who owned the fourth one won't be needing him anymore, either."

Hillman nodded. "All right. Want me to have one o' the hostlers bring the saddlebags over to your office later?"

"That would be fine. I'll go through their gear, see if I can find anything to tell me who they were." If Frank could locate any relatives, he would write to them to tell them what happened. That wasn't too likely, though. Men who were on the dodge often severed all ties with their pasts.

He carried the payroll himself as he and Jack returned to the office. There was a small safe in the marshal's office where the money could be locked up until Tip needed it. And when it was delivered to the Lucky Lizard, Frank intended to go along, just to make sure no one else made a try for the payroll. He was only the town marshal, but he considered himself responsible for everything that went on in the vicinity of Buckskin since there were no sheriff's deputies down here and the sheriff himself rarely made it to these parts.

Frank Morgan's career as a law enforcement officer had been pretty spotty. He had pinned on a badge a time or two before coming to Buckskin, and on several occasions he had pitched in to help a friend of his, Texas Ranger Tyler Beaumont. But that had been on an unofficial basis. A personal quest for vengeance had brought Frank to Buckskin. He'd found that he liked the settlement and the people who lived here, and when Tip Woodford and some of the other leading citizens had asked him to stay and take on the job of marshal, Frank had surprised himself by accepting.

He would have been willing to bet that plenty of other people would have been surprised if they'd heard about it, too. In the eyes of most star-packers west of the Mississippi, Frank Morgan was more of a lawbreaker than a law enforcer.

All because of the reputation he had as a fast gun, a reputation he had never sought nor celebrated.

Once there had been quite a few men like Frank Morgan in the West. Wild Bill Hickok, Ben Thompson, Matt Bodine, John Wesley Hardin, Falcon McAllister, and the man who some said was the fastest there ever was or ever would be, Smoke Jensen. Call them shootists, pistoleers, gunfighters . . . no matter the name by which they were known, they were a dying breed now in the waning days of the nineteenth century. Frank Morgan sometimes felt that he was indeed the last of them—but then somebody else would come along, determined to kill him and make a name for himself as a gunfighter. A part of Frank believed that for him it would never end until he was dead, no matter where he rode or how much he sought peace. He could almost believe he had found it here in Buckskin, but then some ruckus like the one today would break out and the killing would start again. . . .

Frank Morgan was a solidly built, broad-shouldered man with some streaks of gray in his thick dark hair. That gray had been well-earned in the hard, dangerous life he'd led. He wore jeans, comfortable boots, and a faded blue work shirt. A wide-brimmed, steeple-crowned Stetson of gray felt rode squarely on his head. A gunbelt was buckled around his lean hips, and a well-cared-for Colt revolver rode in the attached holster. The gun had walnut grips, but Frank had never carved any notches in them to represent the men he'd killed. For one thing, he wasn't the sort of hombre to do a thing like that, and for another, there wouldn't have been any grips left on the gun by now. They would have been whittled away to nothing.

A few hours after the shootout with the men who had stolen the Lucky Lizard payroll, Frank walked down to the neat little house that was both the residence and the office of Dr. William Garland. The physician answered the knock on the door. Frank asked, "How's that outlaw doing?"

"He's awake now," Garland answered as he moved back and gestured for Frank to come in. "I was about to send for you, Marshal. I figured you'd want to question him."

Frank stepped into the front room and removed his hat as he did so. "Yeah, there are a few things I'd like to know," he said.

He followed Garland to a small room where the wounded bandit was half propped up in a narrow bed. The man's right arm was in a sling, and heavy bandages were wrapped around his shoulder. His beard-stubbled face was pale and drawn. His left wrist was tied securely to the bedpost with a short length of rope.

"Your deputy did that," Garland said with a gesture toward the rope.

"Yeah, I told him to stop by and do that while this fella was still unconscious," Frank said. "I didn't want him taking off for the tall and uncut once he came to."

"I'm not sure a restraint is necessary. He's really too weak from loss of blood to go anywhere or cause any trouble."

"Better not to take a chance. A fella can usually find a little extra strength if it means avoiding a hangrope."

The outlaw's eyes widened. "A hangrope!" he repeated in a hoarse voice. "I ain't done nothin' to deserve hangin'! I never killed nobody in my life!"

"Yeah, well, that's no fault of your own, the way you were throwing lead around in the street this morning with those other three."

"What happened to them? Nobody'll tell me anything, damn it!"

That was another order Frank had given. This man

was to be kept in the dark about what had happened to his companions.

Frank put a tone of bitter disappointment in his voice as he answered, "They're probably way up in the high lonesome by now, along with that payroll money."

"They got away? And with the money?"

"That's right. They couldn't abandon you quick enough, hombre."

The man started to curse in a low, furious voice. Frank let him go on for a few seconds, then cut in with a harsh laugh. "You didn't expect them to stay behind and get caught just because you got shot, did you? They had the money. That was all they cared about."

"The dirty sons. We said we'd stick together. Damn their hides!"

"Tell me who they were," Frank suggested. As expected, he hadn't found anything in the saddlebags that had belonged to the dead men to tell him their identities. "Maybe that would help me track them down."

"I dunno. . . ."

"I imagine they'll be living high, wide, and handsome in San Francisco within a week or two, as much loot as they carried off."

The outlaw cussed again, then said, "All right. They're Johnny Blanco, Matt Higgins, and Ed Wrinkle. Those are the names I know 'em by, anyway."

"And what about you?"

The man's mouth twisted. "I'm Cullen Bradley."

"Where're you from, Bradley?"

"Poplar Bluff, Missouri. That's where I grew up, anyway. I been on the drift for the past few years. That's where I met Johnny and Matt and Ed. On the trails where the night owls hoot, if you know what I mean."

Frank nodded. "I know, boy. I've ridden a few of those trails myself."

Bradley swallowed hard and asked, "You . . . you ain't really gonna hang me, are you, Marshal?"

"Give me one good reason why I shouldn't."

"It wouldn't be right! Like I told you, I've never killed nobody. I've stole before in my life, sure, but I draw the line at killin'. You might not've noticed, but every shot I fired this mornin' went high on purpose."

Frank didn't believe him for a second. He had seen Bradley firing, and the outlaw wasn't aiming deliberately high. If Bradley was right about never killing anybody, it was because he was a poor shot.

But in the absence of proof, Frank didn't intend to try to send the outlaw to the gallows. Bradley didn't have to know that just yet, though.

Frank shook his head. "I don't think a judge and jury will believe that, Bradley. And even if they do, I'm not sure they'll care. The mayor was pistol-whipped—"

"I didn't do that, neither!" Bradley interrupted, his voice rising in panic. "That was Johnny Blanco done it! I never hurt nobody!"

"Folks might be more inclined to believe you if you were willing to help us out a mite."

"What do you want me to do?" The young outlaw looked and sounded desperate. "I'll do anything!"

"Tell me how the four of you knew that payroll money was going to be in the Lucky Lizard office this morning."

Bradley licked his lips and hesitated, but only for a second. Then he nodded in eagerness and said, "It was a fella who works at the bank in Virginia City who told us. He used to ride with Johnny before he went straight. His name's Russell."

"That his first name or last name?" Frank asked.

Bradley shook his head. "Hell if I know. I never heard Johnny call him anything except Russell."

Frank thought about it, then nodded. "All right," he said. "I'll send word to the authorities in Virginia City and let them figure it out. I reckon they can find this fella Russell and see that he gets what's coming to him for helping you."

"What about me? Are you . . ." Bradley swallowed hard. "Are you still gonna hang me?"

"You'll stand trial for robbery, assault, and attempted murder," Frank said. "What the court does with you isn't up to me."

"You . . . you're not gonna just string me up?"

Frank smiled coldly at the young outlaw. "You're lucky Tip Woodford wasn't hurt any worse than he was, and that his daughter wasn't hurt at all. If they had been . . . well, I wouldn't have wanted to be you, Bradley."

The outlaw gulped and closed his eyes in relief. With a snort of disgust, Frank turned and left the room.

"Take care of him, Doc. I'll deputize a couple of men to stand guard over him until he can be moved over to the jail. How long do you reckon that'll be?"

Garland thought about it and said, "Give me a day or two, Marshal, just to make sure he's out of the woods. Then you can take him over and put him behind bars where he deserves to be." The doctor paused. "*Will* he be sentenced to hang?"

Keeping his voice low enough so that Bradley wouldn't overhear, Frank said, "Not likely. He'll be sent to prison, though, that's for sure."

Garland sighed. "It's been peaceful here for a while," he said. "I hope today's events don't signal a return to the sort of violence that used to plague this town."

"You and me both, Doc," Frank said. "You and me both."

But unknown to Frank Morgan, events were taking place far to the south that would have an effect on his desire for peace and quiet. The seeds of brutal violence and deadly peril were already being sown.

Just not in Buckskin, Nevada.

Chapter 2

Despite the heat, the eight men who rode into Tucson wore long dusters over their range clothes. Their hats were pulled down low to shield their faces from the sun—and to make it harder for anyone to get a good look at their features. They reined to a halt in front of the First Territorial Bank, which was a large, redbrick building, and as they dismounted, the long coats swung back a little to reveal guns in low-slung holsters. If anyone had been paying any attention, these eight strangers surely would have aroused some suspicion.

But it was the middle of the afternoon and mighty hot, as it always was in Tucson, and the few folks who were out and about instead of snoozing in the shade somewhere just wanted to finish whatever errands had brought them out and get back to somewhere cooler.

So nobody on the street really noticed the eight strangers. But Randall Berry did as they strode into the bank. He saw the dusters, the tugged-down hats, the way the men pulled bandannas up over the lower half of their faces as they entered the building so that only their eyes were visible. Randall Berry was a teller in the

First Territorial Bank, and as he saw the men he said, "Oh, hell."

Those were his last words, because a second later the man who was in the forefront of the sinister group swept his hand under his duster, came up with a gun, and fired. The bullet struck Randall Berry just above the right eye, smashed his skull, bored through his brain, and exploded out the back of the unfortunate teller's head in a grisly spray of blood, bone shards, and gray matter. The impact flung Berry backward in his teller's cage. He flew off the stool where he had been sitting and crashed to the floor on his back.

The gunshot, and Randall Berry's death, got the attention of everybody else in the bank.

And that was just the way Cicero McCoy wanted it.

The gun in McCoy's hand was rock-steady as he bellowed, "Nobody move! This is a holdup!" He had learned over the course of a career in lawlessness that had lasted for several years that sudden, unexpected death made people freeze at first, so that instinct didn't make them try to fight back. Then fear that they would be the next victim prompted them to cooperate.

True, the sound of a gunshot usually alerted the local law that something bad was happening, but McCoy and his men knew how to clean out a bank in no time flat. They were usually on their horses, galloping out of town, while the star-packers were still trying to figure out where the shot had come from.

Today would be no different. Cicero McCoy was sure of that.

Half-a-dozen people were in the bank, not counting the dead teller—three customers, two more tellers, and the bank manager. They all stared at the outlaws in shock and horror. The duster-clad robbers spread out through the big room. One man covered the manager while another leveled his gun at the pair of terrified tellers. A third man-herded the customers together and warned them not to try anything or they would die. That left four men with canvas sacks to clean out the tellers' cages and the vault, which the manager was forced to open at gunpoint. While that swift looting was going on, the leader of the gang, the rawboned, lantern-jawed Cicero McCoy, strut-ted back and forth keeping an eye on the whole thing, as well as glancing at the street from time to time to make sure it was still clear. With the metronomic certainty of a clock, the seconds ticked away inside McCoy's head. He knew that if they were in and out of the bank in no more than two miutes, they stood a good chance of getting away clean.

Unfortunately for McCoy and his gang, today the sheriff happened to be only a couple of doors away down the street, rather than in his office, which was separated from the bank by several blocks. At the sound of the shot, the law officer jerked his revolver from its holster and ran out of the dress shop where his wife had dragged him so that he could look at the gown she had picked out for a dinner being given by the county supervisors. The sheriff didn't know what was going on, but he figured he would rather face outlaw lead than go through more of the torture he'd been enduring.

He skidded out of the shop onto the boardwalk. A man who was standing nearby pointed and yelled, "Down there, Sheriff! I think that shot came from the bank!"

The lawman had already wondered about that. Tucson had never been as wild and woolly as some of the other settlements in Arizona like Tombstone, and it had settled down even more in recent years as the final decade of the nineteenth century rolled by.

But there were still outlaws in the West, and train robberies and bank holdups still took place. Here and there stagecoach lines still operated, and the stages got held up, too.

So the sheriff figured outlaws had hit the bank, and as he approached the big brick building on the run, he saw that he was right. Men wearing dusters, pulled-down hats, and bandanna masks ran out of the bank and headed for horses tied at the hitch rack in front of the building.

The sheriff, a stocky man with a hawk nose and a bushy mustache, bellowed, "Hold it right there, you bastards!"

Smoke and flame spurted from the muzzles of the outlaws' guns as they opened fire on him. The sheriff felt the jolt as a bullet burned along his left forearm. He yelped in pain and stumbled. More slugs whistled around him. He triggered a shot and threw himself off the boardwalk, landing behind a water trough. He didn't have any idea if his bullet had hit one of the bandits, and at the moment he didn't care. He made himself as small a target as he could as he huddled behind the trough. Right now he wished he was back looking at ball gowns with his wife, no matter how boring that had been.

Cicero McCoy bit back a curse as he swung up onto his horse. That lone badge-toter didn't worry him, but the fact that somebody had taken a shot at them did. Sometimes, if anybody put up a fight, that emboldened the rest of the townsfolk to show some backbone, too. Well-armed citizens were more of a danger to lawbreakers than the authorities were. If anybody ever figured out how to take all the guns away from the people, so that they could no longer defend themselves, then hell would break loose. McCoy and his kind would run rampant, with no one left to stop them.

Right now, McCoy was more concerned with getting himself and his men out of Tucson, along with the money they had taken from the bank. He peppered the trough where the sheriff had taken cover with lead to keep the lawman pinned down. "Let's go, let's go!" he shouted to his men as they leaped onto their horses.

When they were all mounted, McCoy jerked on the reins and wheeled his horse around. The plan was for them to head southwest out of Tucson. There wasn't much but rugged country in that direction between the settlement and the border. Mountains and desert, ravines and towering spires of rock. Ugly country where a man on the run could disappear. That was exactly what Cicero McCoy intended to do.

His spurs raked savagely against his horse's flanks as he put the animal into a run. The other members of the gang trailed behind him. Shots began to blast here and there as townies tried to stop them. When a man ran out in front of them brandishing a shotgun, McCoy shot him down without hesitation, sending a bullet into his chest and catching him in the throat with a second slug. Crimson fountained in the air as the dying man turned in a circle and then collapsed.

A little boy yelled, "Pa!" and ran toward the man, who had fallen in front of McCoy's hard-charging horse. McCoy never slowed. If the brat was going to run in the street like that, then he deserved whatever happened to him.

A woman screamed and ran after the boy. She grabbed him, jerked him back, flung him out of the way of the thundering hooves. But the shoulder of McCoy's mount struck her and spun her off her feet, and a second later the steel-shod hooves of the horses belonging to the rest of the gang shattered her skull and pounded her body into a bloody heap that barely looked human. The kid stood there shrieking in horror as the riders flashed past him.

Being orphaned like that would be good for the little bastard in the long run, McCoy thought. It would toughen him up. Kids these days had it too damned easy.

Killing didn't bother McCoy, had never fazed him. People usually got what they deserved in life, he figured, and if they got in his way, that was their own lookout and not his problem. Up ahead, an old greaser in a sombrero tottered through the open double doors of a livery stable at the edge of town. He carried a pitchfork. He wasn't really a threat, but McCoy shot him in the belly anyway. The old Mexican groaned, doubled over, and fell as the bank robbers thundered past the stable. Blood darkened the sand around his body.

The robbers had left behind two dead men inside the bank. The manager had gotten brave at the last minute and made a grab for a gun in his desk. A couple of McCoy's men had filled him with lead. Five people had died in Tucson as a result of the robbery, including the woman. That would mean a posse.

But there was nothing they could do about it now. McCoy and his men had a good lead. They would be a mile or more out of Tucson before the outraged citizens could get organized enough to come after them.

One of McCoy's men was a half-Mex, half-Apache named Cortez. He had grown up in the rough country where they were headed now and knew every rock, every ravine, and more importantly, every water hole. When McCoy had decided to hit the First Territorial Bank in Tucson, he had conceived an audacious getaway plan.

The gang was headed for Ambush Valley.

Originally the place had had another name, but nobody had used it for a long time. Ten years earlier, while Geronimo and his Apaches had still been raising hell and striking terror into the heart of every white settler in the territory, a company of United States cavalry had ridden into the rugged, arid valley in pursuit of a small band of raiders. The troopers and the officers who led them had no idea that that was exactly what Geronimo wanted them to do. The scout who'd accompanied the patrol had been picked off earlier, and since the soldiers were freshly arrived in Arizona, they had no idea what sort of nightmare they were getting into.

They found out soon enough. The valley was a torturous, twisting maze of rocks and cactus and no water. Unsure how to get back out, the troopers had wandered around for most of a day in the baking heat until they were weak from thirst and dazzled by the blinding sun.

Then the much smaller force of Apaches, who knew every inch of the valley and had been following the cavalrymen all day, fell on them and wiped them out almost to the last man.

They had saved a couple of troopers who weren't badly wounded so they'd have somebody to torture to death. A little light entertainment around the campfire that night.

Amazingly, one of the victims of the Apaches' cruelty lived long enough to be found the next day by another patrol accompanied by Al Sieber, General Crook's chief of scouts, who knew Arizona better than any white man alive and better even than some Apaches. The trooper was horribly mutilated, but before he died he was able to gasp out the story of what had happened.

Ever since then, the hellish wasteland where the attack had taken place had been known as Ambush Valley.

The soldiers probably would have all died of thirst before they ever found their way out of the trap, but there *was* water in Ambush Valley. You just had to know where to find it. Cortez knew, or at least claimed he did, and McCoy tended to believe it because Cortez's life would be on the line, too, just like the rest of the gang's. Ambush Valley was a day and a half's ride from Tucson. All they had to do was stay ahead of the posse until they got there, then Cortez would lead them through the valley. The pursuers wouldn't risk their lives by following. That was what McCoy was counting on, anyway.

Once the outlaws came out at the other end of the valley, they wouldn't be far from the border. They would cross into Mexico, safe from American law, and live a life of ease . . . at least until the loot ran low and they had to start planning another job.

With Cortez to guide them, McCoy was confident they could stay ahead of the posse and make it through Ambush Valley. And if the pursuers were foolish enough to follow them into the valley, McCoy and his men would ambush them and wipe them out just as surely as the Apaches had with the cavalry.

It was a foolproof plan, as long as the outlaws didn't allow the posse to catch up to them before they reached Ambush Valley.

There wasn't a whole lot Conrad Browning liked about the West. It was still rough and uncivilized, and he much preferred Boston. But he had to admit that some things out here weren't too bad, like the idea of a siesta. Stretching out for a while in the middle of the day, on a comfortable bed inside a hotel room, with thick adobe walls to keep most of the heat out . . . that wasn't bad at all.

Especially when you had your beautiful naked wife right beside you.

Rebel was lying on her stomach, dozing. Conrad propped himself on an elbow and ran his fingertips along her spine, following it down to the curve of her hips. His touch made her stir. She turned her face toward him and smiled, although her eyes remained closed. "So soon, Conrad?" she murmured in a sleepy voice.

They had been married for only a few months, so the wanting for each other was still strong in both of them. Conrad moved closer to her, took her in his arms. She turned and found his mouth with hers. Their kisses were eager and even hotter than the sun beating down outside the hotel.

That was when the shooting started.

One shot, actually, but that was enough to make Conrad lift his head and frown. Rebel reached up, stroked her fingers through the blond hair on the back of his neck, and said, "Don't worry about it, Conrad. Probably just some cowboy letting off steam in one of the saloons down the street."

Rebel was a Westerner, so she knew about such things. Conrad had met her a year and a half earlier, over in New Mexico Territory, when trouble cropped up on a railroad spur line one of his companies was building. Conrad's father, Frank Morgan, had been mixed up in that affair, too, but everything had been straightened out in the end and Conrad had found himself falling in love with the wild and beautiful Rebel Callahan. They had been married a year later in Boston.

Conrad felt an occasional twinge of guilt that they

hadn't invited Frank to the wedding. If not for him, the two of them might not have ever gotten together. But Conrad had spent a lot of years hating Frank Morgan, and it took time to get over something like that. They saw each other from time to time and got along all right now, but they would never be close and Conrad was all right with that.

He turned his attention back to kissing Rebel, but a couple of minutes later what sounded like a small-scale war broke out on the streets of Tucson. Conrad couldn't ignore the gunfire, the shouts, the screaming. Rebel was concerned, too. She said, "What the hell's going on out there?" as Conrad got out of bed and yanked a pair of trousers on.

Rebel had managed to bring her plainspoken nature under control while she was living back in Boston with Conrad, but some of her natural bluntness had surfaced again since they'd come West to make a tour of some of the holdings of the vast Browning business empire. She stood up from the bed, wrapping the sheet around her nudity, as Conrad went to the window and thrust the curtain back.

He saw several riders in long coats galloping out of town, shooting as they fled. His breath hissed between his teeth in horror as he watched a woman trampled to death under the hooves of the horses. "It looks like some desperadoes making a getaway," he told Rebel.

And he realized a second later that the First Territorial Bank, which was owned by the Browning Banking Trust and was the reason he and Rebel had stopped in Tucson, was just down the street.

"My God," Conrad said as he reached for his shirt, "I wonder if they robbed the bank!"

"You're going down there?" Rebel asked.

"I have to find out what happened. If the bank was robbed, some of the employees might have been hurt!"

There was a time when Conrad wouldn't have cared so much about the lives of the people who worked for him. They did their jobs, they were paid their wages, and that was the end of it as far as he was concerned. He supposed that being around Frank had caused some of his father's attitudes to rub off on him, at least a little.

"Let me go with you," Rebel said as Conrad dressed hastily.

He shook his head. "No, I want you to stay here where it's safe. They might come back."

"Not if they already robbed the bank, they won't," she pointed out. "They'll want to put as much distance as they can between them and Tucson."

Conrad supposed she was right about that, but he still wanted her to stay there. "I'll be back in a few minutes," he said, and then he hurried out of the hotel room.

When he got downstairs, he found a crowd of people in the lobby, peering out the windows and talking excitedly. When he asked if anyone knew what had happened, a man dressed in the garish suit of a traveling salesman replied, "Somebody said the bank down the street got robbed!"

Conrad had been afraid of that. He pushed through the crowd until he reached the door. A man told him, "Better be careful, mister. They might start shootin' again!"

Conrad wasn't worried about that. He had been shot at before. Anyway, the outlaws were gone.

He yanked the door open and ran outside.

As he turned toward the bank, he spotted a man with a sheriff's badge pinned to his vest climbing to his feet next to a water trough. Obviously, the lawman had taken cover there when the shooting started.

"Sheriff, what happened?" Conrad demanded, not bothering to hide his anger. "I'm told the bank was robbed."

"Who the hell are you?"

"Conrad Browning. I *own* the bank."

The sheriff looked surprised. Conrad knew he didn't fit the popular image of a banker. He was too young, for one thing, and with his fair hair and slender build, he wasn't physically imposing by any means. But that didn't stop him from owning not only banks, but also mines, railroads, factories, and dozens of other business enterprises scattered from one end of the country to the other.

"Yeah, I saw some fellas who looked like bandits come runnin' out of the bank," the sheriff admitted. "I traded a few shots with them, but there were too many of 'em for me to slow them down."

"So you took shelter instead," Conrad snapped.

The sheriff's already florid face flushed even more. "It wouldn't have helped anything to get myself shot full of holes, Mr. Browning. Somebody's got to put together a posse and go after those sons o' bitches. First, I got to find out just what happened."

The lawman strode toward the bank, his gun still gripped tightly in his hand. Conrad fell in step beside him. "I was watching from the hotel as the robbers shot a couple of men and rode right over a poor woman who was in their way." Conrad's voice was grim as he spoke.

"Yeah," the sheriff replied, his tone equally bleak. "I saw that, too."

One of the tellers came stumbling out of the bank before Conrad and the sheriff reached it. Conrad recognized the man from the visit he and Rebel had made to the bank that morning. Conrad had had a long talk with the manager, Arthur Wick. He was satisfied with the report Wick had made. The bank was doing well.

At least it had been until those robbers struck. The teller saw the sheriff coming and said, "Thank God you're here, Sheriff! Those men shot Mr. Wick! I think he's dead. Poor Randall Berry, too!"

The teller was almost hysterical, but he got the information across. In a matter of moments, the lawman's clipped questions had established that there had been eight robbers, that they had shot the teller named Berry as soon as they came into the bank and then the manager, Wick, had been gunned down as the gang was about to leave. They had cleaned out the tellers' cages and the vault.

Conrad tried not to groan. He had seen the figures just that morning. The bank had had upwards of eighty thousand dollars on hand. The robbers had made a good haul.

A little boy stood near the bodies of the woman who had been trampled and one of the men who'd been shot in the street. He was screaming as if he would never stop. The sheriff grimaced and said, "Somebody go see about that kid." A couple of women from the crowd that was gathering in front of the bank went to try to comfort him.

Conrad thought the dead man and woman were probably the boy's parents. His mind flashed back to his own mother's death. Vivian Browning had been the finest woman who ever lived, at least as far as Conrad was concerned, and she had lost her life because of a gang of vicious outlaws, just like that poor woman who'd been trampled. Conrad had been considerably older than that little boy when his mother was killed, but that didn't matter. At such a terrible moment, every man was a little boy again.

Vivian Browning's death had been avenged. Frank

Morgan had seen to that, although it had taken several years to track down all the men responsible. When the last one of them was dead, Frank had written a letter to Conrad telling him about it, although Frank hadn't gone into any great detail. That was all right with Conrad. It was enough for him to know that the score had been settled.

Now, as he watched one of the women pick up the screaming little boy and press his face against her bosom so that his shrieks were muffled, he asked himself who would settle *this* score. Who would see to it that the men responsible for the deaths of that boy's parents paid the price for their evil?

"Shouldn't you get started organizing a posse, Sheriff?" Conrad asked.

The lawman nodded. "Yeah. I'll spread the word that I'm lookin' for volunteers—"

"You'll get more volunteers if you tell them about the reward."

The sheriff looked confused. "What reward?"

"The one that I'm posting for the return of the town's money and the apprehension of the men responsible for this atrocity," Conrad said between clenched teeth. "Ten thousand dollars. Dead or alive."

Chapter 3

When the shooting started, Abner Hoyt was in bed with a woman, too. Unlike Conrad Browning, the woman wasn't Hoyt's wife. She was a whore named Delia he had brought upstairs to her room in the Aces Full Saloon. He was finished with her, so when he heard the shots, he decided he might as well go see what was going on. Might be something interesting. He sure as hell wasn't interested in Delia now that he had done what he wanted with her.

He swung his legs out of the narrow, rumpled bed and then reached back to swat her ample rump. She giggled and said, "You got some time left, mister. Anything else you want to do?"

"Nope," Hoyt said as he stood up and started to get dressed. "We're done here."

Delia pouted like she was disappointed. There was a slim chance that the expression was at least somewhat genuine. Abner Hoyt was a big, muscular man, and while his face was a little too rugged to be called handsome, it did possess a certain strength that most women found attractive. His thick, sandy hair was long, hanging down almost to his shoulders, and his mustache drooped down on both sides of his wide mouth. He slid his long legs into denim trousers and pulled a buckskin shirt over his head. His feet went into high-topped black boots, and he settled a battered cavalry hat on his head. He'd been out of the army for a long time, but he still had the hat.

A gunbelt with a holstered Colt on the right side and a sheathed bowie knife on the left completed his outfit. He'd already put a coin on the scarred dresser before he ever climbed into the bed with Delia, so his business with her was done. He gave her a curt nod and left the room.

Downstairs, the saloon's customers were gathered at the front windows and the batwinged entrance, craning their necks to try to get a glimpse of what was going on outside. There had been a lot of shooting while Hoyt was getting dressed, but it seemed to have stopped now. He shouldered his way through the crowd, drawing a few angry glances. The men who were offended subsided when they saw Hoyt's powerful form, craggy face, and dark eyes that were hard as flint. Everybody got out of his way instead.

It had been a long time since Hoyt had worried about getting shot. He strode boldly onto the boardwalk. Down the street somewhere, somebody was screaming. Sounded like a kid. Men ran here and there, shouting curses and questions. Hoyt heard the words "bank" and "robbed," and his pulse quickened. He didn't get excited about many things in life, but a bank robbery was one of them.

Because it generally meant work for him.

He saw a group gathering and recognized the building behind them as the First Territorial Bank. That must be where the robbery had taken place. Hoyt headed in that direction, his long legs carrying him quickly toward the crowd.

He spotted the sheriff standing on the boardwalk in front of the bank. The man's name was Lamar Fortson. Hoyt had made the sheriff's acquaintance when he came to Tucson a week earlier. In his line of work, it usually helped to know the local lawman.

Fortson was talking to a man Hoyt had never seen before, a young gent who had the look of an Eastern dude about him. Hoyt walked up in time to hear the slender hombre declare that he was posting a ten-grand reward for the men who had robbed the bank.

And that reward was just the way Abner Hoyt liked it.

Dead or alive.

"Now, dadgummit, you don't need to go posting a reward, Mr. Browning," Sheriff Fortson said. "It's my duty to go after those varmints, and I'm sure there'll be plenty of civic-minded folks willing to join a posse. After all, a lot of people in town had money in your bank. Just let me get this bullet scratch on my arm patched up—"

"My men and I will ride now," Hoyt said.

The sheriff and the man called Browning both turned to look at him as he stood there with his thumbs hooked casually in his gunbelt. "Who are you?" Browning asked.

"He's a bounty hunter," Fortson said before Hoyt could answer. The sheriff's voice held a bitter, disapproving edge. "Him and some of his friends rode into Tucson not long ago. I was afraid when you said that about a reward that he'd hear about it." Fortson's mouth twisted. "Didn't figure he'd be right behind you. You got a nose for sniffin' out money, don't you, Hoyt?"

"With a beak like yours, I wouldn't be talking about anybody else's nose," Hoyt said. He stuck out a hand toward the dude. "Abner Hoyt."

"Conrad Browning," the man said, introducing himself, as he returned Hoyt's grip with more strength than Hoyt expected. Browning might not be quite as soft as he looked. He jerked his head toward the big brick building and added, "This is my bank that was just robbed."

"How much did they get?"

"Enough to make the reward I'm offering worthwhile. And they murdered several people, including two of my employees and a defenseless woman."

Probably the screaming kid's ma, Hoyt thought. Somebody had picked up the squalling brat and carried him off. Hoyt was thankful for that. The noise would have gotten on his nerves after a while.

"Anybody get a good look at them, or know who they were?"

Conrad Browning looked over at one of the tellers who had come out of the bank. The man shook his head and said, "They had masks on. I never saw their faces, and I don't think anybody else did, either."

"Could've been Cicero McCoy and his bunch," Fortson said. "I've heard rumors that they're down here in these parts. They held up a train west of Flagstaff a couple of weeks ago, so they've had plenty of time to get here."

Hoyt nodded. He had seen numerous reward dodgers on Cicero McCoy. The outlaw was wanted in Utah, California, New Mexico, and here in Arizona. If McCoy was the one who'd hit this bank, Hoyt stood to collect a considerable amount of blood money for him, in addition to the ten thousand dollars offered by Conrad Browning.

This trip to Tucson might turn out to be profitable after all.

"Do you think you can catch this man McCoy, Mr. Hoyt?" Browning asked.

"I've got six men who're hard as nails," Hoyt replied. "Several of them are good trackers. We'll run those outlaws to ground, whoever they are. Don't worry about that, Mr. Browning."

"Very well. You heard the reward offer. I'll stand behind it."

"Wait just a damned minute," Fortson said. "I haven't deputized you and your partners as members of the posse yet, Hoyt—"

"And we don't give a damn about that," Hoyt responded. "There's nothing in the law says we can't go after the robbers on our own." He gave Conrad a brisk nod. "We'll be riding as soon as I can round up my men and get our horses saddled."

"Damn it!" Sheriff Fortson scurried off. Hoyt didn't know if the lawman was upset because he thought he might miss out on a chance for the reward, or if Fortson really thought that only duly deputized representatives of the law ought to be chasing after owlhoots. Hoyt didn't care, either.

He had a reward to go after. Ten grand, American, at the very least.

Rebel was fully dressed by the time Conrad got back up to the hotel room. That was a shame, he thought, but only briefly. As much as he loved her, his mind was focused now on the outrage that had taken place a short time earlier. The loss of the money, the murder of his employees, the wanton slaughter of other innocents . . . all of it combined to fill Conrad with a smoldering rage.

When Conrad first met Rebel Callahan, she'd been dressed like a man, which was fitting considering that she could ride and shoot as well as or better than most men. Since their marriage, she had started dressing like a lady, as befitted the wife of one of the most important businessmen in the country. Now she wore a pale blue gown that went well with her blue eyes, tanned skin, and thick blond hair. She came over to Conrad and touched his arm. His obviously agitated state caused concern to appear in her eyes.

"What happened?" she asked.

"The bank was robbed, just as I feared," he replied.

"The bank we visited just this morning?"

"That's right." His voice caught a little as he added, "The outlaws killed Mr. Wick, the manager, and one of the tellers."

"Oh, my God." Rebel lifted a hand to her mouth in surprise and horror.

"It gets worse than that. They killed several people on the street while they were making their getaway. They cleaned out the bank, too. I checked on that myself. Eighty thousand dollars gone." Conrad's hands clenched into fists as futile anger filled him. "The worst of it, though, is the loss of life. I hate outlaws. I hate the way they think they can just cut down anyone who's unlucky enough to be in their way!"

That feeling went back to the circumstances of his mother's death, although that tragedy hadn't been entirely accidental. One of Vivian Browning's trusted associates had been behind what happened, although it had been desperadoes working for him who had carried out the actual killing. After that, Conrad had wound up being held prisoner by the same gang of outlaws. Both incidents had left him with an unending hatred for lawbreakers and killers.

"I'm sure the sheriff will go after them and bring them to justice," Rebel said.

Conrad shook his head. "I'm not so certain. The sheriff doesn't strike me as being all that competent. Luckily, there's a group of professional manhunters in town. Their leader has volunteered them to track down the killers."

Rebel's mouth tightened. "Professional manhunters," she said. "You mean bounty hunters, Conrad? You offered a reward for the men who robbed the bank?"

He frowned as he sensed her disapproval. "Well, what was I supposed to do? I want those bastards brought to justice, if you'll pardon my French!"

"Oh, you don't have to apologize," Rebel said. "They sound like bastards to me, too. But bounty hunters aren't much better. They're killers, too. They've just got the law on their side."

"That's an important distinction," Conrad snapped.

"I reckon so," Rebel said, reverting back to the Western manner of speaking that she had grown up with. "Was the reward you offered dead or alive?"

"Of course."

She nodded. "Then if those bounty hunters catch up to the robbers, they'll bring 'em back dead."

"And that won't bother me a bit," Conrad said.

Hoyt's men were scattered all through Tucson in various saloons, whorehouses, and gambling dens, with the exception of Bartholomew Leaf, who was having his picture made in a photographer's studio when Hoyt found him. Leaf was an Englishman, and just about the vainest son of a bitch Hoyt had ever met. He was also a hell of a shot with a rifle.

Jack and Ben Coleman were in a brothel, with only one whore. What the brothers were doing with her, Hoyt didn't particularly want to know. He just knocked on the door of the soiled dove's room, uttered the magic words "Ten grand reward," and went back downstairs. He knew the Coleman brothers wouldn't waste any time following him.

Sure enough, by the time he'd rousted Joaquin Escobar from a cantina where he'd been playing a guitar he'd borrowed from an old man, and called Deke Mantee and Bob Bardwell from their poker game, then headed for the livery stable where they had all left their horses, he found Leaf and the Colemans waiting for him. Mantee, Bardwell, and Escobar showed up moments later. Hoyt already had the stable keeper and both hostlers hard at work saddling the group's horses.

Hoyt looked around at his partners—Leaf in his sober suit and black derby; the stocky, pug-nosed Coleman brothers; Escobar with his deceptively open, friendly face; lean, swarthy Mantee, who looked more like a Mexican than Escobar did; and Bardwell, such an average hombre that you forgot what he looked like two minutes after you'd been talking to him. Bardwell was an excellent tracker, as was Escobar. All seven of them were fairly familiar with the Arizona Territory, having hunted down fugitives all over it.

"You said the reward's ten thousand?" Mantee asked.

Hoyt nodded. "That's right. Sound worth it to you?"

Mutters of agreement came from the men.

Hoyt took his horse's reins from the man who had saddled the animal. "We'll stop at the store and pick up some ammunition and supplies before we ride out," he said. "The outlaws were headed southwest when they left town."

Escobar said, "There's not much in that direction until you get to the border. And then there's nothing over there, either."

Hoyt nodded. "That's why we're taking supplies and water with us. We may be out on the trail for several days, and there won't be any place to stock up again."

"You don't think they'll head for Ambush Valley, do you?" Escobar asked with a frown. Like most Mexicans, he both hated and feared Apaches in roughly equal amounts. Geronimo's surrender to General Crook some nine years earlier had effectively ended the Indian wars in Arizona, but across the border in Mexico, several bands of bronco Apaches were still hiding out in the mountains. Those renegades emerged from time to time to launch a raid across the border, so anybody who had spent any amount of time in Arizona still worried about the Apaches and likely always would.

"My word, I hope not," Leaf said in response to Escobar's question about Ambush Valley. "That's the most un-civilized place I've ever seen."

"If that's where they're headed, we need to stop them before they get there," Hoyt said. "I don't want to have to track 'em through that hellhole. But just in case we do . . . Joaquin, you know where to find water in there?"

Escobar's shoulders rose and fell in an eloquent Latin shrug. "I know where some of the water holes are *supposed* to be, Señor Hoyt. That does not mean they will be, or that they will have water in them if they are there."

"Let's just catch up to the bastards 'fore they get there," Jack Coleman suggested.

Hoyt nodded. "Yeah, we're wasting time." He swung up into the saddle. "Come on."

They were a hard, dangerous-looking group of riders as they left the stable. As they trotted up to the general store, Hoyt frowned. Another bunch of horsemen were gathering there, townies from the looks of them. Hoyt spotted Sheriff Lamar Fortson among them. Fortson had a bandage wrapped around his left forearm. It didn't look like a professional job, though. Looked like the sheriff had just tied a rag around his wounded arm.

"You put together your posse in a hurry, Sheriff," Hoyt drawled.

"You didn't give me any choice," Fortson said. "I couldn't let you ride out after those bank robbers by yourself. Now, these men have already been deputized—" He jerked his head toward the townsmen. "So if you and your men will raise your right hands, Hoyt, I'll swear you in."

"Let's just skip that part of it," Hoyt said. He turned to the Coleman brothers and went on. "Jack, Ben, go in there and gather up the things we'll need. Make it fast."

The Colemans dismounted and hurried into the store to follow Hoyt's orders. Fortson sat there on his horse, fuming and glaring for a few seconds before he said, "You refuse to let me officially deputize you?"

"That's right," Hoyt said. "No offense, Sheriff, but I'll be damned if I'm going to swear to follow orders from you."

"I'm the law around here!"

"And my men and I know what we're doing, probably better than you do."

"Well, I may not be able to stop you from going, but by God, you'd better not get in our way!" Fortson blustered. He turned to his posse, waved his arm over his head, and shouted, "Come on, men! Let's ride!"

Hoyt looked over at Escobar and Bardwell. "Go pick up the trail before those amateurs ruin it," he said. "We'll catch up to you later."

The two bounty hunters nodded, wheeled their horses, and galloped around the posse. The sheriff and his men had started moving, but they were slow about it. A posse made up of storekeepers, freighters, layabouts, and saddle tramps could never be as swift and professional as Hoyt and his men. Escobar and Bardwell had raced out of sight while the members of the posse were all still trying to get headed in the same direction. Fortson yelled orders at them, but it didn't seem to help much.

Hoyt smiled thinly as he watched the posse lumber out of town. Getting ahead of them wouldn't be any problem.

"I hope that by some quirk of circumstances those fellows don't catch up to the outlaws before we do," Leaf said. "They'll probably be wiped out if that happens."

"Not our problem," Hoyt said.

Chapter 4

Cicero McCoy kept his men moving at a fast pace the rest of that day following the bank robbery in Tucson. It would take most of the next day to reach Ambush Valley, a day to make it through the hellish place, and then part of the day after that to reach the border. They could have gotten to Mexico faster by traveling due south after leaving Tucson, but there was nothing in that direction to slow down any pursuit. It would have been a straight race to the border, and McCoy liked to have the odds more on his side than that. That was why he'd decided to follow the route through Ambush Valley.

They would have to stop when darkness fell. When you rode at night it was too easy to get lost and start going in circles in this trackless wilderness. And there would be only a sliver of moon for the next couple of nights. McCoy had taken that into account when he was planning the bank job, too. Any posse that followed them from Tucson would have to call a halt for darkness or risk losing the trail completely.

Things could still go wrong, but McCoy liked their chances. He had planned well and so far it was working.

Cortez was in the lead now, since he knew this country better than any of the rest of them. He decided when to stop, and held up a hand to signal a halt when the sun was down and stars had begun to twinkle into existence in the sable sky above them.

"Cold camp," McCoy ordered. "Tend to your horses before you look to your own needs." That was just common sense, like not building a fire. Without the horses, they'd stand no chance at all. "Two men on guard at all times. Beck, Newton, you'll take the first watch."

These eight men had ridden together for long enough so that they functioned like a well-oiled machine. Within half an hour, the horses had been grained and watered, the men had made a meager supper on jerky and biscuits, and all of them were asleep except McCoy and the two guards.

McCoy should have been asleep, too, but he was too keyed up to doze off just yet. He sat with his back propped against a rock and took off his hat. He ran his fingers through his hair, which was completely white despite the fact that he was only thirty-two years old. His hair had turned white before he was twenty-five. Some hombres were like that. He wasn't vain enough to let it bother him.

A cold breeze blew. Nights cooled off in a hurry in this semidesert country. The rock at McCoy's back retained a lot of the day's warmth, though, and kept him from getting chilly. He wished he could take one of the thin black cigarillos from his pocket and light it, but he had given strict orders that there be no smoking. The smell of burning tobacco could sometimes travel a long way, and he didn't want anybody using such a thing to trail them. Time enough for smoking . . . and tequila . . . and willing, dusky-skinned women, once they were south of the border. McCoy grinned in anticipation.

Without being aware of it, he drifted off to sleep, but

like a wary animal, his slumber was light. He came awake when the guards changed, then dozed off again. He and Cortez would take the last watch. They would saddle up and hit the trail again as soon as the sky grayed enough for them to see where they were going.

Dreams crept in while McCoy was sleeping. He never remembered them when he awoke, but he knew they often haunted him because people told him that he some-times stirred around and muttered in his sleep as if he were angry. Once, in fact, one of the men who had been riding with him at the time had said, "I was afraid you was gonna wake up and start shootin', Boss. You seemed mighty proddy."

That had never happened, but McCoy worried that someday it might. At times he wished he knew what those troubling dreams were about . . . but mostly he fig-ured maybe it was better to remain ignorant.

The men who had the turn before them woke McCoy and Cortez, and then wrapped up in their blankets for a little more shut-eye. An eerie quiet lay over the vast, mostly empty country. The only sounds were the soft sighing of the wind and an occasional rattle of pebbles as some small, nocturnal animal went about its errands. McCoy wasn't worried too much about a posse sneaking up on them. White men couldn't move that quietly. He would hear them coming long before they got there.

But Apaches were another story, and McCoy stiffened as he heard an owl hoot in the distance. Didn't have to mean anything, he told himself. Chances were it was a real owl, not some painted savage. He waited tensely, but didn't hear any more hoots. Finally, he relaxed again, while still remaining vigilant.

Not long after that, Cortez padded over to him. The

half-breed's moccasins made little sound on the sandy ground. "Time to go," Cortez whispered.

McCoy nodded his agreement. He and Cortez woke the other men.

A short time later, after a quick breakfast, the outlaws were in the saddle again, winding their way through the gray shadows toward the southwest. By the time night came again, McCoy thought, they would be in Ambush Valley, and they would be safe.

The posse was half a mile out of Tucson before Abner Hoyt and his remaining companions rode after them. It didn't take long to close that gap. Hoyt and his men were all mounted on fine horses, the best they could afford. Because a man's life often depended on his horse, especially when he was engaged in such a dangerous profession as bounty hunting.

The posse members, on the other hand, rode a mixture of cow ponies, draft animals, buggy horses, and nags whose best days were long since past. Hoyt signaled for his men to follow him, and swung wide around the other group of riders. As they rode past, he glanced over and saw Sheriff Fortson glaring at them. Hoyt couldn't help but grin.

That reward as good as belonged to him and his men.

They left the posse in their dust. Now they could follow the trail of the bank robbers themselves. Farther back, the tracks had been obliterated by the horses of the men from Tucson. Bardwell and Escobar were somewhere up ahead, making sure they didn't lose the trail, but for now Hoyt and his partners had no trouble following it.

Late that afternoon, Hoyt spotted a lone rider coming toward them. He waved his men to a halt. They

waited with their hands near their guns, just in case
that horseman wasn't friendly. A few minutes later
they relaxed as they recognized him as Bob Bardwell.

The nondescript Bardwell rode up and reined in. He
took his hat off, sleeved sweat from his forehead, and said,
"Joaquin's about a mile ahead. He says that we've cut into
their lead some, but they're moving fast, too, and we won't
be able to catch them until sometime tomorrow."

"What if we rode through the night?" Hoyt asked.

Bardwell shook his head "Then we'd risk losing the
trail altogether. Joaquin's waiting for us, and when we
catch up to him we need to stop and make camp."

The delay chafed at Hoyt, but he trusted his scouts. If
you were going to ride with a man, you needed to be able
to trust his judgment. Hoyt nodded and said, "All right.
As long as we stop them before they get to Ambush
Valley, that's all that matters."

"How do you know that's where they're going,
Abner?" Deke Mantee asked.

Hoyt leaned over in the saddle and spat on the ground.
"Where else could they be headed? If all they wanted to
do was get across the border, they could have ridden
straight south to Nogales. Problem is, men on fast horses
might've caught them before they got there. It's a longer
run to Ambush Valley, but they have to figure that if they
make it through there, nobody will come after them."

Ben Coleman laughed. "Stupid bastards'll die o' thirst
in there."

His brother agreed, saying, "They'll be buzzard bait
before they ever get out of that valley."

Hoyt wasn't going to count on that. The way he saw it,
the outlaws had to have someone with them who knew
the way through the desolate region. If they did, then
their daring plan might just work.

"Let's go," he snapped. "We still need to catch up to Joaquin."

They reached the place where Escobar was waiting for them as the sun was dipping below the western horizon. Nightfall was a sudden thing out here. Dusk didn't last very long. It was light, and then darkness had closed down on the rugged terrain. The bounty hunters made camp in the lee of a shallow, rocky bluff where they could build a small fire without running the risk of it being noticed. It was rare for the Apaches to venture into these parts from across the border, but none of the men wanted to take a chance on that.

Some hot coffee and food braced them after the hard ride from Tucson. Bartholomew Leaf took tea instead of Arbuckle's, and as he sipped the steaming beverage, he asked, "Do you think that posse will get this far, Abner?"

"Lord, I hope not," Hoyt replied. "I reckon we're a mile or more ahead of them. I hope they've already stopped for the night. We don't need them blundering around."

A short time later, though, they heard hoofbeats from the northeast, and Hoyt bit back a curse. Fortson should have known better than to try to keep following the trail after dark.

Hoyt took his rifle and climbed to the top of the bluff along with Mantee and Bardwell. A dark mass was visible as it moved across the sandy plains toward them. Hoyt waited until the riders were within hailing distance, then waved his rifle over his head and shouted, "Fortson! Sheriff Fortson! Is that you?"

He heard the lawman's voice calling orders. "Hold it, men!" One of the riders came forward. "Hoyt?"

"Yeah, that's right," Hoyt said, not bothering to keep the disgust out of his voice.

"Reckon we can share your camp?"

Quietly, Bardwell suggested, "It might be better to keep 'em close by so that we can keep an eye on them, Abner."

"Yeah, you're right. They're townies and plowboys and grub-line riders. Nothing's more dangerous than a bunch of amateurs." Hoyt raised his voice. "Yeah, Sheriff, come on in. Just take it easy and don't spook our horses."

Soon the area in front of the bluff was crowded with men and horses. They made enough noise to wake up every Apache within a hundred miles, too, Hoyt thought disgustedly. He just hoped there weren't any Apaches that close.

He went over to Fortson and said, "Listen, Sheriff, if you're going to camp here, too, you've got to keep your posse under control."

"My men are fine," Fortson replied coldly. "If we're going to work together, Hoyt, we need to all get along."

"Nobody said anything about us working together," Hoyt snapped. "We're still going after those bank robbers on our own."

"Suit yourself. Just remember who's the law here."

He had another reason for wanting to nab those outlaws now, Hoyt thought as he shook his head and returned to the fire he and his men had built earlier. He wanted to rub his success in the face of that officious sheriff.

Hoyt worried that trouble might develop between his men and the members of the posse, but the night passed quietly. Early the next morning, while most of the possemen were still snoring, Hoyt and the other bounty hunters were mounted and ready to ride. As the hoofbeats of their departing horses roused the sleeping townies, Hoyt heard Fortson yelling behind him, exhorting the men to get up and get on their horses. Hoyt smiled in the gray dawn. Once again, he and his friends were going to leave the posse behind.

He had to give Fortson credit for one thing—the sheriff was stubborn as hell. All morning long the posse hung back there, half a mile or so behind the bounty hunters. Actually, Hoyt reflected at midday, he had expected them to give up and turn back by now. Evidently, Fortson wasn't going to allow that, though.

Still, the inferior quality of the posse's mounts gradually took its toll, and they dropped farther and farther behind.

The heat in the middle of the afternoon forced a halt. Hoyt and the others found some shade in an arroyo and waited out the worst of it. Hoyt was beginning to worry that the bank robbers would make it to Ambush Valley ahead of them. In that case he would have a decision to make, whether to follow them into that hellish wasteland or give up. He took scant comfort in the knowledge that the fugitives had probably laid up for a while, as well, to escape the heat.

Finally, Hoyt's impatience goaded him to swing up into the saddle and growl, "Move out." Several of the men looked like they would have rather waited until it was a little cooler, but they went along with what Hoyt said.

Only a short time later, Escobar pointed and said, "I see some dust ahead of us. That has to be them."

Hoyt urged his horse to a faster pace. "Let's run them down," he called to the other bounty hunters. The thrill of the chase had him fully in its grip now, and that excitement soon spread to the rest of the group.

They galloped up a long, shallow rise, and when they crested the top of it they could see for several miles across a huge stretch of rocky, arid ground. "See those cliffs on the other side of the flats?" Escobar shouted over the pounding of hooves.

Hoyt saw them.

"That gap is the entrance to Ambush Valley!" Escobar went on. "A canyon runs through there for about a mile and then opens up into the valley! I've been that far into it several times!"

"Look!" Bardwell yelled. "I see them!"

So did Hoyt. Eight tiny figures on horseback raced across the flats toward the gap in the cliffs, which jutted up sheer for a couple of hundred feet and ran as far to the north and south as the eye could see. Ambush Valley was the only way through without going miles and miles out of the way.

Hoyt lashed his horse with the reins and leaned forward in the saddle, urging as much speed as he could possibly get out of the animal. The horse responded gallantly, stretching out into a hard run.

Bartholomew Leaf pulled up alongside Hoyt and shouted, "I say, Abner, perhaps I could pick some of them off if I stopped and set up my rifle!"

"Do it!" Hoyt shouted back, making his decision instantly. Leaf owned some sort of fancy English rifle that could shoot incredible distances when it was set up on its stand and sighted in. He peeled away from the rest of the galloping group and rode to the top of a little knoll where he would have a good field of fire at the fleeing bank robbers.

Hoyt didn't hear the shot, but a few minutes later he saw one of the outlaws suddenly pitch out of the saddle and flop lifelessly to the ground. He knew that Leaf must have brought him down. A moment later, one of the racing horses collapsed, its front legs going out from under it as if they had been jerked by a rope. Leaf's second shot had hit horse instead of rider, but it was effective because the outlaw who had been on top of the horse went sailing out of the saddle and came crashing down on the ground with such force that he was stunned.

The man had barely had time to recover before the bounty hunters were on top of him.

He jerked his pistol from its holster and raised the gun, and that sealed his fate. Several shots rang out and the man tottered backward, jerking as bullets tore through him. He folded up like a rag doll . . . a bloody rag doll.

That made two of the bank robbers who were done for. The others were drawing steadily closer to the cliffs, though, because they had good horses, too. Those mounts were tired from the long run from Tucson, but so were the horses ridden by Hoyt and his companions. It was a good, hard race, with the stakes being that ten-thousand-dollar reward . . . and the lives of the fugitives.

Hoyt saw a cluster of boulders at the mouth of the canyon that led to Ambush Valley. Six of the outlaws were still alive. If they reached those rocks and forted up in them, they might be able to hold off Hoyt's group. In that case, Hoyt and the others would be caught out here in the open, with no cover for hundreds of yards. They would make mighty fine targets. They were risking their lives in this pursuit, too, he realized.

But that danger sure as hell didn't make him turn back or call off the chase. He wanted that reward. More importantly now, he wanted to win. His blood was up. The smell of powder smoke was in his nose. At moments like this, he lived for battle.

The outlaws had good horses . . . but the bounty hunters' mounts were better. Slowly but surely, the man-hunters closed in. Hoyt drew his revolver and leveled it at the fugitives. He was close enough now he could see the desperation on their faces as they turned their heads to glance back over their shoulders. Hoyt and his men began to fire as the cliffs loomed closer and closer, with Ambush Valley just beyond.

Chapter 5

Red rage swam before Cicero McCoy's eyes. He couldn't believe they had come this far, made it this close to their goal, only to have a damned posse catch up to them. He honestly hadn't believed that anybody from Tucson could catch up to them before they reached Ambush Valley.

But two of his men were down already, and the pursuit was closing in. As he looked back over his shoulder, McCoy's lips drew away from his teeth in a furious grimace. Only six or seven men! Damn it! If he had realized that the gang outnumbered the posse, he would have ordered them to turn around and make a stand, rather than running for the gap in the cliffs. Now he had lost two men and the odds were closer to even.

McCoy didn't want to run the risk of a battle, not when he was this close to sanctuary. The loot from the bank had been consolidated into three bags. McCoy had one, Cortez another, and the outlaw called Beck the third.

That meant the three remaining members of the gang were dispensable.

"Newton! Travis! Mulligan! Fall back and slow those bastards down!"

McCoy's shouted order caused the three outlaws he had named to stare at him in astonishment. He waved an arm at them and went on. "Do it now! Extra shares for you!"

Their habit of following his commands—and the promise of extra loot—made the three men slow their mounts. They wheeled the horses around and yanked Winchesters from saddle sheaths. A few rounds of rifle fire might cause the possemen to think twice about their headlong pursuit.

Meanwhile, McCoy, Cortez, and Beck continued galloping toward the gap in the cliffs as fast as they could.

Newton, Travis, and Mulligan began firing. Their horses were used to the sound of shots and stood fairly still, giving them a stable platform from which to shoot. The posse members blazed away at them, but the bullets fell short or went wide.

Then Mulligan's head jerked and blood sprayed from it as a bullet cored through it. He toppled out of the saddle, causing his horse to shy violently.

"They got a sharpshooter back there somewhere!" Newton yelled. "I don't care what McCoy said, I'm gettin' the hell out of here!"

He jerked his horse around and put the spurs to it. Travis didn't hesitate. He followed Newton. As they pounded toward the cliffs, the other three riders reached the gap and vanished into it.

Newton cried out and leaned forward as a bullet creased his shoulder. He managed to stay mounted and kept riding.

McCoy was waiting for the two of them behind the cluster of boulders at the canyon mouth. "Get behind those rocks!" he ordered. "You can hold 'em off from there!"

"I'm hit, Cicero!" Newton said as he clutched his bleeding shoulder.

"That's your left shoulder. You can still shoot!"

Travis asked, "What're you and Beck and Cortez gonna do?"

"We'll ride on into the canyon a little ways and cache the loot, then come back to help you."

"We still get extra shares?"

"Of course."

Travis slid down from his horse with his Winchester in his hand and said, "All right, but make it fast! I don't know how long we can hold off those bastards!"

"Lemme go with you, Cicero," Newton said. "Leave Beck or Cortez here with Travis."

McCoy shook his head. "Just do what I tell you. You'll be all right. We'll be back in a few minutes."

"But, Cicero —"

"By God, do what I said!" McCoy roared. He swung his gun up. "Or I'll shoot you myself! That posse's getting closer all the time!"

Newton had no choice but to dismount and join Travis behind the rocks. "Don't leave us here," he said, a note of pleading in his voice.

"Hell, I never double-crossed you boys before, did I? We're all in this together!"

As Newton and Travis opened fire on the approaching posse, McCoy turned his horse and rode hard after Cortez and Beck. An ugly smile of satisfaction tugged at the corners of his mouth. He knew the two men would be able to slow down the posse. That would give him a chance to make it deep into Ambush Valley with Cortez and Beck . . . and the money.

McCoy had made a rough count of the loot earlier in the day, when the gang was stopped for a few minutes to rest their horses. Upwards of eighty thousand dollars, he made it. That was an even bigger haul than he'd expected.

He chuckled as he followed the twisting canyon. He'd told the truth when he said that he had never double-crossed any of the men he rode with.

But he had never had eighty thousand good reasons to double-cross them, either . . . until now.

A bitter taste filled Abner Hoyt's mouth. So close . . . They had been so close to stopping the bank robbers before they reached Ambush Valley. Now the outlaws had made it to those boulders at the mouth of the canyon, and at least two of them had opened fire on the bounty hunters from the shelter of those rocks.

"Spread out!" Hoyt shouted as a rifle bullet zipped past his head. "Hunt some cover!"

Problem was, there wasn't much cover to be had out here on the flats. All they could do was try to find some slight irregularity in the ground and sprawl out behind it. Failing that, they could pull their horses down and use the animals themselves for cover. That would mean sacrificing the horses, but they could afford to do that because the posse from Tucson was coming up behind them. The posse didn't have any extra mounts, but some of them could double up if they had to. And if Sheriff Fortson didn't like it, that was just too damned bad. Come down to it, Hoyt and his men would just take what they needed, as they always had.

Hoyt spotted a little hummock of ground and headed for it as more shots banged from the rocks at the canyon mouth. Powder smoke puffed from behind the boulders. Jerking his rifle from the saddle boot, Hoyt flung himself off the horse and dropped behind the hummock. Bullets kicked sand and grit into the air. He cursed as the stuff settled down around him. When the shots stopped for a second, he thrust the barrel of his rifle over the top of the little rise and opened fire, cranking off several rounds as fast as he could. The trick to dealing with enemies who were forted up in rocks like that was to pour in enough lead so that a ricochet stood a good chance of hitting one of the bastards.

He settled down to a slow, steady fire, and glanced around to see what had happened to his partners. They were spread out over a hundred yards or so of open ground, but they had all found at least a little cover, as Hoyt had done. Shots came from all five of their locations, telling Hoyt that they were all right, or at least still capable of using their rifles. Several hundred yards to the rear, Leaf continued using his high-powered target rifle to pepper the rocks at the canyon mouth with lead.

The conviction grew in Hoyt that only two men were behind the boulders. Three were down out here on the flats, more than likely dead. But that still left three of the outlaws unaccounted for, and Hoyt realized bitterly that those three had probably gone on through the canyon and were in Ambush Valley by now. No doubt they had the loot from the bank with them, too. They had left two of their bunch behind to slow down the pursuit.

It was effectively slowed down, too. Hoyt had no doubt that he and his men could root the bastards out sooner or later, but it was going to take some time.

Escobar was about twenty yards to Hoyt's left, stretched out behind a rock that couldn't have been sticking up more than a foot from the ground. Hoyt called over to him, "Joaquin! You think if we covered you, you could circle around and get close enough to that cliff to work your way along its base?"

"You mean so I could get at those hombres in the rocks?"

"Yeah, that's right." Another worry crept into Hoyt's mind. Night wasn't more than an hour or two away. "If we don't get rid of them, they'll keep us pinned down out here until after dark. Then they can slip away."

Escobar didn't sound happy about it when he called back, "I'd need a lot of covering fire."

"We'll give it to you," Hoyt promised. Bardwell was the next man to his right. Hoyt turned his head and called, "Bob! Joaquin's going to try for the cliffs! When he takes off, pour as much lead as you can into those rocks! Pass the word to the other men!"

"Right, Abner!" Bardwell replied. "Good luck, Joaquin!"

Escobar was going to need it.

The Mexican set his rifle aside. Carrying it would slow him down too much, and if he couldn't do this job with his pistol and knife, it wasn't going to get done anyway. He looked over at Hoyt, waiting for the signal to begin his desperate run.

Hoyt waited until all the other men had acknowledged his order, then looked over at Escobar and jerked his head in a nod. He yelled, "Now!" and began emptying his Winchester at the rocks as fast as he could work the lever and pull the trigger.

The other men opened fire, too, sending a storm of lead into the boulders. Even at this distance, Hoyt could hear the slugs whining viciously off the rocks. Maybe they would bounce around enough in that nest of stone to take care of the outlaws before Escobar ever got there. At the very least, the bastards ought to be hunkered down, unable to draw a bead on the Mexican bounty hunter who had leaped up from his meager cover and now sprinted toward the cliffs as fast as he could, angling away from the canyon mouth and zigzagging back and forth.

It was maybe 150 yards to the cliff face. Escobar took between twenty and thirty seconds to cover that distance, and the time seemed longer. It must have seemed like an eternity to Joaquin, Hoyt thought as he saw slugs kick up dust around the man's racing feet. Even with the barrage of rifle fire raining down on them, the outlaws were able to get off a few shots. None of them were accurate enough to hit Escobar, though. He reached the base of the cliff and sagged against the rock, his chest heaving as he dragged in huge breaths of air. The sprint had completely winded him.

Hoyt smiled as he saw that Escobar had reached his goal safely. The bounty hunters' guns were falling silent now as their bullets ran out. "Reload!" Hoyt called. "Let's keep it hot for them while Joaquin catches his breath!"

Within a minute or two, Hoyt and his men resumed their fire. Return shots still came from the rocks. The outlaws might have been wounded—there was no way to know about that yet—but they weren't dead.

Escobar began working his way along the cliff. He had only about fifty yards to cover, and it didn't take him long. The two bank robbers holed up in the boulders had to know that he was coming, but there was nothing they could do about it. They couldn't even see Escobar from where they were, let alone draw a bead on him.

But there *was* one other thing they could do, Hoyt realized as he heard the swift, sudden rataplan of hoofbeats.

They could run.

Escobar heard the horses, too, and froze where he was for a moment until Hoyt waved him on. He slipped into the rocks, gun drawn, moving warily in case this was a trick.

It was no trick, Hoyt knew when Escobar appeared in the canyon mouth a few minutes later and waved for the rest of the bounty hunters to come on in. The outlaws had fled.

But before they'd cut and run, they had accomplished what they'd set out to do. They had slowed down the pursuit enough so that the rest of the gang was well on their way into Ambush Valley by now—with that stolen bank money, no doubt. Hoyt stood up and spat in disgust.

The bastards had gotten away—for now. But sooner or later, Hoyt vowed, he would catch up to them.

He wasn't giving up on ten grand that easy.

McCoy had told Newton and Travis that he and his companions were going only a short distance into the valley to cache the loot. McCoy didn't slow down, though, as he and Cortez and Beck made their way deeper into the wasteland.

The canyon ran for maybe half a mile through the cliffs, twisting and turning between sheer rock walls, before emerging into Ambush Valley itself. Two to three miles wide and more than fifteen miles long, the valley ran roughly east and west between two ranges of rough sandstone and granite peaks. The mountains petered out eventually, giving way to desert again, and when they did, Ambush Valley came to an end as well.

Almost no vegetation grew in here. The landscape was an ugly, unrelenting mixture of brown and tan and red. In some places, razor-sharp rocks jutted up from the ground.

They would cut a horse's hooves to ribbons if anybody tried to take a mount across one of those stretches. In other places, sandstone spires rose dozens of feet into the air, tapering to sharp points. Narrow, steep-walled ravines cut across the valley as if a giant knife had slashed them into the earth. Natural stone bridges transversed those ravines, but a traveler had to know where they were; otherwise, he might ride back and forth for hours, searching for a place to cross. Huge boulders balanced atop pinnacles, looking as if the slightest vibration might make them come crashing down.

No doubt about it, Cicero McCoy thought as he looked around. Ambush Valley was about as close to being a true hell on earth as anywhere could be. As close as you'd ever *want* anywhere to be.

"We're following you, Cortez," he said to the half-breed, who was riding a few yards in front of him. "I hope you know where you're going."

"I do," Cortez said with a confident nod as he looked around. "I've been through here before, Boss. Don't worry." He frowned. "But I thought we were going to hide the loot and go back to help Travis and Newton hold off that posse."

"Travis and Newton are fine," McCoy snapped. He could still hear the shots falling farther and farther behind them. "Just keep going until I tell you to stop."

Cortez just looked at him for a second, then shrugged in acceptance of McCoy's decision. Splitting the loot three ways was better than splitting it in fifths. It didn't take a genius at ciphering to figure that out.

The little group's progress into Ambush Valley was slow. If you rushed your horse in a place like this, chances were you'd wind up with a lame horse, at best. At worst, the animal would fall and break a leg, and then a rider would be in a terrible fix. So McCoy, Cortez, and Beck took their time. When the shooting in the distance to the rear came to an abrupt halt, they looked at each other but didn't stop, and sure as hell didn't turn back.

They didn't stop until the sun went down and it grew too dark to keep going. "Reckon it's safe to build a fire?" Beck asked.

McCoy looked to Cortez for the answer. The half-breed said, "As far as I know, all my mother's people are below the border now, holed up in the mountains. But a war party *could* have ridden up here."

Beck gave a grim laugh. "I'd rather keep my hair than have a hot cup of coffee. I can do without a fire."

They found a good level place to stop for the night. A few blades of hardy grass poked out of the rocks and gave the horses a little graze. McCoy sloshed the water in his canteen back and forth and said, "We're gonna need to find a water hole in the morning, Cortez."

"We're not far from one. We may have to dig down a little for water, but it'll be there," Cortez promised.

"I sure as hell hope you're right."

If Cortez was wrong, then the three men faced a long, thirsty—and possibly fatal—day in this hellhole of a valley.

Earlier, while there was still some light, the bounty hunters gathered at the mouth of the canyon and peered into it. Because of the high walls, shadows had already gathered thickly in the canyon. Jack Coleman rubbed his jaw, his fingers rasping on the beard stubble, and said, "I ain't sure I want to ride in there, Abner. Ain't no tellin' what might be waitin' for us."

"Ten thousand dollars reward, that's what waiting for

us," Hoyt snapped. "If you don't want to be part of that, Jack, it's your decision. Always has been." Hoyt looked around at the other men. "You're all free to drop out of the hunt anytime, just like always."

"Now, I never said I wanted to quit," Jack muttered. "All I meant was that I don't like the looks o' that place very much."

"Neither do I," Hoyt said, "but I'm going in there anyway."

He heeled his horse into motion and rode into the canyon.

One by one, the rest of the bounty hunters followed him. Bob Bardwell brought up the rear, not because he was hesitant, but rather because he was the most watchful among them and didn't want any enemies coming up behind them. There shouldn't be anyone back there except the posse from Tucson, Bardwell knew, but you didn't survive in this business by taking unnecessary chances.

They had followed the meandering canyon for about a quarter of a mile when Hoyt reined to a sudden halt and lifted his rifle. The others came up behind him and saw what had made him stop. A figure lay sprawled on the floor of the canyon, unmoving. It was already too dark in here to make out any details.

"Check him out, Deke," Hoyt said to Mantee. "We'll cover you."

The saturnine Mantee didn't protest. He dismounted and strode forward with his revolver in his hand. When he reached the fallen figure, he hooked the toe of a boot under the man's shoulder and rolled him onto his back. There was still enough light in the canyon for the bounty hunters to see the dark stains all over the front of the man's shirt.

"Dead," Mantee announced, somewhat unnecessarily. "Looks like several of those ricochets got him. He was able to get on his horse and start through the canyon, but this is as far as he got before he fell off and died. Or died and fell off." A humorless smile creased Mantee's lean face. "Doesn't really matter which, does it?"

"No," Hoyt agreed. "He's dead either way. I don't see his horse."

"The other hombre probably took it with him," Bardwell suggested.

"One of us can carry his body back to the opening of the canyon where the other bodies are and turn them over to the sheriff. Don't know how much we can get for them, but something's better than nothing." Hoyt looked at the men. "Jack, load him up and take him back."

"Them bodies ain't goin' anywhere," Coleman pointed out.

"No, but I don't want any coyotes to come along and mess them up so bad that we can't identify them."

Coleman nodded. "All right. The rest of you goin' on?"

"That's right." Hoyt hitched his horse into motion again.

They rode on to the end of the canyon without seeing any sign of the second outlaw. As they reached Ambush Valley itself, Escobar pointed to the ground and said, "Look there." The bounty hunters all saw the dark splash on the rocks.

"He's hit, too," Hoyt said. "No telling how far he was able to go, though."

The six men sat there on their horses and peered out over Ambush Valley. Nothing was moving anywhere, probably because there wasn't much life in this place. A few lizards might come out at night, and there were probably some snakes denned up here and there. Some rats around the isolated water holes, maybe, and tarantulas in the cracks in the rocks. That would be about it.

The last of the day's sunlight slanted along the canyon from the far end. Hoyt squinted against it and thought that he had never seen an uglier, less inviting place in his life.

"Are we goin' in there, Abner?" Ben Coleman asked.

Hoyt didn't answer right away. He thought about it for a moment and then turned to Escobar. "Joaquin, what's on the far side of this valley?"

"About five miles of desert and then the border," Escobar replied. "There's a little settlement on this side of the line called Hinkley."

"If we went around, how long would it take to get there?"

"To Hinkley?" Escobar shrugged. "If we pulled out first thing in the morning, we might be able to get there by nightfall."

"And how long will it take what's left of that bunch to get through Ambush Valley and make it to the border?"

"They can get to Hinkley before us, Abner."

"By how much time?"

"An hour? Two?" Escobar shook his head. "The important thing is, they can get across the border before we can catch up to them that way."

"What about if we ride all night?" Hoyt suggested.

Leaf said, "I daresay our mounts will collapse from exhaustion if we attempt that, old boy."

Hoyt reached a decision. "We'll have to try it anyway. If we start through the valley and lose our way, we'll never make it out of there alive."

"I could *probably* find the right trail," Escobar said. "I've talked to some old Indians who've been through there."

Hoyt shook his head and said, "No offense, Joaquin, but I'm not going to risk all our lives on probably. We'll go slow, rest the horses as often as we can, but we're going around and try to beat those outlaws to the border that way." He nodded toward Ambush Valley. "But if anybody wants to try that route on their own . . ."

Nobody did. Hoyt nodded and turned his horse around, putting his back to Ambush Valley.

Chapter 6

By morning, it was obvious that Newton and Travis weren't going to be catching up to McCoy, Cortez, and Beck. That came as no surprise to any of the three remaining outlaws. Even if the two men who'd been left behind had survived the battle at the canyon mouth, they would never be able to find their way through the part of Ambush Valley that the others had already put behind them. If the unlucky bastards were still alive, they would wander around in here until they died of thirst or exposure.

They wouldn't last long enough to starve to death.

McCoy took only a small swig of the brackish water still in his canteen when he got up the next morning. His sleep had been restless, and the heat that began to build up as soon as the sun rose began to get on his nerves right away. "Let's find that water hole," he snapped as he threw his saddle on his horse.

"What about breakfast?" Beck asked.

"You should have some jerky left in your saddlebags. Chew on that."

All three men were in a foul mood as they set out.

Their spirits lifted considerably about an hour later when Cortez led them into a little hollow with a sandy floor. "This is it," he said.

"I don't see any water," McCoy muttered.

"I told you, Boss, we might have to dig for it." The half-breed swung down from his horse and knelt to scoop up some of the sand with his hands. He continued digging for several minutes. His attitude became more frantic as he pawed up handfuls of dirt. "It can't have gone dry," he said under his breath, but McCoy and Beck heard him anyway and also grew tense.

"Get down there and help him," McCoy snapped as he gestured at Beck. The outlaw complied, kneeling beside Cortez and digging into the dirt with him.

A few more minutes passed. Then Cortez let out a relieved whoop. "The sand's getting wet," he told McCoy. "We'll have to dig down a little deeper and then let it seep in for a while."

It seemed to take forever, but eventually they had a hole about a yard deep with a foot of muddy water at the bottom. Cortez scooped up the water in his hat and poured it through a bandanna to filter out most of the sand as he filled the canteens. Then he took the wet bandanna and wiped the noses and mouths of all the horses before he put more water in the hat and let the animals drink sparingly. Other than the grittiness, the water tasted pretty good.

"There's another spring even better than this one, close to the far end of the valley," Cortez explained. "This water will get us that far, and we can fill the canteens again there. That will take us across the desert on the other side of the valley to the border."

When they were finished with the water, McCoy nodded toward the hole and said, "Fill it back in."

"Why?" Beck asked. "After we went to all the trouble of digging it?"

"If anybody's following us, I don't want them finding this place. And if they do, they'll have to work for the water just like we did."

"I reckon that makes sense," Beck admitted. The two men set to work, and it didn't take long for them to fill the hole. Then they mounted up and rode away, once again following Cortez's lead.

McCoy could see where the mountains ran out and the valley ended, and it seemed tantalizingly close. He knew that distances were deceptive out here, though, so he wasn't surprised when long, hot hours dragged by and they didn't seem much closer to the end of their trek than when they'd started out. The sun reached its zenith and began its slow crawl down toward the western horizon.

Around the middle of the hellishly hot afternoon, Cortez led McCoy and Beck down a rocky slope and into one of the ravines. They had been avoiding these slashes in the earth so far, but McCoy assumed that the half-breed knew what he was doing. Cortez had better hope so.

The ravine wound around through the wasteland. In most places it was no more than a dozen feet wide, with sheer stone walls and a sandy floor. After the three riders had been down there for a long time, they rounded a sharp bend and Cortez let out a whoop.

McCoy felt like whooping, too. The ravine opened out into a depression roughly forty feet wide. On the far side was a pool of water with a couple of mesquite trees shading it and some grass along its banks. The pool was fed by a spring that trickled out of a crack in the rocky wall of the ravine. The men had to hold the horses back to keep them from rushing across the clearing and plunging their muzzles into the pool. McCoy understood the temptation all too well.

The ravine continued beyond the pool. Cortez pointed at it and said, "All we have to do is follow that and it'll bring us out only a few miles from the end of the valley."

"Then head due west across the desert to the border?" McCoy asked.

Cortez nodded. "That's right. We can stock up on supplies and water at Hinkley and then head across the border."

"Yeah," Beck said with a laugh. "We got plenty o' money to buy what we need, that's for damn sure."

McCoy had been thinking about that very thing. Now, as they let the horses drink a little, he said, "We're not taking all the loot with us."

The other two men turned to look at him in surprise. "What are you talkin' about, Boss?" Beck asked. "What else can we do with it except take it with us?"

McCoy reached his decision. "We're only going to take a few thousand, just enough to keep us comfortable in Mexico for a while. The rest of it stays here." He pointed to a jumble of rocks next to one side of the pool. "We'll bury it under those rocks."

Beck's eyes narrowed. "Why in blazes would we want to do a thing like that?"

McCoy felt anger well up inside him. He didn't like having his decisions questioned. He snapped, "Who's the boss of this outfit, Beck, you or me?" His hand edged closer to the butt of his gun as he spoke.

Beck held up both hands in a conciliatory gesture. "You're the boss, Cicero. Always have been, and I reckon you always will be. But after we've gone through so much to get this money, I don't understand why you want to ride off and leave it here."

"We're not leaving it for good. I just don't want to carry that much money south of the border. I don't trust the greasers. Things tend to happen down there, especially where *dinero*'s concerned."

Beck looked over at Cortez. "Those're your people he's talkin' about."

Cortez shrugged. "The Mexicans hate the Apache side of me, the Apaches hate the Mexican side of me. I say to hell with all of them. I agree with you, Boss. We can come back here and dig up the rest of the loot when things have cooled down and nobody's lookin' for us anymore."

McCoy grinned. "You're starting to think like me, Cortez. Just don't get too ambitious."

"No chance of that," the half-breed said with a laugh. "Part of me comes from *mañana*-land, remember."

The men spent a while filling their canteens, washing their faces with wet bandannas, and letting the horses drink, but not so much that they'd founder. The shade of the mesquite trees was very welcome, and McCoy wouldn't have minded spending some more time here . . . but he had things to do and places to go.

Beck and Cortez rolled one of the rocks aside and began scooping out a hole in the sandy earth underneath it, while McCoy took some of the money out of one of the canvas bags and stowed it in his shirt. Then he spread his rain slicker out on the ground, piled all the bags on it, and rolled them up inside the garment into as tight a bundle as he could manage. He bound it closed with rope, pulling that tight, too.

When McCoy judged that the hole was deep enough, he told Beck and Cortez to step back. He placed the bundle into the hole. "This place should be easy enough to find again," he said. "And that rock's got a distinctive shape. We'll know that it marks the place where the loot's buried."

"What if it floods down here?" Beck asked with a worried frown. "It sometimes does in these ravines, doesn't it?"

"The money's inside those canvas bags, and they're wrapped up in my slicker," McCoy pointed out. "That ought to protect it even if a little water seeps down there."

"Anyway," Cortez added, "it's probably been two or three years since there's been enough rain in these parts to flood. Chances are it'll be just as dry when we come back to get the money as it is now. We won't wait too long, will we, Boss?"

"Six months," McCoy said. "Maybe a year. No more than that." He gestured toward the hole. "Now fill it up, like you did with that water hole back yonder, and roll the boulder back into place."

As Cortez and Beck got to work, McCoy eased around to the other side of the pool. His hand rested lightly on the butt of his gun. He waited until the other two men had finished filling in the hole and then rolled the boulder into its original position, grunting with effort as they did so, before he slipped the Colt out of its holster.

Cortez and Beck stepped away from the rock. Beck brushed his hands together, obviously satisfied with a job well done. He died that way, as McCoy shot him in the back of the head. The impact of the slug threw him forward and draped him over the boulder that marked the bank loot's hiding place.

Cortez tried to whirl around at the sound of the shot, but he wasn't fast enough. McCoy shot him while Cortez's gun was only halfway out of the holster. The weapon fell the rest of the way out as Cortez toppled onto the ground next to the pool.

McCoy kept his gun trained on them for a long moment, but neither man moved. They never should have trusted him, McCoy thought. No matter what had happened in the past, once a man started double-crossing his friends, it got easier every time. He had discovered that as soon as he realized not splitting the money at all was even better than divvying it up three ways.

He walked around the pool and checked Cortez first. The way Beck's blood and brains had splattered all over that boulder, McCoy was pretty sure he was dead. So was Cortez. McCoy took hold of Beck's shirt and rolled him off the rock, let him flop limply to the ground. The bullet had made a mess of Beck's face when it came out.

He holstered his gun and dragged both bodies to the far side of the clearing, well away from the pool. He might be a thief and murderer, but he didn't want to foul this water hole. He would want to drink from it again when he came back in a year or so to recover the money. By then, there wouldn't be much left of Cortez and Beck except a couple of dried husks that had once been human. Less than that if any coyotes ever ventured in here. Scavengers would scatter the bones.

McCoy had no doubt now that he would reach the border without any trouble. He even had extra canteens and extra horses. And he was confident that none of the posse from Tucson had attempted to follow him through Ambush Valley, not with the reputation the place had as a death trap.

That was exactly what it had turned out to be for everyone in the gang except him, he thought with a wry smile. He was still smiling a few minutes later as he rode away without looking back, following the ravine that the luckless Cortez had told him would lead him out of the valley.

McCoy still had plenty of water, but he was thirsty for something else as he came out of the desert later that afternoon. The little border settlement of Hinkley shimmered into existence out of the waves of heat radiating from the ground, and at first McCoy wasn't sure it was real. Then he heard the braying of a donkey and knew that it was.

Hinkley consisted of a single street with a church at one end, a public well at the other, and a couple of dozen shacks and businesses in between, most of them built of adobe. A big general store was the largest frame building in town. According to the sign on the front of it, the store was owned and operated by one Cyrus Hinkley, who had probably founded the town and named it after himself.

McCoy wasn't interested in the store at the moment, although he would stop there before he left the settlement and headed across the border into Mexico. For now, his attention was fixed on a squat adobe building with crudely painted letters spelling out CANTINA above its arched entrance. McCoy reined to a halt in front, dismounted, and tied the three horses to a ramshackle hitching post. They were the only horses there.

The shadows inside the cantina were a welcome relief from the heat. A couple of old Mexican men in sombreros and the loose white outfits of peasants sat at a table passing a bottle of pulque back and forth. The rest of the tables were empty. Planks laid across whiskey barrels on one side of the room formed a bar. A fat, sweating Mexican stood behind it. McCoy walked over to him and said, "*Cerveza, por favor, hombre*." He dropped a coin on the makeshift bar. "And I damn well hope that it's cold."

"There is nothing cold this side of the snow on the mountains far to the south of the border, Señor," the bartender replied. "But the *cerveza* is . . . less hot."

"I reckon that'll have to do."

The Mexican drew the beer from a keg, filling a mug that wasn't too smeared with fingerprints. He set it in front of McCoy, who lifted it and took a long, deep swallow. The stuff was bitter and watery, but at least it was a little cool and cut the dust that the desert crossing had left clogged in McCoy's throat.

The bartender leaned closer and lowered his voice. "You want a woman, Señor?" he asked in a conspiratorial tone.

It had been a long time since McCoy had enjoyed any female companionship, but he wasn't really tempted. He wanted to finish his business in Hinkley and get across the border. He considered it highly unlikely that any of those possemen from Tucson would stay on his trail this far, but there was no point in taking chances. So he shook his head and said, "*Gracias*, but no."

"Are you sure, Señor?" The bartender leered. "I got a young girl . . . my cousin . . . she is virgin. Innocent, just for you."

McCoy didn't believe that claim for a second. But he still shook his head. He lifted the mug to take another swallow of the beer.

Outside, one of his horses nickered.

McCoy frowned and turned his head. Nobody had better be messing with those animals. The money he'd brought with him from the bank job was still in his shirt, but there were supplies and extra rifles on the horses.

Not to mention the animals themselves. Greasers were natural-born horse thieves.

"I can get you *two* girls, Señor," the bartender said hurriedly. "Both virgins, I swear on my sainted mother."

McCoy turned away from the bar as one of the horses nickered again. He realized now that the bartender was trying to distract him, keep him occupied while some other pepper-belly stole his horses. He'd deal with the thief first, then come back and give that fat bartender something to really sweat about.

Before McCoy reached the door, a large figure appeared there, silhouetted by the late afternoon light. "You're the fella who came out of Ambush Valley," the man said as he stepped closer. McCoy had never seen him before. The stranger was big, craggy-faced, with sandy hair and mustache. Recognition flared in the man's deep-set eyes. "And I know you, too. Seen your face before. You're Cicero McCoy."

Alarm bells were clanging in McCoy's brain. This was a setup of some kind, a trap. But there was only one man between him and the door, and he was confident in his ability to shoot his way of this.

"I don't think we've ever crossed trails before, mister," McCoy said in a hard voice.

"No, we haven't. But I've seen your picture . . . on wanted posters."

Bounty hunter! The big stranger was a damned bounty hunter. Had to be.

McCoy reached for his gun.

The sound of a Winchester's lever being worked came from behind him. "Don't move, mister," a flinty voice ordered.

McCoy glanced over his shoulder. There was another one of the bastards! McCoy didn't know where he'd come from. He must have been hidden behind the bar someplace.

A rear door opened and several more men crowded into the cantina. The bartender crossed himself and then ducked out of the same door, getting out of the line of fire in case any shooting broke out.

The two old men sat at the table watching, their lizard-like dark eyes full of years and the sure knowledge that they didn't care anymore what happened to them. They had already lived out their allotted span, and now they just wanted to be entertained.

"Where's the money, Cicero?" the big, sandy-haired man drawled. "We looked in the saddlebags on all three horses, and it's not there. What did you do, hide it in Ambush Valley?"

Shock coursed through McCoy as the bounty hunter guessed correctly on the first try. McCoy didn't want to let the son of a bitch have the satisfaction of knowing that, though, so he didn't say anything.

"You're going to tell us," the big man said as he came closer. "Taking you back to Tucson is one thing, but I don't know if we'll get the whole reward if we don't bring the money with us."

McCoy tried a bluff, even though he knew it wouldn't do any good. "I don't know what you're talking about. You've got the wrong hombre, mister."

"I don't think so. We've been waiting for you. You're the only one who's showed up from the direction of Ambush Valley. And like I told you, I know who you are. That job in Tucson wasn't the first bank robbery you've pulled, McCoy."

McCoy couldn't take it anymore. He ran out of patience and his lip curled in an angry snarl. To be this close to escaping, this damned close . . .

"Go to hell," he said. "I'll never tell you anything."

Then he grabbed for his gun despite being surrounded. He'd rather force them to kill him than be taken back and thrown behind bars.

But before he could clear leather, the man with the rifle slammed the weapon's butt against the back of McCoy's head. Red starbursts exploded behind the outlaw's eyes. He was driven forward by the blow.

That brought him within reach of the sweeping punch that the big sandy-haired man threw. His fist crashed against McCoy's jaw. McCoy's gun slipped from his fingers and thudded to the floor. The room spun crazily around him and he felt himself falling. As he sprawled on the floor, he reached for the gun he had dropped, but a boot heel came down on his hand and ground it against the planks. McCoy screamed. Another kick smashed into his ribs and rolled him onto his side. A red-tinged darkness crept in from the edges of his vision, and he knew he was losing consciousness.

The last thing he was aware of before that darkness claimed him was the big bounty hunter saying, "Don't kill him. We still need him to tell us where that money's hidden."

That'll be the day, McCoy thought, and then he was gone.

Chapter 7

McCoy's lawyer, a stocky, red-faced man named Mitchell, probably hadn't been fully sober since the days when Geronimo had been terrorizing the Arizona Territory. He only took the case because the judge insisted that McCoy have legal representation instead of acting as his own lawyer. And because McCoy had had a couple of thousand dollars on him when he was captured, and the judge could order that part of that money to go to the lawyer as his fee.

As far as McCoy could figure, it didn't matter a damn whether he had a lawyer or not. What was there to say? He was guilty. He knew it, the judge knew it, the whole blasted town of Tucson knew it. Five people had died because of that bank robbery, most of whom McCoy had killed personally. By all rights, he ought to hang.

But he knew that wasn't going to happen.

Sure enough, the trial didn't take long. Folks testified that they had seen McCoy leading the bank robbers. The prosecutor entered the money into evidence. The jury filed out of the courtroom, filed back in a few minutes later, and rendered their verdict. Cicero McCoy was guilty as sin. Guilty of bank robbery and murder.

For which the judge sentenced him to twenty-five years at hard labor in the territorial prison at Yuma.

Yuma . . . a real hellhole. Men who went in there seldom came out again, no matter how long their sentences were. Yuma had a way of grinding its inmates down until there was nothing left of them.

McCoy's face showed no emotion as the verdict was read and the judge passed sentence on him. That was just about what he had expected. They couldn't hang him because he was the only one who knew where that money was. So they had to send him to prison in hopes that somewhere along the line they could force him to talk. Eighty grand was a fortune. It meant more than justice, which should have had McCoy swinging from the end of a hangrope.

As he was led out of the courtroom, McCoy's eyes met those of one of the spectators. One of the guards was talkative and had mentioned him to McCoy earlier. The hombre's name was Browning. He didn't look like much—a scrawny, fair-haired Eastern dude who hadn't been out in the sun enough in his life. But he owned the First Territorial Bank of Tucson, and as McCoy's bad luck would have it, he'd been in town when the robbery took place. Browning was the one who had put the ten-thousand-dollar reward on the head of the gang.

Without the prospect of collecting that big reward, Abner Hoyt and the rest of those damned bounty hunters wouldn't have come after them, McCoy knew. And if all he'd had to worry about was the posse led by Sheriff Lamar Fortson, he would have gotten away clean. He'd be down in Mexico right now, sipping tequila and fondling some eager, brown-skinned gal . . . instead of being led out of a hot, stuffy Tucson courtroom, shuffling along with leg irons locked around his ankles and shackles on his wrists.

But he could still grin, so that's what he did. He grinned right at Conrad Browning, and the message was clear.

I've got your money, you rich bastard. I know where it is and you'll never see it again, because no matter what you do to me, you can't make me talk.

McCoy laughed at the frustrated anger that darkened Browning's face. He was still laughing when the guards hustled him out and prodded him at gunpoint into a prison wagon. The barred door slammed shut and the vehicle lurched into motion. Several outriders fell in around it. McCoy gave a mocking wave to Conrad Browning as the young man stepped out onto the porch of the courthouse. McCoy waved, too, as the wagon rolled past a saloon and the group of bounty hunters who had captured him stepped out of the place to watch him go by. From the way they glared at him, McCoy knew that Browning had refused to pay the full reward. They had gone to all that time and trouble, and they hadn't even gotten the ten grand.

It was one hell of a good joke as far as McCoy was concerned. Almost as good as that sanctimonious judge thinking that he was actually going to stay in Yuma Prison. The stone walls and iron bars hadn't been made that could hold him.

Somehow, sooner or later, Cicero McCoy was going to escape.

He knew it in his bones.

Abner Hoyt looked across the desk in the borrowed office in the First Territorial Bank and said, "I can make him talk. I know it."

Conrad Browning didn't look convinced. "You had plenty of chances to do that on the way back here to Tucson with the prisoner, Mr. Hoyt, and yet McCoy never divulged where he hid the rest of that money."

"I was trying to take it easy on him," Hoyt said with a glare. "I didn't want to mark him up a lot, because I knew he'd have to come back here and stand trial. Might've looked bad."

Browning leaned back in the bank manager's chair, steepled his fingers in front of his face, and frowned. "No offense, Mr. Hoyt, but you don't strike me as the sort of man who would worry a great deal about appearances."

"I'm not," Hoyt growled, "but I didn't want my partners to get carried away and kill him, either. That way he'd never talk."

It had been a chore, too, convincing the Coleman brothers not to use the old Apache torture of cutting strips in a man's hide and peeling them off one by one on McCoy. They wanted that reward.

So did Hoyt, and he'd been mad as hell when Browning refused to pay the whole ten grand. Browning had ponied up a thousand for McCoy, but that was all. He said that he would pay the rest of the bounty when the money was recovered, but not before.

"What do you propose to do now?" Browning asked.

"I'm going to Yuma. McCoy just *thinks* he's gotten away from me."

Browning shook his head. "What can you do to him in prison? There'll be guards and other officials around. You can't—"

"The hell I can't," Hoyt broke in. "I never saw an official yet who couldn't be paid off."

"You're talking about a bribe."

Hoyt shrugged. "Call it an investment. Spend a thousand dollars or so paying off the warden and a few guards in order to find out where that eighty grand is."

Browning's frown came back. He said, "What you're talking about is illegal."

"Do you want your money back or not?"

"It's not *my* money. It's the bank's money. But yes, I want it back. You're damned right I do." Browning's head jerked in a nod as he made up his mind. "All right. We'll do like you suggest, Mr. Hoyt I'll even pay your expenses to travel to Yuma. But the effort had better pay dividends this time."

"Oh, it will," Hoyt said with complete confidence as he nodded and thought about the things he would do to Cicero McCoy. "It will."

The trip from Tucson to Yuma took several days in the prison wagon. McCoy was the only prisoner, which was fine with him. He'd never cared that much for company anyway. It was hot during the day, but at least the roof of the wagon gave him some shade. At night, though, the chilly wind blew through the bars on the sides of the wagon and he lay there shivering since he had no blanket or any other cover. There was a bucket in which he could relieve himself, but that was the only item inside the wagon. He couldn't stand up, either, because the roof wasn't high enough.

McCoy didn't waste his breath complaining. He knew it wouldn't do any good. He just sat there and endured the misery, knowing that it would be over sooner or later. Of course, once he got to Yuma, things would be even worse, he supposed. But at least there he could start making plans to escape, once he'd had a good look at the place.

The prison sat atop a hill that overlooked the town of Yuma. All around was ugly, rugged terrain scored by ravines and dotted with sandstone ridges and buttes, similar to Ambush Valley but not as inhospitable. The prison offices and guards' quarters were frame buildings that sat in front of the main compound. They were what McCoy saw first as the wagon trundled up the hill. Then, as the vehicle reached the top of the slope, the prison itself came into view. McCoy couldn't see anything except a high, whitewashed adobe wall with an arched entrance midway along it. The entrance was closed off by a huge wooden gate. The wall was even thicker around the gate, bulging out like a pus-filled blister.

The wagon came to a halt in front of one of the administration buildings. The prison authorities must have been waiting for McCoy to show up, because two men in sober suits emerged from the building, followed by three guards in dark blue woolen uniforms that had to be miserably hot and itchy in weather like this. No wonder the guards at Yuma had a reputation for brutality, McCoy thought.

One of the suited figures was short, fat, and balding, with a graying brown beard that jutted out from what was no doubt a double chin. The other man was younger and thinner, with spectacles that perched on his nose. He had a subservient air about him as he followed the fat man over to the wagon.

"I'm Warden Eli Townsend," the fat man said as he stared through the bars at the prisoner. "Welcome to Yuma Territorial Prison, McCoy."

"Don't reckon you'll mind if I don't say I'm glad to be here," McCoy drawled, summoning up a smile.

Warden Townsend's lips tightened petulantly. "You won't be so arrogant once you've been here for a while," he promised. "But if you follow the rules, you'll be treated humanely. I'm aware that Yuma has a . . . less-than-sterling reputation, shall we say. But we're fair and we ask nothing except that you cooperate and do as you're told. Do you understand that, McCoy?"

McCoy understood that he didn't give a damn what this fat little toad said about anything. But he just jerked his head in a curt nod. He was ready to get on with it, and didn't need a lot of jabber from some stinking warden.

Townsend looked up at the man driving the wagon and nodded. The man slapped the mules with the reins and got them moving again. "Remember what I told you, McCoy!" Townsend called after the vehicle as it circled the administration buildings and headed for the prison's main gate.

When it drew to a stop in front of the gate, one of the guards on horseback dismounted and used a big key to unlock the heavy padlock on the door at the rear of the wagon. Leaving the door closed, he backed away and leveled his rifle at McCoy. All the other guards took the same precaution. Half a dozen guns were pointed at him.

"Come on out, McCoy," the guard who had unlocked the door ordered.

McCoy pushed himself up from the filthy planks that formed the wagon bed and hobbled to the door, bent over because of the low roof. He pushed the door open and climbed down to the ground. His movements were awkward and unsteady, and as he straightened from his crouch, muscles that were stiff from being cramped up for days screamed in protest. He didn't allow that to show on his face, but kept his expression as stony as ever instead.

The big wooden door had a square, barred grate in it. Another guard peered through that opening, and then McCoy heard the sound of numerous bolts and bars being withdrawn. The door swung open. Four more guards

waited just inside it, each carrying a pistol. McCoy saw
that the entrance was an old-fashioned sally port like
something from a fairy-tale book with castles in it. The
wall here was a good twelve feet thick, with a passage cut
through it from the gate into the prison compound. At the
far end of the passage was a second door, this one made
of thick iron bars. It was closed and locked at the
moment. The inner door wouldn't be unlocked and
opened until the outer one was secure again. It was a
good setup, a double layer of security.

A rifle barrel prodded McCoy in the back. "Get in
there," one of the guards who had accompanied the
prison wagon growled.

Still stiff from his confinement, McCoy shuffled into
the sally port. "So long, you bank-robbing bastard," one
of the other guards called after him. McCoy didn't look
around to see which one it was.

The outer door shut with a crash. When all the bolts
had been thrown again, one of the blue-uniformed
guards took a key ring from his belt and unlocked the
inner, barred door. McCoy had already looked through
the bars and seen the long, low stone cell block inside the
compound. The walls around the outside were high and
steep, and their thick coating of whitewash would make
them too slick to climb. There were guard towers at each
corner of the compound, too, and McCoy had no doubt
sharpshooters were posted in each of those towers. If a
convict ever made it over the wall somehow, at least a
couple of riflemen would have a clear shot at him wherever he ran. There was no cover within two hundred
yards all around the prison. If there ever had been any,
it had been cleared away.

The guards took him to the cell block. The place actually had several wings, McCoy discovered as he was led

inside. It was laid out something like a maze, probably to confuse the inmates and make them less likely to attempt a breakout. Each cell had a thick wooden door with a tiny barred window in it.

The fact that the guards still had their guns told McCoy that the whole prison had been locked down for his arrival. The guards wouldn't have carried firearms in if the prisoners had been loose inside the compound, as they were sometimes. At those times, the guards would rely on the thick bludgeons they carried in loops on their belts to maintain their authority, as well as on the threat of the sharpshooters in the towers.

One of the guards unlocked a cell. As the door swung open, McCoy saw that the chamber inside was no bigger than eight feet by ten feet, and maybe not quite that big. A bunk with a thin mattress and one threadbare blanket was bolted to the wall. The ubiquitous bucket was there for his wastes. That was all.

"Inside."

McCoy held up his shackled wrists. "How about taking these off, and those damned leg irons, too?"

"Warden didn't say nothin' about takin' your chains off," the guard said. "When he's ready for 'em to be off, he'll let us know."

"You can't expect me to wear them from now on," McCoy objected. "They're already rubbing sores on my wrists and ankles."

"Well, now, ain't that too bad?" The guards all laughed. "Not as bad as bein' shot down by some damn snake-blooded, bank-robbin' killer like you, though."

"Go to hell," McCoy muttered as he shuffled into the cell.

"Why? So's I can visit you? Because that's where you are now, McCoy, whether you know it or not." The door slammed shut, and the lock fastened with an awful, metallic finality. "You're in hell."

The bastard wasn't telling McCoy anything he didn't already know. And for the first time he felt a thread of panic worming its way around inside him. What if he *couldn't* escape? What if he was doomed to spend the rest of his life here, however long that might be? One thing was for sure—he couldn't stand to be locked up for the full twenty-five years of his sentence. He would go stark raving mad long before that time was up.

McCoy took a deep breath and steeled himself. He sat down on the bunk and swung his legs onto it. The leg irons clanked as he straightened out and lay there staring at the stone ceiling. Not much light came in through the lone window in the door.

Would he ever see the light of day and feel the sun on his face again?

Once again he forced himself to take a deep breath. Think, Cicero, he ordered himself. There has to be a way out. Think.

And slowly, even though he had no idea yet how he would get out of here, his confidence began to return. He would escape because he had to. He had eighty thousand dollars waiting for him.

It was as simple as that.

Time dragged inside the walls of Yuma Territorial Prison. McCoy wasn't sure how many days had passed. Three, he thought, based on how many times the slot in the door had been opened and a tray with food and water had been thrust into the cell. The food was simple and there wasn't enough of it, but at least the bread wasn't moldy and he didn't see any worms in the meat. Could have been worse, he supposed. He still wore the shackles and the leg irons. Looked like they were going to be lifelong companions.

Then one day, footsteps came down the long aisle in the cell block when it didn't seem like it was time for a meal yet. They stopped outside his cell, and a key rattled in the lock. McCoy sat up and swung his legs off the bunk. He wasn't sure what was about to happen, but a sudden chill went through him as he realized that the odds were it wouldn't be good.

That big, sandy-haired bounty hunter, Abner Hoyt, stood there when the door opened. A couple of his men were with him—the Mexican and the one called Mantee, who looked more like a greaser than Escobar did. Hoyt smiled at McCoy, and it was one of the ugliest things McCoy had ever seen.

"Thought we'd come and pay you a visit, Cicero," Hoyt said.

"Where are the guards?"

Hoyt shook his head. "Not here. It's just the four of us."

"The warden—"

"Was only too happy to cooperate," Hoyt interrupted. "You saw him, Cicero. How do you think he reacted when we told him we wanted to talk to you alone?"

McCoy fought hard to keep his face and voice under control. "I think the slimy little bastard took the bribe you offered him and told you to do whatever you wanted."

Hoyt took a step into the cell, followed by his partners. "That's exactly right." The Mexican shut the door behind them. Hoyt went on. "He said it was all right if you screamed some, too." He chuckled. "They're used to it here."

Chapter 8

Conrad said, "So he still didn't talk." His voice had a flat, bitter finality to it.

"We pushed it far as we could without killing him," Hoyt said. He sounded as gloomy as Conrad did. "Escobar's a Mexican. He knows something about making a man talk. And Deke Mantee's worse than Joaquin is. He's got ice water in his veins." Hoyt shook his head. "If I didn't know better, I'd almost say that McCoy doesn't even know where that money is."

"But he *does* know. He has to. He went into Ambush Valley with it but didn't have it when you captured him in Hinkley."

Hoyt nodded. "You're not telling me anything I don't already know, Mr. Browning. McCoy knows damn good and well where the loot's hidden. Probably buried somewhere. I could see it in his eyes. Just a hint of a smirk. He thinks he's beaten us." Hoyt's voice hardened with anger. "Beaten *me*."

"It appears that he has." Conrad's tone was cool. He wasn't over his disappointment, but he was trying to move past it, trying to think of what to do next. The one thing he knew for certain was that he wasn't going to give up. The people who had deposited that money in his bank had put their faith in him. He wasn't going to let them down.

Hoyt sighed. "I can go back to Yuma and try again. Maybe it's just a matter of time before McCoy breaks."

Conrad shook his head and said, "I don't think so. I saw the man myself, during his trial and as he was being taken away. I think that no matter how long you torture him, he won't talk. He'll die before he gives us what we want."

"Then that's the end of it. He's the only one who came out of Ambush Valley. The rest of the gang has to be dead, somewhere in there. That means McCoy is the only man alive who knows where the loot is."

"Therefore we have to keep him alive if we want to have any hope of recovering the money." Conrad suddenly leaned back in his chair and smiled. "Maybe there *is* a way."

"You thought of something?"

"Perhaps. But it may take some time to arrange."

A short, humorless bark of laughter came from Hoyt. "McCoy's in Yuma Prison. He's not going anywhere. Time is the one thing we've got plenty of."

Conrad hadn't liked the idea of bribery and torture to begin with. He had learned over the years to be pragmatic when it came to business . . . but he couldn't help but wonder what his mother would have thought of the tactics he had tried—unsuccessfully—to use here. Vivian Browning had been hardheaded and determined when she needed to be, but Conrad had to believe that she would have drawn the line at torture. He wished now that he had, too. Even though Abner Hoyt hadn't gone into detail about what had been done to Cicero McCoy, Conrad would have a hard time forgetting the grisly scenarios his own imagination came up with. And in all likelihood, he knew, what had really happened was probably worse than anything his civilized Eastern mind could imagine.

So more torture was out of the question.

Deception and subterfuge, on the other hand . . .

Hoyt left the office in the bank after Conrad promised to remain in touch. The bounty hunter hadn't given up on the hope of earning the rest of that reward, and that was good because if Conrad was able to put the plan that had begun to form in his mind into motion, he would certainly need the assistance of Abner Hoyt and the rest of those bounty hunters.

First, though, he had to secure the assistance of someone else. Someone without whom the plan had no chance whatsoever of succeeding.

He left the office and returned to the hotel. Rebel was waiting in their room, and he saw the impatience on her face as soon as he came in. Growing up in the West, she had always lived an active life. Sitting around and doing nothing, staying in one place for too long, even as nice a place as this hotel, those things didn't agree with her.

"How much longer are we going to stay here, Conrad?" she asked.

He smiled. "You'll be glad to hear, darling, that we'll be leaving as soon as I can arrange things for us to travel."

"Thank God. Nothing against Tucson, but it's hot and dusty here. Are we going back to Boston?"

"Not just yet. There's somewhere else I have to go first. I think you'll like it there, though. It should be much cooler, and the scenery will be more picturesque."

She stood up and came over to him, a slight frown of suspicion on her pretty face. "Does this have something to do with the money that was stolen from the bank?"

"Well . . ." Conrad couldn't bring himself to lie to her. He had never been very good at that.

"Well, we can't be going to Yuma, since you said it was going to be cooler than here."

"We're going to Nevada," Conrad said.

Rebel's eyes widened. "Nevada?" she repeated. "That means . . ."

Conrad nodded. "That's right." He took a deep breath. "I'm going to see my father."

Things had been pretty quiet in Buckskin in the weeks since the attempted robbery of the Lucky Lizard payroll. Frank Morgan's duties as marshal had been confined to breaking up the occasional saloon fight between miners from the Lucky Lizard, the Alhambra, and the Crown Royal, which was the operation owned by the Browning Mining Syndicate. Each of the big mines employed several dozen men. Like cowboys who rode for the brand, miners tended to be loyal to their employers, too, and that loyalty led inevitably to rivalry, and rivalry combined with whiskey led to punches being thrown and chairs being busted over rock-hard skulls. But as long as nobody got hurt too bad and the combatants paid for the damage they caused, Frank didn't come down too hard on the brawlers. A night in jail and a small fine were punishment enough, especially when those things were usually accompanied by a hell of a hangover.

The only serious trouble had been a couple of instances when intense young men rode into town determined to make a reputation for themselves by gunning down the infamous gunfighter known as The Drifter. It didn't matter to them that Frank was trying to settle down and put all that behind him. They were determined to force a showdown, to make this old man who was past his prime hook and draw.

One of them, in trying to goad Frank into a fight, had gotten close enough for a swift blow from the marshal's iron-hard fist to knock him out. He had come to, disarmed and with an aching head, in one of the cells in Buckskin's small jail. Frank had given him a good talking to, and as a result the young man had decided that he didn't want to risk his life slapping leather against The Drifter.

The other youngster had been more experienced. He'd been in gunfights before. He had kept his distance, and nothing Frank said to him had done any good. In the end, he had lost his patience and yanked his iron first, leaving Frank no choice.

That young man now rested in Buckskin's boot hill, dead from the single shot Frank had fired. The bullet had gone right through the tag hanging down from the tobacco sack in the young man's shirt pocket. Frank hoped the hombre was at peace now . . . but that was sort of out of his hands.

So the way things had been going, Frank didn't really expect any trouble as he leaned against one of the porch posts in front of Leo Benjamin's general store and watched the stagecoach roll past. The coach was coming in on its regular run from Virginia City. Most of the time, the only passengers were traveling salesmen. Occasionally, someone looking for work in the mines arrived that way.

Catamount Jack was sitting on one of the porch steps,

whittling on a block of wood. As the stage went past, he let out a low whistle. "Did you see that, Marshal?" he asked.

"See what?" Frank responded. "The stagecoach?"

"The gal *inside* the stagecoach. I just caught a glimpse of her, but she looked like one o' the prettiest fillies I've seen in a long time."

Frank hadn't noticed a girl inside the red-and-yellow Concord coach, but the dust from the hooves of the team had blocked his vision to a certain extent. It didn't surprise him that Catamount Jack had noticed her; the old-timer had an eye for a pretty girl, you had to give him credit for that.

A cool, pleasant wind blew the dust away as the stagecoach stopped at the depot down the street. Frank straightened from his casual stance and looked in that direction. The shotgun guard hopped down from the driver's box and came around to open the coach door. A slender hombre in a brown tweed suit and a bowler hat climbed out. Something about him struck Frank as familiar, but he just figured the fella for a drummer who had come to Buckskin before.

But then the stranger turned back to the coach and helped a woman out, and as Frank saw her shapely, graceful form and shining blond hair, he knew her and knew why the man with her had seemed familiar, too.

"There she is," Catamount Jack said. "Weren't I right, Marshal? She's a real looker, ain't she?"

"That she is," Frank agreed. "She's also my daughter-in-law."

Jack's head jerked around in surprise. He looked up at Frank and repeated, "Your daughter-in-law? You mean that dude with her is your boy?"

"Yep," Frank said. "That's Conrad."

He walked toward the stagecoach station, taking his

time since Conrad and Rebel hadn't seemed to notice him yet. He wanted to get a good look at his son and the girl Conrad had married.

Frank had known when they met Rebel over in New Mexico Territory, during all that trouble about the railroad spur line Conrad was building, that she was the genuine article. Smart, tough, able to ride and shoot and fight . . . To be honest, Frank had thought that maybe Rebel Callahan was really too much woman for his son.

But the experiences of the past few years had forced Conrad to grow up some, so Frank wasn't too surprised when he heard that they had gotten married. He was a mite surprised that he hadn't been invited to the wedding, but he wasn't the sort to dwell on such things. Besides, the youngsters had gotten hitched in Boston, and Frank didn't care much for it or any other big town in the East. His one and only trip to Boston had been on a mission of vengeance, the same quest that had in the end brought him to Buckskin.

Now as he looked at Conrad and Rebel, he saw that both of them appeared to be healthy. Rebel was as beautiful as ever. Conrad didn't look particularly happy, though. He had a worried expression on his face as he turned toward Frank. When he spotted his father, a smile replaced the frown. That made Frank feel pretty good. There had been a time, not all that long ago, really, when Conrad Browning hated him.

"Frank," Conrad said as he stepped forward and extended his hand. "It's good to see you again."

The times when Conrad called him "Pa" or even "Father" were few and far between. Frank had learned to accept that, too. He gripped Conrad's hand and said, "It's mighty good to see you, too, son."

No harm in a little reminder every now and then, just so the boy didn't forget.

As Frank let go of Conrad's hand and turned toward his daughter-in-law, Rebel threw her arms around him in a big hug. "Frank, how are you?" she asked.

He patted her on the back. "I'm doing fine, I reckon. Better since you and Conrad are here."

Rebel stepped back and looked around. Buckskin was surrounded by thickly wooded hills, and not too far away were majestic, snowcapped peaks "It's beautiful here! Conrad and I should have come to visit you before now. I can see why you decided to settle down here."

"It's a pretty nice place," Frank agreed. He saw Diana Woodford standing on the boardwalk not far away. She had been walking along the street when she saw Rebel hugging him, Frank realized, and she had stopped to look at them with a slight frown on her pretty face. There was a certain similarity between the two young women. They were about the same age, and both were blond and very attractive. Frank couldn't tell if Diana was curious about the newcomers—or annoyed that the good-looking one had been giving him a hug. He was pretty sure she had realized that there would never be anything romantic between her and Frank, but that didn't mean she couldn't feel a mite jealous to see some other gal hugging him.

So he smiled at her, motioned her over, and said, "Diana, I want you to meet my son and daughter-in-law."

"Oh," Diana said. She put a smile on her face. "Of course."

Frank performed the introductions. Diana shook hands with both Conrad and Rebel.

"Diana's pa owns the Lucky Lizard Mine," Frank explained. "It was the first big strike in this area. Without

Tip, I don't reckon Buckskin would even exist. He's the mayor here, too, which makes him my boss."

Diana laughed and said, "I don't think any man is truly Frank Morgan's boss."

"I'd agree with that," Rebel said.

The driver came around the coach and said, "I expect you folks want your bags unloaded? You're gettin' off here, ain't you?"

"That's right," Conrad said. He looked around. "Is there a porter . . .?"

Frank suppressed the impulse to laugh. You could take the dude out of Boston, but you couldn't take Boston out of the dude, at least not all the time. He said, "I'll help you with the bags, Conrad. The hotel is just down the street. I'd ask you to stay with me, but my cabin's pretty small and anyway, I sleep in the back room at the marshal's office most of the time."

Catamount Jack had followed Frank down the street. He cleared his throat loudly now and said, "I'll give you a hand, Marshal . . . that is, if you'll introduce me to these here folks."

This time Frank did laugh. "Sorry, Jack," he said with a chuckle. "Conrad, Rebel, this is my deputy, Catamount Jack."

Conrad extended his hand. "I'm pleased to meet you, Mr. Jack. Catamount is a bit of an unusual first name, isn't it?"

"That ain't my first name," Jack said as he shook hands. "It's just what they call me."

"Come to think of it," Frank mused, "I'm not sure I've ever heard your last name, Jack."

"Been so long since I used it, I sort of disremember. It don't matter, no how. Let's get them bags out o' the boot and take 'em down to the hotel."

By the time the teams were changed and the stage-coach rolled out of Buckskin, Conrad and Rebel were registered at the hotel and their bags had been taken up to their room on the second floor. Conrad suggested, "Frank, why don't we go somewhere and have a drink?"

Something about the young man's tone made suspicion stir inside Frank. He recalled the worried expression he had seen on Conrad's face earlier. He couldn't stop a hard edge from creeping into his voice as he said, "You didn't come here just to pay a visit to your old pa, did you, Conrad?"

Conrad and Rebel glanced at each other, and Conrad said, "I'd really rather discuss this somewhere private, over a drink."

"You know I'm not much of one for whiskey. Or secrets, either."

Rebel said, "I'm sorry, Frank. We should have come to see you before now. And we should have made sure that you were at our wedding. It's just that we didn't know exactly where you were at the time. . . ."

He had been down in Arizona Territory, in the Mogollon Rim country, trying not to get his damn fool head shot off in a range war, Frank recalled.

"Anyway," Conrad said, "*you* didn't come to see *us* when you were in Boston last year."

Frank grunted. "Know about that, do you?"

"I keep my ear to the ground. I know what happened to Charles Dutton."

Dutton was the reason Frank had gone to Boston. Once he had been one of Vivian Browning's lawyers, before his treachery led to her death.

"You were in the same town with him, and you didn't do a damned thing about it," Frank said. He didn't like the anger he felt roiling around inside him, but he couldn't do anything about it. "The man was responsible for what happened to your mother."

"Yes, well, I'm not a gunman," Conrad said in a cool voice. "I knew you'd take care of the situation sooner or later. I didn't expect that it would bring you out here, but . . ." He shrugged. "At any rate, all that's in the past."

"And now you need my help again, don't you?" Frank guessed. He supposed he would have to resign himself to the fact that his son wasn't going to have much to do with him . . . except when Conrad needed help with something.

The kind of help that only a gunfighter could provide.

"Do you want to hear about it or not?" Conrad asked.

A grim smile appeared on Frank's face. "Might as well," he said. "Who do you need me to shoot this time?"

Chapter 9

They went to the marshal's office instead of one of the saloons. If Conrad wanted a drink, it could wait until after he'd explained what really brought him to Buckskin.

Frank listened in silence as Conrad told him about the bank robbery in Tucson and the eighty thousand dollars that had been taken from the First Territorial Bank.

"I know that's a lot of cash to have on hand," Conrad said. "There were a couple of payrolls in the vault, plus a shipment of cash from the reserve bank in Denver that would have been distributed to some of the smaller banks in the area . . . if that bastard McCoy hadn't waltzed off with it," he added bitterly.

Frank waited for Conrad to go on, and after a moment the younger man did so.

"Since I happened to be in town when the robbery took place, I immediately offered a sizable reward for the capture of the outlaws and the return of the money, of course. A man named Abner Hoyt was also in Tucson, along with some of his friends. They're bounty hunters." Conrad grimaced. "Probably not much better than the men they hunt, but I couldn't afford to be too particular about such things. The local sheriff organized a posse to go after the bank robbers, too, but by the time they got around to riding out, Hoyt and his friends were already on the trail. They followed McCoy and his gang to Ambush Valley."

Frank's expression had been pretty impassive so far, but that bit of information caused him to raise his eyebrows in surprise. "I've heard of the place," he said. "Supposed to be pretty much hell on earth."

"Quite possibly. Hoyt and his men caught up to the gang just before they reached the valley. They were able to shoot down a couple of the outlaws, but the rest of them reached the valley. Two of them fell back to fight a delaying action while McCoy and the others escaped into the valley."

Frank grunted. "Wonder how McCoy talked them into doing *that*."

"I have no idea. All I know is that the only member of the gang who emerged from the other end of Ambush Valley was Cicero McCoy. Hoyt caught him in a little town called Hinkley, right on the border between Arizona and Mexico."

"But he didn't have the money with him," Frank guessed.

Conrad shook his head. "No, he didn't. I don't know what happened in Ambush Valley—"

"I can make a pretty good guess," Frank broke in. "McCoy hid the loot from the bank, or more than likely had his men hide it. Then he killed them so he'd be the only one who knew where the money was."

Conrad's eyebrows rose. "Could any man be so treacherous as to do a thing like that?"

"We're talking about an outlaw," Frank pointed out.

"How many people did you say were killed in Tucson when McCoy and his gang hit the bank?"

"Five," Conrad replied, his face grim. "Including two men inside the bank and two men in the street, both shot down mercilessly by Cicero McCoy."

"There's your answer. I wouldn't put it past McCoy at all to double-cross his partners. Not with eighty grand at stake."

"I suppose you're right."

"What happened to McCoy after Hoyt caught him?"

"He was brought back to Tucson, put on trial for robbery and murder, convicted, and sentenced to twenty-five years in Yuma Prison."

"I suppose somebody tried to get him to tell where the money's hidden."

"Yes. Both before the trial . . . and after it."

Frank sat up straighter in the chair behind the marshal's desk. "You sent a man into the prison to question him?"

"Well . . . I wouldn't put it exactly that way. . . ."

Frank's jaw clenched. He came to his feet without really thinking about it and leaned forward to rest his fists on the scarred top of the desk. "You sent a man into Yuma Prison to *torture* McCoy."

"I won't mince words about it," Conrad snapped. "Abner Hoyt went to Yuma. He bribed the warden and some of the guards and tried to force McCoy to talk." The young man's narrow shoulders rose and fell in a shrug. "He failed."

"McCoy stood up to the torture, eh?"

"Evidently, he *really* wants to hang on to that money," Conrad said. "Although what earthly good he thinks it will do him, locked up for the next twenty-five years as he is—"

"You see, that's not where you're thinking the same way McCoy is," Frank pointed out. "He's not planning on spending that long in prison. Fact is, he probably started thinking about possible ways to bust out as soon as the door of his cell closed behind him. Maybe before that."

"And if he were to succeed in escaping, then he could return to Ambush Valley and retrieve the money."

"Exactly," Frank said. "Before he got caught, he probably planned to leave the loot cached for a year or so, until all the pursuit died down. A lot of outlaws will do that, especially if they're going to be holed up somewhere they think the money might not be safe."

"That was my thinking, too," Conrad said. "And that's why I'm here. Since things haven't worked out for McCoy as he planned, if he escapes, he'll head right for that money and get it as soon as he gets the chance. He won't want to risk being recaptured before he puts his hands on it."

"So what are you going to do?" Frank asked. Before Conrad could respond, he held up a hand and went on. "No, wait a minute. Let me tell you what you're going to do. *You're going to let McCoy escape.*"

"That's right," Conrad said. "And you're going to escape with him."

The way Frank saw it, there was one thing wrong with Conrad's plan.

He wasn't in prison.

Nor did he intend on doing anything that would get him thrown behind bars, especially in a place like Yuma Territorial Prison. He might not spend the rest of his life here in Buckskin—it was too soon to say about that—but he didn't figure on setting out on a rampage of lawlessness, either.

"Of course not," Conrad said. "I'm aware that we haven't spent a great deal of time together, but I know you well enough to say that that thought never entered my mind, Frank."

"So you thought I'd just *pretend* to be an owlhoot."

"That would serve our purpose."

"*Your* purpose."

Conrad's expression hardened. "Allow me to remind you that you own part of that bank, too, Frank. It's your loss as much as it is mine."

Upon Vivian's death, ownership of her numerous business holdings had been split between Frank and Conrad. The difference was that Frank had never had any interest in helping to run the Browning empire, while Conrad took to it naturally. Frank had been content to leave it to his attorneys in Denver and San Francisco to see that everything was done fair and aboveboard, while he continued to live as he always had, with no outward sign that he was one of the richest men west of the Mississippi. Maybe one of the richest in the entire country, although not in the very top level like Carnegie, Mellon, J.P. Morgan, and hombres like that. The way he saw it, a man who had good friends, a good horse, and a good dog was just as well off as one with millions of dollars in the bank. Better, even.

Frank had all of those things, so if Conrad intended on making a financial appeal to him, the boy was out of luck. He could lose all of his share and go right on with his life.

"Take the eighty grand out of my half of the business," he said.

Conrad stared at him. "What?"

"I said, take the money out of my half of the business. Put it back in the bank. That way, the folks who put it in there to start with won't lose anything. Simple as that."

"No!" Conrad burst out. "McCoy—"

"McCoy's already behind bars where he belongs. You told me that yourself." Frank shook his head. "You roped me into that railroad business because of my ties to the company, Conrad, and lots of folks got killed."

"More would have died if you hadn't been there," Conrad pointed out. "Anyway, I didn't come to you for help this time because of the money."

"Then how come you're here?"

"Because it's not right for McCoy to get away with it!" Conrad leaped up from his chair as if he couldn't contain himself any longer and began to pace back and forth. "The man walked into my bank—our bank—and shot one of the tellers in the head. Murdered him for no reason at all, unless he was trying to get the attention of everyone else and show them that he meant business. That man had a wife and a young child, Frank. Then someone in the gang shot the bank manager. Then, outside in the street, McCoy gunned down another man and his gang trampled a woman to death. A husband and wife, with a son who's now been left an orphan. The boy . . . the boy saw his own mother ridden down as if she were less than nothing!"

"McCoy's in prison, and the other members of the gang are dead," Frank pointed out, thinking about how Conrad had seen *his* mother killed by outlaws, too.

Conrad swung around toward him. "It's not enough! You said yourself that he's probably planning to escape."

"Doesn't mean he'll succeed in doing it," Frank said with a shrug.

"No, but if he does, I don't have any confidence in the

law being able to catch him again. If it wasn't for Hoyt and his friends, McCoy would be in Mexico by now, out of reach of justice." Conrad sighed. "Anyway, it doesn't really matter whether or not McCoy escapes. He already thinks that he's won, simply because he kept me from getting the money back. You didn't see the man, Frank. As they were leading him away to take him to prison, he grinned at me. He was practically gloating. The only way to beat him is to recover that money and show him that he can't . . . he can't . . ."

In a quiet voice, Frank said, "I know what you're trying to say, Conrad. You don't like the way outlaws ruin the lives of honest folks. Neither do I."

"Then you'll help me?"

Frank's eyes narrowed. "Are the authorities in Arizona really going along with this harebrained scheme?"

"The only one who has to go along with it is Eli Townsend. He's the warden at Yuma."

"You bribed him to let Hoyt torture McCoy. You figure you can bribe him to let me pretend to be a convict."

Conrad flushed. "I'm not proud of what I did. It was probably wrong. But by God, it would be wrong to let McCoy get away with what he's done, too!"

Frank looked across the desk at his son for a long moment, trying to decide what he wanted to do. He was a little surprised that he was actually considering going along with the crazy plan . . . but he liked the spirit that Conrad was showing. For once, it wasn't all about the money with Conrad. There was an element of, yes, personal vengeance in what the boy was proposing. Frank knew from experience that vengeance was seldom as satisfying as a fella thought it would be.

But sometimes there just wasn't anything else a man could do except try to set things right.

"How would this thing work?" he finally asked.

Conrad's face lit up. "You'll do it?"

"I didn't say that. Just tell me what you had in mind."

"All right." Conrad started pacing again. "You'll be put in the prison at Yuma as a convict. Not as Frank Morgan. We'll come up with a different identity for you, a false identity. Once you're there, you befriend McCoy and offer to help him escape in return for a share of the loot that you've heard about. That's not too far-fetched, is it? Surely every outlaw in this part of the country has heard about what happened."

"More than likely," Frank admitted. "What makes you think McCoy's going to take me on as a partner just like that?"

"Well, I don't know how you'd manage that. I suppose you'd have to get him in your debt some way. Then it would seem reasonable for you to suggest that the two of you should escape together."

"Reckon I'd have to figure out the details once I got in there." Frank rasped a thumbnail along his jawline as he frowned in thought. "Who all would know about this?"

"Warden Townsend, of course. And I suppose we'd have to let the guards in on it—"

Conrad stopped as Frank shook his head. "If the guards know that I'm not a real convict, McCoy will tumble to it, too. They wouldn't be able to fool him."

"But if the guards didn't know about it, they'd treat you like any other prisoner," Conrad said. "You might get hurt."

Frank chuckled. "You want me to bust out of prison and go on the dodge with one of the worst bank robbers and killers north of the Rio Grande, and you're worried about the guards. Let's say the trick works and McCoy and I *do* bust out. What's to stop him from double-crossing me just like he did the members of his gang? He might shoot me in the back the minute we're clear of the prison."

"Well . . . I was counting on you not letting him do anything like that. After all . . . you're Frank Morgan."

This time Frank had to put his head back and laugh out loud. When he was done, he said, "I'll give you another reason the guards can't know what's going on. If they did, they'd probably make it too easy for McCoy to escape. He'd get suspicious from that, too. The only way for this to work is if it's damned hard for me and McCoy to get out of there, as hard as it would be for anybody else to escape from Yuma."

"That's going to be dangerous, too."

Frank shrugged. "No way around it. But if everything goes like that . . . well, it's still a harebrained scheme, but it just might work. What happens after we're loose?"

"McCoy heads for Ambush Valley to recover the loot, you go with him, and Abner Hoyt and his men trail along behind to give you a hand if you need it. Once McCoy has the money, you take him prisoner and rendezvous with Hoyt." Conrad looked intently at his father. "Does this mean you'll do it, Frank?"

Another moment went by before Frank nodded. "Looks like I'm going to prison," he said.

Of all the damn fool stunts he had pulled in his life, this just might be the craziest, Frank Morgan thought as he swayed back and forth in the back of the prison wagon while it made its long, slow way up the hill toward the fortresslike stone and adobe compound at the top. The miserable heat sure as hell made him miss the cool breezes of the mountains in Nevada.

It had taken several days to reach Yuma by stagecoach and train. During that time Frank hadn't shaved, so now a heavy coating of dark beard stubble covered his cheeks and jaw. His hair was uncombed. He had what seemed to be a permanent scowl on his face, as if he were angry at the entire world.

In other words, he looked like most of the other convicts this wagon carried up the hill to Yuma Territorial Prison.

In fact, one of the two men in the back of the wagon could have almost been his brother, except that the man had coppery red hair. The third convict was bigger, with huge, brawny shoulders, long arms, and a bald, bullet-shaped head. As he rocked back and forth, he glowered at Frank and the other prisoner.

When the guards from the prison arrived at the Yuma city jail to pick up Frank, the other two prisoners were already in the wagon. They had been picked up at other places for transport to the prison. Frank didn't know their names or why they were being sent to Yuma. Conrad and Warden Townsend thought it would look more natural for Frank to arrive at the prison along with other convicts. They'd had to let the local marshal in on the plan, so they could use his jail, but the man had been sworn to secrecy and Frank didn't figure that he would want to cross Townsend, whose position as warden made him an important man in these parts. Other than Townsend and the marshal, nobody around here knew who Frank really was or what he was doing here. That was the way Frank wanted it, even though he realized it might cause him to be in even more danger.

Up in Buckskin, Frank had let Catamount Jack in on the plan. He felt like he owed that much to the old-timer, since he was counting on Jack to hold down the fort while he was gone. Jack was perfectly capable of keeping the peace in Buckskin for a while, and he had also agreed to look after Stormy and Goldy, Frank's horses, and the big wolflike cur called Dog. Frank wouldn't have minded having Dog with him, since the shaggy varmint had fought side by side with him many times in the past, but he couldn't very well take an animal to prison with him.

Tip Woodford and many of the other citizens hadn't been happy about Frank taking a leave of absence from his duties as marshal, but when Frank explained that he had some important personal business to take care of, they had grudgingly gone along with the idea. They knew it had something to do with Frank's son, Conrad Browning, but they didn't pry . . . although Frank had been able to tell that Diana Woodford was dying to do so.

Rebel knew what was going on, of course, and she wasn't happy about it, either. In fact, she had tried to talk Frank and Conrad out of it, to no avail. "All right," she had said as she hugged her father-in-law good-bye, "but if you go and get your damn fool head shot off, don't expect me to cry about it."

"I don't," Frank had told her with a smile. "I expect you'd go after the son of a buck who shot me and try to even the score."

Conrad had looked horrified at that comment. "For God's sake, Frank, don't give her any ideas!"

They were both far behind him now. Conrad had returned to Tucson to set up the rest of the plan with Abner Hoyt. Frank had never met the man, but he vaguely recalled hearing Hoyt's name before. He knew the bounty hunter by reputation, and it was a tough, ruthless one.

He came out of his reverie as he realized that somebody was talking to him. Looking across the wagon in the stifling heat, he saw the big, bald-headed convict glaring at him. "Yeah, you, mister," the man said. "What the hell's wrong with you? You deaf?"

Frank shook his head. "Nope. My mind was just somewhere else, I reckon."

The red-haired man laughed. "I wish my body was somewhere else. Damn near anywhere else except halfway up the hill to Yuma Prison." He extended his shackled hands toward Frank. "Name's Nash. Jim Nash."

Frank shook hands with Nash as best he could, since his wrists were shackled, too. "Fred Morton." The initials were the same, and the name wasn't too far from his own.

The bald-headed man didn't offer to introduce himself. Nash laughed and said, "Don't mind Jessup over there. He's just got a natural-born hate for everything that lives and breathes. Ain't that right, Jessup?"

"Keep runnin' your mouth and I'll show you how much I hate you, Nash," Jessup said.

"Yeah, he's so full of hate he strangled his own wife and kids, then burned down their house around them. You wouldn't think that a son of a bitch as ugly as him would even *have* a wife and kids, would you?"

An animal-like growl came from Jessup's throat. "That does it, you carrot-topped bastard!" He launched himself from the other side of the wagon, his gorillalike arms outstretched as if he meant to grab Nash by the neck and choke the life out of him.

Somehow, though, he crashed into Frank instead. The close quarters in the prison wagon weren't big enough for a brawl. Jessup's massive weight bore Frank to the floor of the wagon like a mountain falling on him, and suddenly the man's sausagelike fingers were around Frank's neck in a killing frenzy.

Chapter 10

The violence was so sudden, so unexpected, so shocking, that Frank had had no time to prepare for it, either mentally or physically. From here on out, as long as he was in prison, he needed to remember that trouble could come at him any time, from any direction, with no warning whatsoever. Keeping that in mind might just save his life.

Assuming, of course, that he lived through this little ruckus.

With Jessup's weight pinning him to the floor of the wagon, he wouldn't have been able to breathe even if the monstrous bastard's hands hadn't been wrapped around his throat. A red haze was already beginning to form in front of his eyes. Frank was vaguely aware of shouted curses and orders from the guards on horseback around the wagon. The vehicle lurched to a halt. The guards would pull Jessup off him.

But Frank figured he would be dead by the time they got the rear door unlocked and climbed in there. If anybody was going to save his life, it would have to be him.

Just like always.

He brought a knee up, aiming it at Jessup's groin, but the big man was expecting that. He twisted aside and took the blow on his thigh. His ugly face was made even more hideous by the vicious leer that was plastered on it as he looked down at Frank from a distance of only a few inches.

When Jessup twisted away from Frank's knee, that had shifted his weight just enough so that Frank could get his right arm free—just as Frank had planned. There was enough play in the shackle chain so that his hand could shoot up and grab Jessup's right ear. He hung on for dear life and twisted as hard as he could. He was willing to tear the ear right off Jessup's head if it came to that.

Jessup howled in pain and jerked his head back, but Frank didn't release his grip. Jessup's movement just put more agonizing pressure on his ear. He had to let go of Frank's neck in order to grab Frank's wrist and try to pry his fingers free from the ear, which was now bleeding where it was torn partially loose.

Frank's left hand was free now. Because of the shackles he brought the fist up in a necessarily short but still powerful blow that landed solidly on Jessup's jaw. That jaw was built like an anvil, and that was about what it felt like when Frank hit it.

He punched again and again, though, as he continued to tear at Jessup's left ear. Finally, he had to let go or Jessup would have broken his wrist. Frank couldn't afford to have that happen, especially to his gun hand. Jessup snorted and bellowed and shook his head like a maddened bull. Droplets of blood from the injured ear sprayed through the air like crimson rain.

Frank knew he wasn't doing much good punching Jessup in the jaw. All the bones in his hand would break before he did much damage to the big man. But those blows, along with the excruciating pain from his ear, distracted Jessup enough so that when Frank tried again to drive his knee into Jessup's groin, this time it landed with brutal effectiveness. Jessup screamed and doubled over as best he could in the tight confines of the crowded prison wagon.

Frank had always been stronger than his compact build suggested. He grabbed Jessup by the shoulders and shoved him backward. He put all of his considerable strength behind the pile-driving move and rammed Jessup's head against the iron bars that formed the walls of the enclosed wagon bed. Because of the shape of Jessup's head, his skull went halfway through the bars before the ears stopped it. Jessup shrieked and convulsed as the left ear tore again. It was still attached to his head, but more than half of it had been ripped loose.

Frank heard the clanging of the door being thrown open, and the next second something crashed against his head. He was driven to the planks. Strong hands grabbed him and pulled him away from Jessup. He flew through the air and then slammed down on his back. The sun stabbed into his eyes. He was outside the wagon, lying on the rocky hillside. A particularly sharp-edged stone gouged painfully into his back. One of the guards stood over him, rifle lifted and poised to strike a blow. "Settle down or I'll bust your skull wide open with the butt of this Winchester!" the man ordered.

Frank's eyes flicked toward the wagon. The other guards ringed it, all of them with their rifles leveled at Nash and Jessup in case either of the convicts made an attempt to escape.

Frank was breathing hard. His pulse hammered in his head like the pounding of a drum. He was too old for fights like this. When he had gulped down some air, he asked the guard, "What was I . . . supposed to do? Just let that big ape Jessup . . . choke me to death?"

One of the other guards said to the man standing over Frank, "He's right, Chet. I saw when the fight started. Nash said something to Jessup, and then Jessup jumped Morton there. I couldn't tell which one of 'em he was really goin' for, but once he got his hands on Morton, he didn't care. He was gonna kill him."

"You blasted fool!" the guard called Chet snapped. "Nash and Jessup are partners! Jessup wouldn't have tried to kill him."

Frank sat up and gave Nash a hard look. The redhead shrugged and said, "We figured we'd see what sort of stuff you're made of, Morton." He grunted. "Never figured you'd nearly rip one of Jessup's ears clean off, though."

"It was all a setup," Frank said. "That business about Jessup killing his family—"

"Is that what he told you?" Chet interrupted in a disgusted tone. "Hell, Nash and Jessup have held up stagecoaches and rustled cattle and worked as hired killers all over Arizona Territory and probably other places, too. Neither of them ever even had a family, as far as I know. The law finally caught up to them and sentenced them to life in prison." Chet nodded toward the top of the hill. "Yuma Prison."

Frank felt as disgusted as Chet sounded. Nash and Jessup had been playing a rough game with him. Jessup probably wouldn't have killed him. But Frank hadn't had any way of knowing that.

"All right if I get up?" he asked.

Chet regarded him suspiciously. "You gonna cause any more trouble?"

"I didn't cause *this* trouble. I just defended myself."

"All right, Morton. Back in the wagon."

Nash had helped Jessup work his head free of the bars. The big man was sitting up now, holding one hand over his injured ear and cradling his throbbing privates with the other. Blood from his ripped ear coated the left side of his head and neck. His deep-set eyes never left Frank.

"You want me to get back in there with *them*?"

"They won't try anything else," Chet said. "Because if they do, I'll shoot them. They won't ever be leaving Yuma alive, anyway. You reckon anybody will care if we have to dig two more holes in the prison graveyard now or later?"

Frank knew the words were directed as much at Nash and Jessup as they were at him. He climbed wearily to his feet and walked over to the wagon under the watchful eyes of the guards. When he climbed into the vehicle, he hunkered on his heels in a rear corner, as far away from the two convicts as he could get. If either of them made another try for him, he was going to see them coming this time.

Nash and Jessup just sat there, though, as the door at the back of the wagon was closed and padlocked again. The vehicle lurched into motion again and continued its slow journey up the hill toward the prison.

As the wagon circled around what appeared to be several administration buildings and barracks, Nash finally spoke up, saying, "No hard feelin's, eh, Morton? We had to find out what sort of hombre they were puttin' us in there with. We know now that you're plenty tough. Might be you'd want a couple of partners like us in there."

"I'm not looking for partners," Frank bit off.

"Just want to do your time and get out, eh?" Nash laughed. "I don't know how much you know about Yuma, friend. Once you go in, chances are you won't ever come out."

Chet had mounted up along with the other guards. Now he edged his horse closer to the wagon and leaned over a little in the saddle to say, "You're wastin' your breath, Nash. Morton knows he won't get out. He's a lifer, like the two of you. Killed a sheriff and four deputies, up in the Mogollon Rim country, when they caught him with a running iron."

That was the story Warden Townsend had concocted, and the legal documents he'd had drawn up reflected it. Frank had been to the Mogollon Rim country several times and knew it well, so no one would be able to trip him up on matters of geography or anything like that. He hoped that his appearance was different enough so that if there was anyone inside the prison who had run into him up there, they wouldn't recognize him.

It wouldn't do for "Fred Morton," the vicious killer of four lawmen, to be revealed as Frank Morgan, the notorious gunfighter known as The Drifter, currently employed as the marshal of Buckskin, Nevada.

With luck it wouldn't come to that. Frank kept his face stonily vacant as the wagon drew to a stop in front of the prison's main gate.

Warden Eli Townsend was waiting there. Frank had met him several days earlier. The fat, bearded official looked at him as if he'd never seen Frank before. Then Townsend's gaze moved over to Nash and Jessup, and the warden was genuinely shocked as he saw the blood on the big, bald-headed man.

"Chet!" Townsend barked. "What the hell happened here?"

Chet, who was apparently the leader of the guard detail, said, "Jessup and Morton got in a little scuffle down the hill, Warden. Jessup, show the warden your ear."

Townsend's breath hissed between his teeth in surprise

as Jessup lifted his hand away from the mutilated ear. "He'll have to have medical attention for that," Townsend said. "I'll have the cell block guards take him to the infirmary." He looked over at Frank. "You did that, Morton?"

Frank just stared straight ahead and didn't acknowledge the warden's question either way. That was the way he was going to play this—hard as nails. As harrowing as the fight with Jessup had been, Frank might be able to turn the incident to his advantage. He knew that the story of what had happened would make its way through the prison in no time. That was the way things worked behind bars. By tonight, everybody in there would know that Fred Morton was a tough, ruthless hombre who was dangerous to cross.

Just the sort of man, in other words, who might make a good compadre for somebody like Cicero McCoy. . . .

"Open the sally port and get them inside," Townsend ordered. As the guards covered them, Frank, Nash, and Jessup climbed out of the wagon. While they were doing that, the heavy wooden outer door was swung open. The three of them were herded into the entrance passage at gunpoint, where the cell block guards took over. When the outer door had been closed and locked again, the inner, barred door was opened. The three prisoners walked in . . .

And with a harsh clang, the inner gate slammed shut behind them.

It was at that moment that the knowledge of his situation finally, completely sunk in on Frank Morgan.

He was in prison. And no one inside these walls—not the guards, and not the convicts—none of the men with whom he would be spending his days had the slightest idea that he didn't truly belong here.

* * *

The walls of the eight-by-ten cell were bare rock, as was the floor. A man could chisel away at those rocks for twenty years, provided that he had something to chisel with, and still not get very far. The ceiling was made of beams that were a foot thick. The iron bars along the front of the cell were set in holes drilled into the rock itself. Nothing short of dynamite would budge them, and Frank wasn't sure if even that would do the job. The only way in or out of the cell was the barred door, and it was not only locked, but chains were wrapped around it also and secured with as heavy a padlock as Frank had ever seen.

So he and McCoy wouldn't be escaping from their cells, Frank decided. When they made their break, it would have to be while they were outside. Surely the convicts were taken out for work, or at least for some exercise and fresh air. Frank would have to bide his time.

In fact, there was no limit on how long this job could last, but as a practical matter, Frank didn't want to spend any more time behind bars than he had to. He had been a drifter for most of his life, hence the nickname that followed him. Being locked up rankled his fiddle-footed nature.

He wasn't sure how long he'd been sitting on the hard bunk in the cell when he heard footsteps coming along the passageway. An hour or so, Frank guessed, but that might be wrong. He was already beginning to realize that time passed differently inside these stone walls.

His cell was at the very end of one of the prison's wings, so there was no cell to his right. The chamber across the corridor was empty at the moment. He wondered if that was by design.

He could tell by the footsteps that several men were headed his way. When they came into view, he saw Warden Eli Townsend, accompanied by a couple of guards. Frank didn't move. He continued sitting on the bunk, staring stonily ahead.

"When the warden comes to see you, you get on your feet, damn it!" one of the guards lashed out. "Show some respect or you'll regret it, mister."

"What are you going to do?" Frank asked, tight-lipped. "Put me in jail?"

"You'll get a taste of the Dark Cell if you keep that up," the guard raged. Frank guessed that the Dark Cell was Yuma's version of what was called in some prisons The Hole. A cramped, lightless chamber, possibly even underground, where convicts were placed as punishment for their infractions of the prison rules. "A taste? Hell, you'll *live* in it!"

Townsend raised a hand to silence the guard. "You two can go back to your stations and leave me to have a word with Morton," he said.

"You sure about that, Warden?" the other guard asked worriedly.

"Of course. He can't get out, and I don't intend to stand close enough to the bars so that he can reach me."

Frank frowned. He wasn't sure this was a good idea. Townsend didn't need to treat him any differently than any other prisoner. That could just lead to suspicion. And even though the cell across the way was empty, the ones to the left weren't, and the men in them would be able to hear anything Townsend said. The warden couldn't be foolish enough to give away the plan already, could he?

Although reluctant to do it, the guards left Townsend there. Their steps receded down the corridor. Townsend put his hands in his pockets and rocked back and forth on the balls of his feet. It was dim and shadowy in the passageway, since the only light came from the door at the far end of the cell block. Frank couldn't read the expression on Townsend's face.

But the icy scorn in the warden's voice was easy to hear. "Listen to me, Morton," he said, and his use of the phony name told Frank that Townsend was still playing a part. Frank was grateful for that, at least.

Townsend went on. "I know you probably think you're a dangerous man because you killed that sheriff and his deputies. But you should know that things are different now. You're in our power. We hold the reins. And I'm making it my personal responsibility to see to it that your stay here is as miserable as possible. Do you understand me, Morton?"

Frank didn't say anything. He just sneered and maintained the pose of his own.

Townsend roared, "I said, do you understand me, damn your murdering soul! If you want to go to the Dark Cell right now, I'll send you there! It's already justified, considering what you did to Conner Jessup on the way up here."

So that was what Townsend was doing, Frank thought— helping to spread the word that the new inmate Fred Morton was a very dangerous man. That might be overdoing it a bit, but Frank supposed it wouldn't hurt anything.

"I understand you," he answered in a clipped, hostile tone. He might have to spend some time in the Dark Cell before he got out of here, just to make things look real, but he wanted to postpone that until he grew more accustomed to prison life. Just being locked up in a regular cell was hard enough right now.

"Good. You'll lose all that arrogance sooner or later,

Morton, or else it will kill you. Because I intend to make an example of you, you murderer. Remember that."

Townsend turned away, but as he did so, a flick of his wrist sent a small, folded piece of paper sailing between the bars and into Frank's cell. It landed silently on the stone floor. Because Townsend had shielded the move with his body, it would not have been visible to any of the other convicts in adjacent cells.

Frank waited until the warden had stalked away before he reached down and picked up the paper. The door at the far end of the cell block clanged shut behind Townsend as Frank unfolded the note. He stood up and moved closer to the bars, angling the paper to catch what little light there was so he could read it. The penciled words on it were printed in a precise hand.

You will be placed on work detail after a week. McCoy will be on the same detail.

That was all the note said, but at least Frank knew where things stood now. He had to wait a week before he would have the chance to make Cicero McCoy's acquaintance. He supposed that was all right, since it would make things look less suspicious.

But as he looked around the bare, stark cell that was going to be his home for the time being, Frank Morgan thought that this was going to be a *long* week. Yes, sir, one hell of a long week.

Chapter 11

Frank was right about that. The days passed with agonizing slowness, and the nights were worse. When the utter darkness closed in, unrelieved even by the faintest glow of starlight, the temptation to madness crept in with it. Frank spent hours pacing back and forth in his cell until it seemed that he should have worn a path in the stone floor. In his mind he was riding the high country, with the big Appaloosa Stormy underneath him and Dog trotting alongside, surrounded by snowcapped peaks with a vast blue cathedral of sky arching overhead, the air crisp and cool and clean in his lungs.

That was just a fantasy, of course. The reality was that he was locked up in a cramped stone cell, behind iron bars, and the air was hot and foul with the stench of human waste and sweat that permeated this place.

But the darkness faded each morning and the days dragged by, and the time passed as time will, impervious to mankind's efforts to slow it down or speed it up. Frank had no mirror in which to look at himself, but he figured that he was pretty haggard and hollow-eyed when the guards finally came to get him one morning. They were armed with sawed-off shotguns, terrible weapons that could literally blow a man into bloody, quivering pieces at close range. That was the only way sawed-offs were any good; they were grossly inaccurate at any distance over a few feet.

"Come on, Morton," one of the guards said. "Time for you to start earnin' your keep around here."

So far Frank's "keep" had consisted of a hunk of stale bread, beans, and occasionally some boiled beef twice a day. He didn't figure he'd have to work very hard to earn that. But he didn't say anything, just trudged sullenly ahead of the guards, shuffling his feet because of the leg irons they put on him as soon as he stepped out of the cell.

"If you try to make a run for it, you'll get a ball and chain for your trouble," another guard warned.

"And he ain't talkin' about a wife!" the first guard added with a chuckle. "Fact is, you'll be doin' good to ever see a woman again, Morton, let alone touch one. Think about that for a while, why don't you?"

Frank didn't have to think about it. But his mind went back involuntarily to the women he had known . . . Mercy, Vivian, Dixie, Roanne . . . A couple of them he had married, and those two were dead now, as if being wed to Frank Morgan carried a curse with it. Sometimes, during particularly dark nights of the soul, he had found himself wondering if that could be true. Unlike many gunfighters, he wasn't really a superstitious man by nature. . . .

But considering everything that had happened, it wasn't hard for him to reach a decision that he would never marry again. Any woman who got involved with him would just have to live with that, because he wouldn't lie about it.

You're getting ahead of yourself, old hoss, he thought with an inward smile. Like the guard said, he wouldn't even see a woman here in Yuma, let alone court one.

The little procession emerged from the cell block into sunlight that was blinding after all the time Frank had spent in darkness and near-darkness. To tell the truth, that desert sun likely would have been blinding anyway, no matter where he'd spent the past week.

They joined a group of convicts and guards that was forming up near one of the side walls of the prison compound. Most of the prisoners wore gray trousers and shirts of some coarsely woven material. A few, including Frank, still wore the clothes they'd had on when they were brought to Yuma. One of the guards had some of the gray uniforms with him. He tossed the clothes to the men who still wore their civilian duds and growled, "Put those on."

One of the prisoners asked, "How are we supposed to do that with these shackles and leg irons on?"

"They'll be taken off one wrist and one leg at a time," the guard explained. "Try anything funny and you'll be sorry, especially when you wake up and find yourself in the Dark Cell for three days."

Nobody tried anything, funny or otherwise. While Frank was waiting for his turn to change into the prison uniform, he tried to study the faces of the other convicts without appearing to do so. The note from Warden Townsend—which Frank had torn into tiny strips and dropped into his slops bucket—had said that Cicero McCoy would be in the same work detail as Frank. Although Frank had never seen a picture of the bank robber, Conrad had given him a very detailed description of McCoy. Now Frank had little trouble picking out the man from the other convicts. Many of the prisoners were rangy and rawboned, and several had lantern jaws. But only Cicero McCoy had that shock of prematurely white hair. The outlaw paid no attention to Frank or any of the other new prisoners.

The prison uniform was scratchy and didn't fit too well, but Frank figured that was the least of his worries at the moment. When he had the garb on and his shackles and leg irons were fastened back in place, a shovel was thrust into his hands and he was pointed toward a long trench that was being dug near the wall. He shuffled over to it, contriving to place himself near McCoy's position. He couldn't get right next to the bank robber, not without shouldering another man aside, and he didn't want to draw attention to himself by doing that. He watched what the other convicts were doing, and soon fell into the rhythm of the work.

Some of the men had shovels, others had picks. The ground was too hard and rocky to dig in normally. The men with picks had to break it up first, and then the ones wielding shovels moved in and scooped up the chunks out of the ditch, tossing them onto the area between the ditch and the wall.

Frank spoke under his breath to the man beside him. "What're we digging here? An escape tunnel?"

The man laughed. "Don't I wish, mister. No, this is a new shit ditch, I reckon you'd call it. The trusties who gather up the buckets from the cells dump 'em here, or they will when we're done with it, anyway. We have to dig a new one when the old one fills up, and they fill up pretty fast. You put a few hundred convicts in a place like this, one thing you're gonna have is a bunch o' shit."

Frank couldn't help but smile a little. The guards didn't seem to mind if the prisoners talked while they worked, as long as it didn't slow them down. Low-voiced conversations were going on all along the ditch. So he said, "My name's Fred Morton."

"Oh, I know who you are, Morton," the man said. "I reckon everybody in here knows who you are. You're the fella who pert' near tore an ear off that bruiser Jessup. You can call me Gideon."

"I'd say that I'm pleased to meet you, Gideon, but I'm not pleased about any of this."

Gideon laughed softly. "I know what you mean." After a moment, he went on. "Did you really kill five lawmen? You don't have to answer. The rule in here is, don't ask anything you're not ready to have thrown right back at you."

"I don't mind answering. Yeah, I killed that damn sheriff and his deputies. They caught me with a fire, a running iron, and some cows that didn't belong to me. What would you have done?"

"Well, I damned sure wouldn't have tried to shoot it out with five men. I ain't no gunman. But even if I lived through a fight like that, I'd have five murder charges hangin' over my head."

Frank shrugged. "Where I come from, they'll hang you for rustling just about as fast as they will for shooting somebody, even a lawman. I didn't figure I had a whole hell of a lot to lose."

"Been in trouble with the law before?"

"No. Never got caught like that before." Frank gave a low, bitter laugh. "Hell of a way to get started, wouldn't you say?"

One of the guards came along and barked, "Stop flappin' your gums and get busy, you two."

Frank and Gideon went to work with their shovels. McCoy was only a few paces away, leaning on the handle of his pick for the moment while the men with shovels cleaned out the section of ditch where he'd been breaking up the ground. He'd been close enough to hear everything Frank and Gideon had said, but didn't appear to be paying any attention to them.

Frank thought that was a pose. Most men in this situation would be interested in what was going on around them. And they'd be especially interested in newcomers, given the crushing boredom and loneliness of prison life. Frank figured that McCoy had taken note of every word.

Time passed faster out here, but not any more pleasantly. The sun scorched down on the convicts, baking them. Sweat soaked the gray uniforms, turning them black. And then, even worse, the men stopped sweating. When that happened, they were ordered to drop their picks and shovels and were marched over into the shade of one of the cell block buildings. They sat down and leaned against the stone wall, which seemed blessedly cool after being out in the sun all morning.

Trusties with water jugs passed among the work detail, giving drinks to the men and cautioning them not to guzzle down too much water. Some of the newcomers were too overwhelmed by thirst to pay heed to those warnings, and soon they were vomiting the water they had swallowed back up onto the dry, rocky ground.

Frank knew better. He took it easy, using a sip to moisten his lips and wash the dust out of his mouth before he spit it out. Then he swallowed a couple of sips and passed the jug along to Gideon, who sat beside him. McCoy was on the other side of the tall, lanky Gideon.

The break wasn't a long one. The men weren't given any food, just the water. Then they were put to work again.

When Frank trudged toward the ditch to pick up his shovel, this time he was able to hang back a little and then move forward so that he was between Gideon and

McCoy. Neither of the other convicts seemed to think that there was anything unusual about his actions. McCoy didn't even glance in Frank's direction as he started swinging his pick again, driving the sharp head into the earth, leaning on the handle to break up the ground, then pulling the pick free to start all over again.

The prisoners were too tired to talk now. They labored in sullen silence. Frank let a couple of hours go by before he grunted and said in McCoy's direction, "Is it this bad every day in here?"

For a moment he thought that McCoy wasn't going to reply or even acknowledge the comment, but then the bank robber said with a touch of sardonic humor, "This isn't as bad as usual."

"No?" Frank found that hard to believe. "Why not?"

"At least it's cloudy today."

Frank glanced up toward the sun, thinking that the heat must have made McCoy lose his mind. That was worrisome, because if McCoy was a lunatic, he might not be able to find that hidden loot again.

But to Frank's surprise, he saw that a thin, almost transparent puff of cloud had appeared in the sky. Even though it had floated in front of the sun, it didn't seem to be blocking many, if any, of the murderous rays. Frank realized then that McCoy was making a joke. He grinned and nodded to show that he understood.

It was a small thing, but it was a connection between him and McCoy.

It was a start.

The shit ditch, as Gideon called it, was finished in a couple of days. Frank worked with Gideon and McCoy both days, conversing with them until they both seemed comfortable with him. McCoy didn't talk much, but the garrulous Gideon made up for that.

Several times while they were working, Frank saw other groups of convicts being taken out of the prison through the sally port. "Where are they going?" he asked on one of those occasions.

"Outside work detail," Gideon explained. "Those boys maintain the stagecoach roads runnin' through these parts. Keep the ruts from gettin' too deep and rebuild the roads when they wash out."

"I wouldn't think that it rained enough around here to wash out a road."

"It don't rain often," Gideon said, "but when it does, it's a real toad-strangler. You ever ride on a stagecoach, Morton?"

"Plenty of times," Frank said.

"Bet you never wondered who kept the roads up, though, did you?"

Frank had to shake his head and admit that he hadn't.

"In a lot of places, it's convicts just like you and me who do the work." Gideon grinned. "Hell, I don't reckon this country could get along without its lawbreakers. We're doin' society a service by bein' a bunch o' jail-birds."

"You never did tell me what you did to get put in here, Gideon."

"Yeah, I guess I owe you that much, since I know what you done." A mournful expression came over Gideon's long face. "I killed a woman."

"Your wife?"

"Not hardly. I never got hitched. I was just a poor cowboy lookin' for a good time, so I stopped off in town to find me a whore. I found one, all right, but I made the mistake o' dozin' off after we'd done our business. Woke up to find that gal tryin' to steal my whole poke, not just what I'd paid her earlier."

"So you shot her?"

Gideon shook his head. "Lord, no. I didn't mean to kill her. I just grabbed her and shook her a mite, and she come out with a knife from somewhere and tried to stab me. I grabbed her wrist and we both fell down and that knife . . . well, it ended up planted right in her heart. Never my intention at all, but she was just as dead as if I'd meant to do it. The judge and jury didn't believe me, neither, so here I am, owin' the next fifteen years o' my life to the territory of Arizona. It ain't right, but what can you do?"

Frank just shook his head, indicating that he agreed about the futility of it all.

A few minutes later, Gideon asked for and received permission from the guards to go move his bowels. While he was gone, McCoy edged closer to Frank and said in a low voice, "Don't believe that line of bull Gideon was just handing you, Morton."

"What do you mean?" Frank asked, glad that McCoy was talking to him alone now, instead of just joining in the general conversation while Gideon was there.

"The way I heard it, it was no accident that Gideon killed that whore. Somebody who was still outside when it happened told me he took that knife to her on purpose. Cut her up real good with it, too. Said there was blood splattered all over the girl's room in that whorehouse, and they found Gideon sitting in the middle of it, laughing."

Frank thought about Gideon's easygoing manner and ready smile and found it difficult to believe the gossip that McCoy was telling him. And yet he was well aware that it was almost impossible to look at a

man and know what he was like inside. Some of the
most brutal-appearing men had the kindest, gentlest
natures, while others who seemed to radiate innocence
had nests of evil snakes where their brain and heart
should have been. Maybe McCoy was right about
Gideon, maybe he wasn't. It was hard to say.

But what was certain was that as far as the job that had
brought Frank here was concerned, it didn't matter a
damn one way or the other.

As the group was being taken back to the cell block
late that afternoon, Frank asked, "Now that this job is
finished, what will they have us doing next?"

"Not much telling," Gideon replied. "Maybe nothin'.
We might sit in our cells for a month or more before they
come up with somethin' for us to do again. There's a
heap o' convicts here, and not that much work."

"I can't sit in that damned cell," Frank said with a
growl in his voice. "I'll go crazy if I do. I'd rather be out
working on just about anything."

"I want on one of those road details myself," McCoy
said. "Anything to be outside the walls of this place." He
gave a short, humorless bark of laughter. "I don't reckon
that's going to happen, though."

"Why's that?" Frank asked.

"They've got good reasons for not letting me outside."

McCoy didn't offer any details, but Frank understood
what he meant. As long as he was the only one who
knew the hiding place of that stolen money, the authorities didn't want to take a chance on him escaping.

At least, that was the way it was as far as McCoy
knew. He had no idea what plans were really afoot.

Frank wondered if he could somehow get a message
to Warden Townsend. It would help matters if Townsend
assigned McCoy to one of those road details—and

Frank, too, of course. An escape could be made to look real if they were outside the prison. Hell, it would *be* real, Frank reflected. The guards wouldn't know any different, and if any shots were fired, it would sure enough be real bullets buzzing through the air around them.

If he could pull that off, Frank thought, then McCoy would have no idea that he was actually working for the law. It was still going to take some work before such a ploy was possible, though.

And if he could, he'd like to get McCoy to trust him even more before then. . . .

They entered the cell block and passed another group of convicts being taken the other way. Frank felt eyes on him and glanced in their direction. He spotted two familiar faces in the other group—redheaded Jim Nash and bald Conner Jessup. The brutish Jessup glared at him. A bandage still covered the big man's ear. Frank didn't know what the injury looked like under that dressing, but he would have been willing to bet that it wasn't pretty. Jessup mouthed something as he went by, and Frank had no trouble deciphering the words.

I'm gonna kill you. . . .

Frank kept his face expressionless, but he didn't really mind the threat.

In fact, he thought, there might even be a way to make it work to his advantage.

Chapter 12

Once a month, the prisoners who hadn't caused any trouble were allowed out of their cells to spend an afternoon in a large common area. An awning that jutted out from one of the buildings provided shade, and the men were given cigarette makings. They could sit in the shade, roll quirlies, and smoke, or they could walk around the common area. Those who had been confined and hadn't been on any work details for a while generally chose to stretch their legs.

Gideon explained all this to Frank as they were herded into the common area along with fifty or sixty other prisoners. It had been almost a week since the ditch was completed, and during that time Frank had been stuck in his cell, unable to talk to McCoy or make any other progress on his plan. The time had been deadly dull, but at least he'd had a chance to figure out how he wanted to proceed. He would need a little luck . . .

And he was about to get it, he saw as he and Gideon and the other men in their group walked out into the common area. Cicero McCoy was already there, sitting under the awning with his back against the wall of the building, a cigarette dangling from his lip.

On the other side of the large open space, about fifty yards away, Jim Nash and Conner Jessup strolled along, talking quietly to each other. The bandage was gone from Jessup's ear. Even at this distance, Frank could see that although the damage was healing, it had left an ugly scar and Jessup's ear would never really look right again. Of course, the man hadn't been any prize to look at to start with . . . but the mutilated ear didn't help matters any.

Frank and Gideon went over to join McCoy, who still had a packet of papers and a tobacco pouch. He offered the makin's to Frank first, who shook his head and said, "No, thanks." Gideon took the tobacco and papers and began rolling a cigarette. His fingers were deft and quick at the task. He set fire to his gasper with the quirly that McCoy was smoking. Another convict passing by took the pouch and papers and carried then down to another part of the shaded area. Nobody was going to fight over the makin's, because they didn't want even this once-a-month privilege taken away from them.

Frank leaned his back against the cool stone wall and gazed around. He saw at least ten blue-uniformed guards around the perimeter of the common area, keeping their eyes on the prisoners. The guards weren't carrying guns today, not with this many convicts loose, without even any leg irons or shackles. Instead, the guards carried stout wooden clubs, and they were all big, powerful men. No doubt they could shatter a skull with a single blow from one of the bludgeons. Of course, outnumbered by five to one as the guards were, the convicts *could* have overwhelmed them . . .

If not for the fact that the first man who made a threatening move toward a guard would get a bullet through the head from one of the marksmen in the towers, and they all knew it.

Gideon pulled deeply on his cigarette, making the tip glow a bright orange. He gave a satisfied "Ah . . ." as he blew the smoke back out.

"They watch us like hawks, don't they?" Frank said.

McCoy grunted. "What do you expect? The warden prides himself on the fact that hardly anybody has ever escaped from this place."

"But they *have* escaped, haven't they?"

McCoy nodded. "Yeah. But there's nowhere to run except desert and badlands. Townsend sends guards after the men who get away, and nine times out of ten they come back with bodies. Mostly it's the desert that kills the poor bastards." He shrugged. "At least that's what I've heard. I haven't been here all that long, but nobody's busted out since I got here so I don't know for sure."

"A man who knew his way around the desert might be able to make it, though," Frank said in a deliberately thoughtful voice.

"I've heard that it's been done," McCoy agreed. "It would be a long shot."

Frank grinned. "Hell, that's the best kind of shot. What fun is betting if you don't have anything to lose?"

McCoy looked over at him and said, "You're a real hardcase, aren't you, Morton? You thinking about trying to bust out of here?"

"Do you ever think about anything else?"

"Women," Gideon said. "All the damn time."

Frank and McCoy both chuckled at the wistful note in the lanky killer's voice.

Then Frank grew serious again as he saw that Nash and Jessup were approaching. The two outlaws had continued to make their circuit of the common area. They were going to pass by about ten feet in front of the spot where Frank, McCoy, and Gideon lounged.

Frank laughed and raised his voice. "Look at the ear on that one," he said. "You wouldn't think anything could make a bullet-headed bastard like that even uglier, but by God, I think I did it."

Jessup swung his head toward Frank and glared. Nash snapped, "Lay off, Morton. Don't try to start trouble with us."

"You two started the trouble with your damned game," Frank shot back. "As far as I'm concerned, Jessup got what he deserved. You're the one who got off easy, Nash. I should've ripped your ear off, too."

Jessup bunched his hamlike hands into fists, but Nash nudged his arm with an elbow. "Morton's just runnin' his mouth," Nash said. "Better move on. One of those guards is watchin' us pretty close."

Jessup kept walking, but he sent another murderous glare back over his shoulder at Frank as he and Nash continued on their way. Gideon let out a low whistle and said, "I don't know if I'd be baitin' that big son of a bitch like that if I was you, Fred. Jessup's half grizzly bear and half curly wolf, I reckon."

Frank shook his head. "He doesn't scare me. I've already whipped him once." He raised his voice, since Nash and Jessup were still within earshot. "Yeah, I whipped him good."

McCoy muttered, "You're a crazy bastard, you know that, Morton? Maybe you better go sit somewhere else. I don't need any trouble."

"No trouble," Frank said, sitting back and crossing his arms over his chest. "That big galoot just gets under my skin, is all."

He pretended not to watch Nash and Jessup as they circled the common area again, but really Frank was keeping an eye on them. As they approached for a second time, he saw Jessup muttering something and Nash making a heated response. Nash took hold of Jessup's arm, but the big man shook him off. He turned and strode into the shaded area.

Frank came to his feet, bristling with belligerence just as Jessup was. Behind him, Gideon muttered, "Uh-oh."

"What do you want, Jessup?" Frank demanded.

Jessup pointed a blunt finger at him. "You and me are gonna have it out one of these days, Morton. We're both gonna be in here for a long time—"

"The rest of our lives, if Arizona Territory gets its way," Frank drawled.

Jessup went on as if he hadn't been interrupted. "—and sooner or later I'll get my chance to settle the score with you. I'll never forget what you done to me."

Frank gave him a sneering grin. "I reckon not. You'll remember it every time you go to lay on that bad ear."

"I'll do more than give you a bad ear. I'll twist your head right off your shoulders, little man."

Frank shook his head. "You couldn't do it before, and you can't do it now or any other time. The only way you could beat me is if you and Nash and probably two or three of your friends ganged up on me. That's the kind of cowards you are."

Jessup stepped closer, his face reddening. "You son of a bitch. You wouldn't talk so big if you didn't have *your* friends with you."

"McCoy and Gideon don't have a damned thing to do with this," Frank said with a shake of his head. "If you start the ball, they'll stay out of it."

McCoy put in coolly, "That's right, Morton. We won't

take a hand if Nash doesn't. But maybe you better think about this, anyway. Jessup's mighty big."

"Yeah, but he's hollow inside," Frank said. "No guts. And no brains in his head, either. Reckon they all leaked out when I tore his ear half off."

He saw rage flare in Jessup's piggish eyes and knew that he had finally pushed the big man too far. It had taken damned long enough, he thought as Jessup rushed forward, swinging a sledgehammer fist. Nash made a grab for his sleeve but missed. Jessup was consumed by fury now, and he wasn't thinking about the guards or anything else except battering his enemy's face into a crimson ruin.

Frank hoped the sharpshooters didn't make a habit of killing prisoners who got into fights with each other, only the ones who threatened the guards. But it was a little too late to worry about that possibility now. . . .

Jessup was fast for a man of his massive size. But Frank Morgan had lived as long as he had because he possessed a rare combination of speed and instinct and reflex. He ducked under Jessup's sweeping blow and stepped in to smash a right and a left into the big man's belly. Hitting Jessup in the stomach wasn't quite as bad as punching that granitelike jaw, but his torso was overlaid with slabs of muscle and Frank could tell that his blows didn't do much good. While Jessup was still off balance, Frank stomped one of his feet as hard as he could.

Jessup yelled and hopped backward. That told Frank a lot. The bruiser had bad feet. That didn't really come as a surprise. Those feet had to carry around a lot of weight. And if the feet were bad, the knees might be, too.

Jessup recovered and came at him again, flailing another roundhouse punch. Frank moved with desperate speed, knowing that if one of those huge fists ever connected with all of Jessup's strength behind it, the fight would be over. As it was, the blow clipped the outside of Frank's shoulder and still had enough power to jolt him halfway around.

He turned the movement to his advantage, spinning away from another charge. As he did so, he saw Nash standing there tensely with his fists clenched and knew the redhead was thinking about jumping into the fight. McCoy and Gideon were on their feet now, though, and Nash had to be recalling what the bank robber had said about staying out of the fight as long as he did. Nash held back.

Frank heard guards yelling, too, and knew that he had only seconds before they would arrive and break up the fight. If it was over now, the guards might not do anything except throw him in the Dark Cell. They might not even do that. He could wind up back in his regular cell, locked up there for weeks. He couldn't take that chance.

He darted to the side again as Jessup lunged at him. The move put him to the giant's right. Frank leaned to his left, lifted his right foot, and drove the heel of his work shoe into the side of Jessup's knee as hard as he could. A Cajun gambler in New Orleans had taught him that move years ago, and while he hated fighting like a Frenchman, sometimes it worked.

This time it did. Frank could have sworn that he heard something ripping inside Jessup's leg. Then he couldn't hear anything except the big man's agonized screams as Jessup collapsed and started rolling around on the ground, clutching his ruined knee. He might never walk again and he sure as hell wouldn't ever walk right, and Frank might have felt a tad sorry about doing that to him . . . except for the fact that Jessup was a brutal son of a bitch who had murdered numerous people during his career as an outlaw and hired killer. Frank figured he had a little pain coming to him.

Besides, it would get Frank what he wanted, too.

He tried to bear that in mind as one of the guards hammered a club across his back and knocked him to the ground. Several more of the blue-uniformed men closed in around him and hit him again and again. He didn't fight back, just lay there and absorbed the punishment they were dishing out, even though doing so went against the grain for him. Through the legs of the swarming guards, he caught glimpses of McCoy and Gideon standing there and watching the beating with grim looks on their faces. But they didn't make a move to interfere, and Frank was glad of that. He didn't want any complications.

After a while, the guards had had enough. They stopped clubbing him and grabbed hold of him to drag him to his feet. Frank was only semiconscious as they hauled him out of the common area. He struggled to focus his eyes and his thoughts as he realized he wasn't being taken back to the usual cell block. That was good. But not good enough yet.

"Take him to the infirmary," one of the guards ordered. "We'll let the surgeon look him over, and then the warden'll want to have a talk with him before we throw him in the Dark Cell."

If they had been paying any attention, they would have seen the grin that flickered briefly across Frank's bloody, battered face.

His plan was working.

Warden Townsend was aghast as he walked into the front room of the infirmary, a stout adobe building set off to one side of the massive cell block wings. Two armed guards followed him. Frank sat on a table while the prison surgeon wrapped bandages tightly around his torso. The surgeon thought Frank might have some cracked ribs, so he was binding them up as a precaution. Frank had had cracked ribs before and didn't think that was the case this time, but he didn't argue with the man.

Moans and whimpers and an occasional scream came from another room in the rear of the building. That was where Jessup was.

The surgeon had already cleaned and bandaged the wounds on Frank's face, arms, and shoulders. Huge bruises had started to appear everywhere he had been struck with the clubs. Townsend stared at him, then paled as more shrieks of pain came from Jessup.

"Good God, man, what have you done?" the warden demanded.

"Defended myself," Frank said. "Jessup attacked me, just like before."

"But you goaded him into it. I've talked to Nash, and he confirms it. So do the guards."

The surgeon stepped back, finished with the job of binding up Frank's ribs. Frank shrugged as best he could and grimaced as pain shot through him.

"He threatened me. Said he was going to get me sooner or later. I figured I'd rather have it over and done with, right then and there, out in the open."

Another of Jessup's screams trailed away into a bubbling whimper.

Townsend wiped a hand over his face and said to the surgeon, "Can't you do anything for him?"

The surgeon shook his head. "I can't repair his knee. It's torn to pieces inside."

"Then for God's sake, can't you shut him up?"

"I've already given him as much laudanum·as I dare. Any more and I run the risk of it killing him." It was the surgeon's turn to shrug. "He's so big the stuff is taking a long time to take effect. But he should go to sleep soon."

"Lord, I hope so," Townsend muttered. He turned back to Frank. "The punishment for fighting is twenty-four hours in the Dark Cell, Morton. The next time it'll be forty-eight hours, so I'd advise you not to cause any more trouble. Some men crack after forty-eight hours in there."

Frank wasn't worried about that. He said, "I've got something to tell you, Warden. You, personal-like."

Townsend glared and shook his head. "Impossible."

"It's important."

"I'll go check on Jessup, even though it's not going to do any good," the surgeon said. He left the room, going down a hall toward the room where Jessup still moaned and cried while waiting for the laudanum to make the pain in his knee go away.

Townsend thought about it for a minute, then told the guards, "Step back."

The guards looked dubious. "I ain't sure that's a good idea, Warden."

"Look at Morton," Townsend snapped. "He's so beaten up that he doesn't pose any danger to anyone right now. And the two of you will still be right here in the room if he tries anything. Now step back."

The guards exchanged a glance and then followed orders, moving back until they were just inside the door. Townsend came closer to Frank and said, "Now what is it?"

Townsend's broad body blocked the guards' view of Frank's face. He whispered, "When I get out of the hole, put me and McCoy on road detail. Got it?"

Townsend nodded, the motion so slight as to be almost imperceptible. But Frank saw it and knew the warden understood. He went on in a louder voice. "Lean closer, Warden, so you can hear me better."

Townsend did so.

Frank spat in his face.

Townsend recoiled in disgust as Frank laughed and the guards leaped forward. The warden's reaction was genuinely surprised, which was what Frank wanted. One of the blue-uniformed men cursed and swung a fist, crashing it against Frank's jaw and knocking him back off the table. The surgeon rushed in as Frank sprawled on the floor and shouted, "What the devil's going on here? You can't brawl in here! This is the infirmary!"

Townsend pulled out his handkerchief and with a trembling hand wiped Frank's spittle from his face. "Take Morton to the Dark Cell," he ordered in a voice that shook with rage. Some of it was a sham, Frank thought as the guards grabbed him and jerked him to his feet, but some of it wasn't. Townsend was really upset. That was perfect. "Lock him up in there," the warden went on.

"For twenty-four hours?" one of the guards asked.

Frank cut his eyes back and forth, hoping Townsend would understand what he meant. They had to make it look good, and this would do the trick.

"No," Townsend said coldly. "For forty-eight."

"Warden, are you sure—"

"I gave the order, didn't I? Now carry it out!"

The guards nodded and hustled Frank out of the infirmary. Outside, several more guards closed in around them. He was marched rapidly toward the rear of the prison where another slope rose. As they approached it,

Frank saw a dark hole gaping in the caliche hillside like an open mouth waiting to swallow him.

"I haven't had anything to eat since breakfast," he protested as they shoved him toward the open door of the Dark Cell.

"Should've thought of that before you started a fight and spit in the warden's face, you stupid bastard," one of the guards grated.

They practically threw him inside the hole in the hill. He tripped, stumbled, and lost his footing. The cell was only about five feet deep, so he hit his shoulder against the rear wall when he fell. He landed in a huddled heap on the stone floor and twisted around toward the door just in time to see it swinging shut. It closed with a slam of finality, cutting off all light in the windowless cell. Frank wondered how air got in here. There had to be some tiny cracks here and there, enough to let some air in so prisoners wouldn't suffocate, but not enough to admit any discernible light. Or maybe there was some sort of chimney arrangement in the roof that blocked the light but let air in. He hadn't had time to get a good look before he was tossed in here.

Not that it mattered. A thick bar dropped across brackets on either side of the door outside the cell, sealing him in here good and proper. He wouldn't be going anywhere until someone let him out. That would be forty-eight hours if Warden Townsend stuck to the original punishment he had decreed. Frank hoped that he would. Townsend couldn't afford to make it look like he was taking it easy on this troublemaking new prisoner "Fred Morton." Not if they wanted the plan to work.

The cell was too small for Frank to stretch out. He sat with his back propped against the wall instead and put a hand to his jaw, working it back and forth. The guard's punch hadn't done any real damage, but it hurt. That didn't matter much, either, because he wouldn't be eating anything for a couple of days. By then some of the bruises would have healed.

"Conrad," Frank said in a voice so low that only he could hear it, "I sure as hell hope that you appreciate all this."

Chapter 13

Forty-eight hours or forty-eight years . . . Frank Morgan wouldn't have taken bets on which was the correct answer when the door of the Dark Cell finally swung open again and guards stood outside the cramped chamber to wait for him to crawl out. They wouldn't come in and get him, one of them explained. The rules said he had to come out under his own power. Frank figured that was because he hadn't had any place to relieve himself, and none of the guards wanted to enter the cell until some of the trusties had taken buckets of water in there and washed down the stone floor.

He didn't crawl. Knowing that was what they expected, he forced himself to his feet. He was already bent in what felt like a permanent crouch, so he had no trouble getting through the low door. He staggered forward, blinking against the light that seemed more harsh and blinding than ever. As he lifted a shaking hand to shield his eyes, a blurred shape moved in front of him. He couldn't see well enough yet to tell who it was, but he recognized the voice as Warden Eli Townsend said, "I hope you've learned your lesson, Morton, and won't have to go in there anymore. But just to make sure that you don't have enough energy left to start trouble in the future, we're going to work you like you've never been worked before." An angry and vindictive edge came into Townsend's voice as he added, "You'll be on the road gang until you drop!"

Frank didn't allow himself to chuckle or even smile. Townsend's words were perfect. Even after the hellish two days he had spent in the Dark Cell, Frank's brain was still clear enough for him to realize that.

He could think about the plan later. Right now he just wanted some food and water, and to stretch out muscles that had been cramped in unnatural positions for far too long.

But he was still proud enough to wave the guards away as a couple of them moved forward to give him a hand. Like an old, old man, he tottered toward the cell block on his own two feet, without any help.

With the guards surrounding him, he walked all the way to his cell without any help. As he passed along the aisle between the barred, stone-walled chambers, the prisoners stepped up to watch him go by. Some of them spoke low, encouraging words to him, like Gideon, who said, "That's showin' 'em, Fred." Others just looked on in silence. But all of the convicts seemed to be impressed that he had not only survived the ordeal, but come through it in better shape than those unlucky enough to get thrown into the Dark Cell usually did.

The door of his cell slammed shut behind him, cloaking him in gloom once more. It was positively bright in here, though, compared to where he had spent the past two days. He stumbled over to his bunk and collapsed on it. A groan escaped from his lips as he stretched out. He couldn't hold back the sound as his stiff muscles tried to unkink themselves. His whole body was one giant throbbing ache.

Frank wondered how long it would be before Warden Townsend assigned him and Cicero McCoy to the road gang. It couldn't be soon. Frank needed at least a little time to recover. No matter how much resolve he had, he was in no shape to be out working on a stagecoach road in the hot sun.

He pondered that for a few moments, but those were the last coherent thoughts that went through his head.

After that, he was sound asleep, utterly drained and exhausted by the hellish experience.

Frank roused enough that evening to eat and drink a little, then fell asleep again. By the next morning he felt better, though he was still only a shadow of his normal self. The prison surgeon came by the cell to check on him and see when he would be fit to go back to work. When the surgeon was finished with his examination, he said, "I'll tell the warden that you can resume your normal activities in a couple of days."

Frank nodded. His active, outdoor life had given him an iron constitution that enabled him to recover quickly. He wanted to get on with the plan. The less time he had to spend behind bars, the better.

Besides, the idea of getting out in the open air and working appealed to him, even though he would probably have to do it wearing leg irons and shackles.

The two days passed fairly quickly. Frank slept a lot, ate the food that was brought to him, and let strength flow back into his body. By the time several guards showed up on the third morning to unlock his cell and lead him out, he was most of the way back to normal. Not there yet, but getting better all the time.

He joined a line of other convicts assembling in the courtyard. Gideon was among them—and so was Cicero McCoy. The white-haired bank robber said under his breath to Frank, "I've been wanting to get put on road detail ever since I got here. You made it almost right away, Morton."

"What's better about this job?" Frank asked. "Besides being out in the open, I mean."

"That's it. When you're working on the road, you're not behind these damned walls anymore." One of McCoy's eyes closed for a second in a lazy wink. "That makes it easier to get away, like we were talking about that other time."

Frank gave a knowing nod. He hoped McCoy wouldn't be impetuous enough to try to make a break for freedom right away. Frank still needed a little time to work his way in with the outlaw, so that there was no question they were partners and would make their escape together.

Of course, if McCoy *did* get away and Frank didn't, the charade could be ended. He wouldn't have to spend any more time behind bars. But that would mean that his mission to Yuma had been a failure, and Frank didn't like the notion of failing. Never had, and never would.

Gideon was one of the men being sent to work on the stagecoach road, too. As they were climbing onto wagons to be taken out of the prison, he grinned at Frank and McCoy and said, "Here we are, together again, boys. We're gettin' to be sort of like the Three Musketeers, ain't we?"

"Who?" McCoy asked with a puzzled frown.

"Characters in a book," Frank explained. During his

drifting days, he'd nearly always had a book or three in his saddlebags and had spent many an evening reading by the light of a campfire. He knew the work of Dumas quite well. "The musketeers were good friends, three soldiers in France."

McCoy shook his head. "I never cottoned to the idea of taking orders like a soldier, and I don't like Frenchies."

"Well, I didn't say we had to be just like them," Gideon said as he sat down in the wagon bed with his back propped against the driver's seat.

Frank noticed that several of the convicts had heavy iron balls attached to their leg irons by means of a chain that was long enough for the men to carry the balls as they were walking. They were men who had tried to escape in the past, he reasoned. If they tried to run with one of those balls chained to them, they wouldn't move very fast or get very far. The guards could run them down without any trouble.

The road gang had two dozen men in it. They rode twelve to a wagon. Ten guards accompanied them—one man riding point, one bringing up the rear, and two on either side of each wagon. The guards were armed with rifles and pistols. In addition, a smaller wagon rolled along about fifty yards behind the vehicles carrying the prisoners. Three men rode on that wagon, which had something sitting in the bed. Frank couldn't tell for sure what the object was since it had a canvas tarp draped over it, but he could make a guess.

Gray-uniformed trusties drove the wagons carrying the prisoners. In the event of trouble, they would probably stay out of it, not taking either side. Their lot in prison life could hardly be called comfortable, but at least they were better off than the regular convicts, and they would want to protect the extra privileges they had.

The wagons rolled down the hill and headed east out of the settlement of Yuma, following the stagecoach road. The sun grew hotter as it rose. Almost an hour went by before the wagons stopped where the road swung around a rocky outcropping topped by boulders to the left. To the right the ground fell away at a fairly steep angle into a dry wash that followed the curve of the road. The gully had a gravelly floor dotted with large rocks that looked like no water had run there for years.

That wasn't the case, though. A torrent had poured through the wash recently enough so that the edges of the road were ragged and washed out in places. As the wagons came to a halt, the guard who had led the procession out here waved his hand at the damaged road and called, "That's what you'll be workin' on! Grab your shovels and build up the side o' that road until it's good and solid again. Wouldn't do for a stagecoach to come along and have a wheel go off the edge and tip it over."

Several of the guards had brought along bundles of shovels tied together with cord. They untied the cords and the tools dropped to the ground with a clatter. The convicts climbed down from the wagons and each man picked up a shovel.

The man in charge of the details shouted, "Give me or any of the other guards any sass, and it'll be in the Dark Cell you go as soon as we get back to the prison!" He grinned at Frank. "Morton there can tell you that ain't no picnic, just in case you were thinkin' it was. Ain't that right, Morton?"

Frank didn't answer. He stood there in stony silence.

The guard brought his horse closer. "Maybe you didn't know it, Morton," he said with a dangerous edge to his voice, "but the warden put me in charge o' this detail. That means you do what I tell you, just like you would if the warden told you to do it. And that means you don't ignore me, either."

With that he leaned forward and slashed the quirt that he carried across Frank's chest. It hit gray uniform instead of bare skin, but it still hurt like blazes. Frank hissed and his jaw tightened. It was all he could do not to reach up, haul that bastard out of the saddle, and throw him on the ground like the mean varmint that he was.

"I said the Dark Cell ain't no picnic. Ain't that right, Morton?"

"Yeah," Frank grated. "That's right. No picnic."

The man laughed and straightened in the saddle. "Now that we've settled that, I'd best point out somethin' else for those of you who ain't been on road detail before. You may think that since we're outside the walls o' the prison now, it'd be easy to run away. Well, we got a couple of special deals for anybody who wants to try that. First we put a ball and chain on you." The guard nodded toward the prisoners who carried heavy iron balls. They stared sullenly back at him. The guard went on. "And if that don't work . . ."

He gestured toward the smaller wagon, which had come to a stop, still keeping its distance of approximately fifty yards. Two of the men who had ridden on it had climbed into the back, and now they removed the canvas tarp from the object carried there.

Frank grunted as the canvas slid smoothly over metal and then fell away into the wagon bed, exposing the sleek lines of a Gatling gun. He wasn't surprised. He had guessed from the general shape under the tarp that the hidden object might be one of those deadly, rapid-fire repeaters.

"That's right," the guard who was in charge of the detail said. "We got us a Gatling. If we need to, we can mow down the whole lot of you in less than half a minute. And we'll do it, too, if it looks like you're gonna get away. Don't you doubt it for a second."

Frank didn't doubt it at all. From the sound of the guard's voice, the man would have enjoyed watching the bodies spout blood and fall as the multiple barrels of the Gatling gun revolved and its deadly chatter filled the air.

The trick for an escaping convict would be not only to get away, but to somehow silence that Gatling gun while he was making his escape.

Either that, or somehow turn the Gatling's stuttering roar to his advantage somehow . . .

The guards didn't hunt some shade and neglect their duties; Frank had to give them credit for that. They stayed out in the sun like the convicts and watched alertly as the work got under way. The prisoners shoveled up wheelbarrows full of rocky dirt, then wheeled those barrows along the road to the washed-out spots and dumped them there. Other men used their shovels to tamp down the new dirt and make it solid enough to support the weight of a stagecoach wheel.

It was hard labor, especially under the merciless rays of the sun. Frank quickly discovered that he hadn't recovered as much of his strength as he thought he had. Weariness threatened to overwhelm him. He forced himself to keep working, but after a couple of hours his head suddenly started spinning, and before he knew what has happening, he found himself on the ground where he had fallen.

He heard the ominous sound of numerous guns being cocked.

Squinting against the sun, Frank looked up to see himself surrounded by guards. "What's wrong with you,

Morton?" one of them demanded. "If this is some sort of trick, you'll regret it."

Gideon hustled forward. "It ain't a trick, boss, and he ain't fakin'! You know he just done two days in the Dark Cell not long ago. Shoot, he probably shouldn't even be out here workin' yet—"

Frank waved off Gideon, even though the man was just trying to stick up for him. "Just give me a second to . . . catch my breath," he told the guards. "I'll be all right." He picked up the shovel he had dropped when he collapsed and used it to help himself climb back to his feet.

But when he tried to take a step, he swayed and almost fell again. "For God's sake," McCoy muttered as he stepped forward. "Let me give you a hand, Morton." He grasped Frank's arm to steady him.

One of the guards said in a grudging voice, "Take him over to the wagons, McCoy. I reckon he'll have to sit in the shade for a while, and get him a drink."

"Yeah," another man put in. "The warden don't like it when a man dies on work detail."

Frank was about to mutter his thanks, when McCoy leaned closer and whispered so that only he could hear, "Keep it up. The bastards believe it. I won't forget how you helped me get away, Morton."

No! Not yet . . . McCoy was about to try something, and Frank was in no shape to stop him, let alone escape with him. They had to wait—

The guards' horses were picketed next to the wagons. The teams were still hitched up. If McCoy jumped onto one of the wagons and whipped up the team, then stampeded the saddle horses, he'd stand a chance of getting away, Frank realized as he forced his brain to work as fast as it could.

That is, McCoy would stand a chance of getting away . . . if it hadn't been for that Gatling gun. When the guards manning the gun opened up, hundreds of slugs would chop the wagon to pieces, and McCoy with it.

"McCoy," Frank muttered. "Don't . . ."

"They're not paying any attention," McCoy insisted. "I'll never get a better chance."

They had reached the closest wagon. McCoy lowered Frank to the ground.

"So long, pard," the bank robber whispered with a grin. Before Frank could stop him, he sprang to the wagon seat and grabbed the reins that were looped around the brake lever.

"Hey!" one of the guards yelled. "McCoy, what're you—"

"Hyaaahhh!" McCoy shouted as he slashed the rumps of the team with the reins. The startled horses leaped into motion.

But even as that was happening, Frank forced his muscles to work, no matter how much they protested. He twisted around, lunged up, and grabbed the back of the wagon as it went past him. He was pulled off his feet, but he didn't lose his grip.

McCoy must have felt the added weight. He looked around and saw Frank trying to pull himself into the back of the wagon. "Morton!" he shouted. "Let go!"

Frank didn't release his hold on the wagon. Instead, he hauled himself into the bed, sprawling on his stomach. He looked back over his shoulder and saw the Gatling gun swinging toward them with its deadly circular array of barrels. In a matter of seconds, flame and lead would begin spitting from those barrels, and McCoy wasn't anywhere close to being out of range of the weapon.

Moving automatically, not thinking about what he was

doing, just acting, Frank scrambled to his feet as McCoy sent the wagon careening through the group of saddle horses, just as Frank expected him to do. And also as expected, the horses spooked, jerked loose from their pickets, and scattered in a wild stampede. The guards would have to spend some time rounding them up again.

But that didn't matter, because by then McCoy would be riddled with bullets from the Gatling gun, unless Frank could somehow prevent it. And with McCoy's death, the chances of ever finding that hidden loot would die as well.

Frank launched himself in a dive over the back of the seat. He slammed into McCoy. Wrapping his arms around the outlaw's shoulder, he drove both of them toward the side of the wagon. McCoy howled curses as Frank shoved him right off the seat. Both men tumbled to the ground, landing hard and rolling over and over in the dust.

And as they did, a hail of bullets gouted from the Gatling gun and tore into the wagon with devastating force. Splinters flew as the slugs chewed their way through the vehicle. Wagon spokes snapped. The two horses in the back of the six-horse team screamed and stumbled as they were hit. One of the wheels flew off, and the wagon came to a lurching, shuddering, skidding halt. The two wounded horses collapsed in their traces.

Frank and McCoy lay there, unhit by the bullets, as the Gatling gun fell silent. After the terrible chattering roar that had filled the air, the quiet was almost eerie. Then the guards started yelling as they ran toward Frank and McCoy. They trained their rifles on the two prisoners and ordered them not to move.

"You son of a bitch," McCoy grated. "Why'd you do that, damn you? I could've made it!"

"No, you couldn't have," Frank told him. "Look . . . look at that wagon, McCoy. The seat's . . . shot to hell. . . . You'd have . . . forty or fifty bullet holes in you right now . . . if I hadn't knocked you off of there."

McCoy pushed himself into a sitting position and glared at the wrecked wagon. What Frank had said was beyond dispute. McCoy would be dead now if not for what Frank had done.

"All right," he said in a grudging growl. "I reckon it was a fool play. But I've been in here longer than you have, Morton. And I got more waiting for me outside."

He didn't say anything else, but Frank knew he was talking about that eighty grand.

The guards reached them then, surrounding them. One of the men screamed curses as he stepped behind McCoy and drove the butt of his rifle into the bank robber's back, right between McCoy's shoulder blades. McCoy grunted in pain as he was driven face down on the ground by the vicious blow.

Frank and McCoy were both hauled to their feet. "You'll go in the Dark Cell for a month for this, McCoy!" the guard who had struck him threatened.

Frank hoped not. He didn't want to spend a month waiting for McCoy to get out of that dismal hole. Warden Townsend would have to punish McCoy for this attempted escape, though. It would look too odd if he didn't. And after this, it would look a mite strange, too, if Townsend turned around and assigned McCoy to the road gang again.

This was the worst break so far, Frank thought. McCoy's impulsive act had set everything back, at best, and made the plan unworkable, at worst. If only McCoy had waited . . .

It looked like Frank would have to be mighty patient if he wanted to have any chance of pulling this off, he told himself.

But being patient was easier said than done . . . especially when a man was in prison.

Chapter 14

One of the guards caught his horse and rode back to the prison with the news of McCoy's attempted escape. He brought back another wagon to replace the one that had been heavily damaged by the Gatling gun. In the back of the new wagon was one of the heavy iron balls, which was soon chained to McCoy's leg irons. The warden had ordered that because he couldn't treat McCoy differently than he would any other prisoner.

McCoy didn't say anything else to Frank during the afternoon. His sullen silence was enough of an indication that he hadn't completely forgiven Frank's interference—even though it had saved his life and McCoy had to be aware of that.

Gideon said to Frank, "You came damn close to gettin' yourself killed, Fred. What were you thinkin'?"

"McCoy's my friend," Frank answered. "I knew he'd be killed if I didn't get him out of the line of fire of that Gatling gun."

Gideon shook his head. "You can't afford to be too friendly in here. You never know when it'll get you in more trouble'n it's worth."

Frank didn't say anything. He wanted McCoy to know that he considered him a friend. It was likely that Gideon would say something about it to McCoy sooner or later.

Frank wasn't going to give up just because of this bad break. Something might be salvaged from the situation eventually.

When the wagons returned to Yuma late that afternoon, Frank and McCoy were both taken under heavy guard to the warden's office. Townsend glared across his desk at them. "I'm disappointed in you, McCoy," he snapped. "You've been a good prisoner while you were here. I suppose that was all an act, wasn't it? You've just been biding your time, waiting for a chance to escape."

McCoy didn't say anything, but his chin jutted out in defiance as his jaw tightened. He stared straight ahead without looking at the warden.

Townsend shifted his angry gaze to Frank. From the looks of it, it almost appeared that Townsend had forgotten Frank wasn't a real convict. He seemed genuinely mad.

"And as for you, Morton, were you trying to escape, too?" Townsend demanded.

"Is that what the guards told you?" Frank asked.

"Never mind what the guards told me! Just answer the question!"

Frank shrugged. "I didn't think McCoy was going to make it before that Gatling gun got him. So I knocked him off the wagon to save his life."

Townsend snorted and said, "A likely story. I think both of you tumbled off the wagon by accident. You thought you'd get away, too, Morton. Well, I'm tired of your troublemaking. You're going back in the Dark Cell."

That jolted a response out of McCoy at last. "Hold on, Warden," he said. "Morton's telling you the truth. He was just trying to help me. He just got out of the Dark Cell a few days ago. You put him back in there now, it's liable to kill him."

"And what is that to you?" Townsend asked in a cold voice.

"Well . . . he *did* save my life."

Townsend sat back in his chair and glared at both of them again. After a moment, he gave a curt jerk of his head and said, "All right. Since you two are friends . . . you can go in the Dark Cell together."

Frank knew from the startled expressions the guards wore that this was unusual. The Dark Cell was so small it was possible that two men had never before been put in there at the same time. With both of them in there, the space would be more cramped and uncomfortable than ever.

"Twenty-four hours," Townsend went on. "I think that will be enough time."

Maybe the warden was being canny after all, Frank thought. By putting them both in the Dark Cell, Townsend was cutting down the time that McCoy would be out of commission, and yet there was nothing all that suspicious about it.

"What about the ball and chain?" one of the guards asked.

"It stays on McCoy," Townsend snapped. "Now get them out of here."

The guards hustled them out of the office and back through the sally port into the prison itself. McCoy carried the iron ball attached to his leg irons, grunting now and then from the effort. Word of the attempted escape had gotten around. Some of the convicts were out in the large open area, and they watched with avid interest as Frank and McCoy were taken to the Dark Cell. Frank spotted redheaded Jim Nash, and beside him bald Conner Jessup limped along on a pair of crutches, his injured knee still heavily bandaged. Both men grinned in pleasure at the prospect of Frank and McCoy being tossed into the hole in the hillside.

The guards unlocked and unbarred the door of the punishment cell and stepped back to motion with the barrels of their rifles. "Get in there, you two," one of them grated. "This'll teach you never to try runnin' again."

Frank and McCoy shuffled into the chamber. As they turned back toward the door, it swung shut, cutting off the light. Awkwardly because of the darkness, they lowered themselves to the floor and sat with their backs against the walls as the heavy bar and the chains were put back in place. Then they heard the guards walking away.

Neither man said anything for a while. Then McCoy spoke in a taut, angry tone. "If you're waiting for me to apologize for you being thrown in here, you're wasting your time, Morton."

"I don't give a damn whether you apologize or not," Frank said. "Anyway, you don't have anything to be sorry for. What I did was my own choice. I could've stood back and let them shoot you to pieces with that devil gun."

"Yeah," McCoy said. "You could have." Again he was silent. The moment stretched out for a while; then McCoy finally said, "That damn warden was wrong. You weren't trying to escape with me."

"This time," Frank said.

McCoy grunted in surprise. "What's that mean?"

"Just what I said. I wasn't trying to escape with you this time. But maybe next time . . . if we plan it out and don't act on the spur of the moment . . . it might be a different story."

"You want to bust out of here, too?"

"Hell, what do you think?" Frank gave a humorless laugh. "I never wanted to get locked up in the first place, and now, with Nash and Jessup in here hating me so bad, I sure as hell don't want to be here. Sooner or later those two will try to kill me."

"Yeah," McCoy agreed, "you're right. Jessup's got a powerful hate for you, and Nash will go along with him and help him. If you stay in here, it's a death sentence, not a life sentence."

Frank laughed again. "So what do you say, McCoy? We come to an agreement and figure out a better way to get out of this place?"

"Maybe." McCoy hesitated. "But there's something you're not saying. An agreement about what?"

Frank was glad McCoy had picked up on that. He had figured that the bank robber would.

"If we're going to be partners in an escape, we're going to be partners right down the line," Frank said. "I heard about you, McCoy. You're famous. You're the fella who stole eighty grand from a bank in Tucson, and the authorities never got the loot back."

"And you want a share of it," McCoy said, his voice taut again.

"I want half," Frank said. "If I help you escape, and both of us get out of here, I get half the loot from that bank job."

"Go to hell," McCoy responded curtly. "That money's mine."

"Yeah, and it's doing you a lot of good while you're in here and it's out there somewhere, isn't it?"

Frank couldn't see the sneer, but he could hear it in

McCoy's voice as the outlaw said, "I'll escape on my own. I don't need your help, Morton."

"Without my help you'd be dead now, remember?" Frank pointed out. "Your first attempt on your own was so successful, that Gatling would've chopped you to pieces."

McCoy didn't say anything, but Frank knew he had to be turning things over in his mind. It was McCoy's nature to bargain, so Frank wasn't surprised a few moments later when he said, "Half's out of the question, but I'll give you a fourth of the bank money."

"A third," Frank countered.

"Thirty percent. Not a damn penny more."

Frank was silent as if he were thinking over the proposal. Then he said, "Twenty-four grand. I can live with that."

"We have a deal?"

"Yeah," Frank said. "We have a deal."

"Then shake on it."

Frank would have preferred that they didn't do that. It went against the grain for Frank Morgan to give his word to anybody, even a vicious murderer and bank robber, knowing full well that he was going to break it. Shaking on it just made him even more uncomfortable.

But he didn't have any choice in the matter. He put out his hand and felt around in the darkness until he encountered McCoy's hand. They shook to seal the deal.

Now there was the little matter of figuring out exactly *how* they were going to make that escape. . . .

The Gatling gun was the key. That and being outside, working on the road detail. During the time they were locked up in the Dark Cell, Frank and McCoy spent hours talking about how the prison was run and how the work details assigned to the stagecoach road operated.

"We have to get our hands on that Gatling some way," Frank said, "or at least fix it so that they can't use it against us."

"The guards are bound to know that's how the convicts think. That's why the wagon with the Gatling gun on it stays back a good ways. I'll bet if a prisoner even starts toward it, they'd chop him down like a weed."

Frank nodded, even though McCoy couldn't see him in the darkness. "More than likely. Let's put that aside for a minute and think about what we're going to do for transportation. Taking one of the wagons and scattering the guards' horses wasn't a bad idea, but it would be better if we could get our hands on a couple of those horses for ourselves."

"And stampede the rest so they couldn't come after us?" McCoy asked.

"Well, we'd almost have to, or they'd be on our trail too quick."

"They could unhitch the horses from the wagons and ride them," McCoy pointed out.

"Those are draft animals, not saddle horses. I reckon we can outrun them."

Frank heard a faint rasping sound and figured that McCoy was rubbing his fingertips over the beard stubble on his lantern jaw as he thought over the problem. After a few minutes, McCoy said, "What we need is a distraction. Something to keep all the guards so busy that we could get to the wagon with the Gatling gun before they realized what we were doing."

"That would work, all right," Frank agreed. "But what could it be?"

"That's going to take some more thinking," McCoy said.

The heat inside the Dark Cell made it difficult to think or even stay awake. Eventually, both men dozed off. Frank had no idea how long he was asleep, but when he awoke there was the germ of an idea in his mind. He thought it over for a while before bringing it up to McCoy, fleshing it out and trying to consider all the angles. When he did broach the subject again and started talking about what he had come up with, McCoy saw right away what Frank was getting at. He laughed softly and said, "It might work. With a little bit of luck, it just might work, Morton."

They continued talking about the escape plan, and the time in the Dark Cell passed faster than either man would have dreamed that it could.

That didn't mean that they weren't damned glad to get out anyway when the time came. Both were cramped up and weak from hunger and thirst, and they blinked against the harsh light as they stepped from the Dark Cell.

But even though they were the only ones who knew it, they firmly believed that those were their first steps toward freedom, no matter how unsteady they might be.

As Frank had expected, neither he nor McCoy were put back on the road detail right away. For Warden Townsend to do so would make it look too much like he *wanted* them to escape. But that was all right because the delay gave them both time to recuperate from the time they had spent in the Dark Cell.

And to recruit the help they would need to make their plan work.

Gideon was the first one they approached. "It's simple," Frank said to him one day when they were in the prison yard. "A fight breaks out among the men working on the stagecoach road, and while the guards are trying to deal with that, we grab some horses, stampede the other mounts, and take off for the tall and uncut."

Gideon frowned. "It's been tried before. Some fellas did that while they were comin' in through the sally port. There was enough confusion that they were able to slip away, but the guards ran 'em to earth pretty quick and brought 'em back in chains."

"That's because they were right here at the prison when they made their escape. We'll be out away from it. And if we scatter the other horses, we'll be long gone before any pursuit can get started after us."

Gideon rubbed his jaw. "Well . . . it might work. You say McCoy's part of this?"

"That's right."

"I reckon we can give it a try. We'll need more men involved, though. And the guards'll have to believe it's a real fight, not somethin' that we staged."

A grim smile played over Frank's face. "That's why it's *going* to be a real fight. I'm counting on Jessup and Nash to see to that."

Gideon's eyebrows rose. "Jessup and Nash? They hate your guts, Fred. And with that bum knee you gave him, Jessup ain't gonna be put on no road gang."

"He might drive one of the wagons. He's getting around pretty good now, and they're going to have to find some sort of work for him to do. That's about the only chore he can handle."

"Yeah, they might do that. Could be a long time before everything lines up just right, though."

"Then we'll wait," Frank said. There was nothing else they could do.

More time passed. Days stretched into a couple of weeks. A dozen men agreed to take part in the riot in hopes that they could escape during the confusion. When he was alone, Frank worried a little about that. He didn't want to be responsible for freeing any vicious criminals back into the territory. For that reason, he tried to recruit men whose crimes hadn't been particularly violent. Yuma housed more thieves than any other sort of criminal, so there wasn't any shortage of men who were more than willing to break the law, yet didn't have any history of wanton cruelty. Anyway, if everything worked out as Frank hoped, he and Cicero McCoy would be the only ones who actually escaped.

He managed to catch Warden Townsend's eye one day when the warden was making his rounds of the prison. The next day, Townsend sent his bespectacled assistant to fetch Frank. A couple of guards escorted him to Townsend's office. Since Frank's two visits to the Dark Cell, he had been a model prisoner. He believed that the guards figured his spirit was broken now and he wasn't as much of a threat to cause trouble or attempt to escape.

"You have a visitor, Morton," Townsend said when Frank was ushered into the office. He waved a hand toward a man who wore a dusty black suit and the white collar of a priest. As the man turned toward him, Frank recognized the face of Bob Bardwell, one of Abner Hoyt's crew of bounty hunters. With his bland, unmemorable face, Bardwell had no trouble passing for a priest.

"Howdy, Padre," Frank muttered.

"My son," Bardwell said, then put his arms around Frank and hugged him. "It's good to see you again, Uncle Fred."

Townsend motioned for the guards to leave. When they had done so, he said in a low voice, "What the hell's going on here, Morgan? You've been in here for more than a month now!"

"You don't have to tell me that," Frank said. "I remember every single miserable day of that time. But I think I've just about got everything set up the way we want it. McCoy trusts me."

"You've befriended him?" Bardwell asked.

"I didn't say that. I'm not sure a man like McCoy ever has any real friends. But he thinks he can use me to help him escape, and that's all he really cares about." Frank shrugged. "He's liable to double-cross me as soon as we get out . . . but we've known that was a possibility all along."

"What do you need me to do?" Townsend asked.

"Send these men out to work on the stagecoach road." Frank gave the warden the names of the men he and McCoy and Gideon had convinced to join them. "It doesn't matter who else you put on the detail . . . as long as two of them are Jim Nash and Conner Jessup."

Townsend looked surprised. "Nash and Jessup!"

"Who are they?" Bardwell asked.

Quickly, Frank explained about the trouble he'd had with the two men. "As much as they hate me, no one is going to question that the fight is real."

"Then what?" Townsend asked. "You can't count on something as simple as a riot to provide enough of a distraction."

"Yeah, I know," Frank said with a smile. "That's where the avalanche comes in."

"Avalanche!"

"When we were working out there before, I spotted several boulders up on top of the bluff that borders the road. There were others down in the bed of that wash on the other side. They told me that rocks roll down the slope sometimes. The wagon with the Gatling gun on it was parked right in the path of some of the boulders that are still up on the bluff."

Bardwell nodded slowly as he frowned in thought. "So when the trouble breaks out, you're going up the hill to start those rocks rolling. They crash into the wagon with the Gatling gun, which has been abandoned by the guards when they see the boulders coming at them."

"That's right," Frank said. "I thought for a while about trying to capture the gun, but we can't risk that. McCoy might open up with it and slaughter a bunch of folks, guards and convicts alike."

"I don't want a bloodbath out there," Townsend said with a stern frown.

"That's why we're doing it this way. Once I've eliminated the threat of the Gatling gun, McCoy and I will grab a couple of horses and take off. As soon as we're gone, the extra guards who are going to be waiting nearby can move in, quash the riot, and get everything back under control."

"Extra guards?" Townsend repeated. Then a look of understanding appeared on his face. "I see. It won't matter then if the other prisoners figure out it was all a setup. You and McCoy will already be gone."

"On your way to that eighty thousand dollars," Bardwell said. "And Abner and the rest of us will be trailing you."

"Just don't get too close," Frank warned. "We don't want to tip McCoy off to the fact that we're being followed."

"We won't have to get close. We know the general area where you'll be heading."

"That's right." Frank nodded. "Ambush Valley."

Chapter 15

"What was that about?" McCoy asked when Frank was brought back into the prison and joined the men in the yard. "The warden's not going to throw you in the Dark Cell again, is he? He seems to like doing that."

Frank gave a grim laugh. "No, not with the way I've been careful to behave myself. All of us need to make him and the guards think that starting more trouble is the farthest thing from our minds . . . until the right moment comes to get the hell out of here."

McCoy and Gideon nodded in agreement with that.

"I had a visitor," Frank said, explaining why he had been taken to the warden's office. "My nephew."

"It ain't visitin' day," Gideon said. "Anyway, you never had nobody come to see you before, Fred."

"The boy's a priest," Frank said, deliberately putting some scorn in his voice. "He's my sister's boy. He thinks he's doing the Lord's work by coming to see his poor convict uncle. Townsend went along with him, even though it's not the regular visiting day."

Those days happened once a month, on the first Sunday. It made sense that someone who was a priest wouldn't be able to come to the prison on that day. The Sabbath wasn't a day of rest for men of the cloth.

"Something interesting did happen while I was in the warden's office," Frank went on. "Townsend mentioned that he's going to put us all back on the road detail soon. If enough of the men who are in on our plan are part of the same detail, we'll be out of here before you know it."

"Can't be soon enough to suit me," McCoy said. He gave Frank a meaningful glance, and Frank knew the bank robber was thinking about that eighty thousand dollars. They were the only ones who had talked about it. They didn't know if Gideon was aware of the loot or not. The man had never mentioned it. All Gideon was really interested in was his freedom.

The next couple of days dragged even more than usual. But at last, the guards came and marched Frank, McCoy, Gideon, and nearly two dozen more men out of their cell blocks and got them loaded onto wagons. Frank saw the men whose names he had given to Townsend among the group. And Conner Jessup sat on the driver's seat of one of the wagons, just as Frank had requested. Nash was there, too, sitting right behind the seat.

At long last, everything was falling into place.

The wagons rolled out, surrounded by guards as usual. The wagon with the Gatling gun mounted in the back trundled along behind, also as usual. There was nothing to indicate that this was anything other than a normal work detail going out on a normal day—just the way Frank wanted it.

The men swayed back and forth in the wagons as they rocked along the road. Even though the weather had been bone-dry at the prison, there had been a downpour in the hills about a week earlier, which meant the stage-coach road along the arroyo could have been partially washed out again. That must have happened; otherwise, the work detail from the prison wouldn't be sent out like this. Frank looked at McCoy and Gideon and gave a tiny nod. They passed it along to the other members of their escape plot. If any of them found it suspicious that so many of them had been assigned to this detail, none of them showed it. Everybody worked hard at Yuma Prison. Being given a chore like this was nothing unusual.

It took a couple of hours for the slow-moving wagons to reach their destination. When they came to a stop, it was in the same place as they'd been before, on the stretch of road between the dry wash and the rocky bluff. Frank eyed the slope and tried to pick out the best route to the top. He'd have to cover that ground in a hurry, and if any of the guards noticed what he was doing, he'd probably have to dodge some bullets on the way, too. But if he made it, there were several of the boulders perched precariously enough that he thought he could put his shoulder against them and get them rolling with a good hard shove.

The prisoners climbed down from the wagons, claimed their shovels and wheelbarrows, and got to work. Frank noticed that several of the convicts seemed to be friendly with Jim Nash and Conner Jessup. That was good. Having two distinct factions among the prisoners would make the fight look more real. Hell, it would be real. He intended to make sure of that.

He also studied the place where the Gatling gun wagon was parked in relation to the boulders on the outcropping above it. He knew which rocks to push; now he just had to wait for the chance to start them rolling. It wouldn't be much of an avalanche, he thought . . . but he wouldn't need much of one. Just enough to wipe out that Gatling gun.

On the way out here, Frank had kept an eye on their back trail, too. He didn't want a cloud of dust from the hooves of the horses ridden by those extra guards to give away the game. The men had hung back far enough so that no one would notice them. Frank gave a little mental nod of satisfaction. Everything was ready.

He looked at McCoy and Gideon and gave them a real nod. Gideon would accompany Frank up the hill and help him shove the boulders down. McCoy couldn't do that because of the heavy iron ball still chained to him. They passed along the signal to the others. One of the convicts sauntered over to Nash and said something to him. Frank couldn't hear the words, but they must have been pretty vile because Nash jerked around with a surprised glare on his face.

"What the hell did you just say to me?" Nash demanded.

The other convict repeated it, with even more emphasis this time. Several of the other men lowered their shovels and looked around. They started drifting toward the confrontation. Some of them were part of Frank's plan; others were Nash's friends.

Make it fast, Frank thought. The guards were already starting to notice that something was going on.

Nash suddenly lost his temper and swung his shovel at the convict who'd been baiting him. The man sprang back and blocked the blow with his own shovel. The tools rang together with a loud clang that drew even more attention. Somebody yelled, "Fight!" and instantly men were shouting and hurrying to join in the fracas. Nothing broke up the monotony of hard work like a good fight.

And this was a good one, a yelling, fist-swinging melee that spread like wildfire. The guards who had been spread out around the work detail rushed in to try to break it up. The men with the Gatling gun were alert, but didn't make a move. They held the trump card in case this was more than the mere ill-tempered brawl that it appeared to be.

Frank dropped his shovel and started up the slope toward the boulders. Gideon was right behind him, he saw as he glanced over his shoulder. They had to use their hands for balance, and the leg irons attached to their ankles made it even more difficult to scramble up the bluff. But desperation gave them speed they might not have had otherwise.

With all the shouting already going on, Frank didn't hear it when one of the guards spotted him and Gideon and bellowed a warning. He knew that must have happened, though, because a bullet suddenly whined off a rock near him as he climbed. More bullets thudded into the hillside as other guards opened fire on them. They were easy targets up here on the slope, but luckily, they were almost at the top. Frank drove hard with his legs and hauled himself over the lip of the bluff. Gideon sprawled on the ground beside him a second later.

They rolled over, sprang to their feet, and lunged behind the rocks. The boulders provided some cover for them now, at least for the moment. "Come on, Gideon!" Frank called to the convict as he put his shoulder against one of the rocks he had chosen to start the avalanche. He shoved as hard as he could, but the boulder didn't budge.

Then Gideon threw his weight against the stone, too, and it rocked forward. With grunts of effort, Frank and Gideon pushed harder, and they almost fell down as the boulder suddenly rolled forward and tipped over the edge of the bluff. Its great weight carried it straight down the slope.

Straight toward the wagon with the Gatling gun.

Frank couldn't hear the shouts of alarm from the guards manning the gun, but as he threw himself behind another boulder, he caught a glimpse of them swinging the deadly repeater around and opening fire. That wasn't going to do any good, though. Bullets wouldn't stop an avalanche.

Frank and Gideon threw themselves against the second boulder, which was a little smaller. It rolled over the edge and started bouncing and rumbling down the slope, taking dirt and gravel and other rocks with it. The horses hitched to the wagon snorted and whinnied and jerked around in their traces as the rocks descended toward them, faster and faster. With frightened yells, the guards finally abandoned the wagon, leaping off frantically and running toward the riot, which was still going on along the road above the wash.

The first boulder landed perfectly, smashing down on top of the wagon, shattering the bed and the wheels and putting the Gatling gun out of commission permanently. The other rocks pelted down around it, but they no longer mattered. The damage had been done.

Frank headed for the edge of the bluff. He had to slide down now, join McCoy, and get both of them on horseback so they could gallop away from here.

A weak voice called him back, though. He paused and turned his head, saw that Gideon had fallen to his knees. The convict pressed a hand to his chest. Blood welled between his fingers. Gideon coughed and more blood welled from his mouth. He managed to grin and said, "Got hit . . . on the way up . . . looks like I won't be . . . gettin' away. Have a . . . hell of a good time . . . for me, Fred."

Frank realized that Gideon must have already been

mortally wounded when he was helping push those boulders over the edge of the bluff. Even though he was dying, he had still pitched in to do his part in the escape plan. One of these days, Frank might feel a little bad about the man's sacrifice.

But there wasn't time right now. Gideon groaned and toppled forward on his face. Frank grimaced and turned back to the slope, stepping over the edge and sliding down to the road, raising dust and scattering gravel in front of him in a miniature version of the avalanche that had wiped out the Gatling gun.

One of the guards trying to break up the fight heard him coming and turned around just in time for Frank to smash clubbed fists into his face. The man went down, out cold, and Frank snatched up his rifle. He put the barrel of the Winchester against the chain that ran between his leg irons and pulled the trigger. A shot blasted out. The chain parted as the slug fired at such close range tore through it.

Frank's legs were free now. Carrying the rifle, he ran along the fringes of the melee and looked for McCoy, who was supposed to be making his way toward the horses. He spotted the bank robber. McCoy had the chain attached to his wrist shackles looped around the neck of a guard from behind. The guard's face was already purple as McCoy choked the life out of him. Before Frank could do anything, McCoy heaved hard on the chain, and the guard's neck snapped. He went limp all over.

McCoy dropped him and snatched up the dead man's rifle. Frank trotted up and told him, "Pull back on the chain attached to that ball!"

McCoy did so, and Frank blew the chain in half with

a single shot. McCoy blasted his ankle chains apart. Now both men could move around much more freely.

They still had to grab a couple of horses and stampede the others, though, and by now the guards were beginning to realize what was going on. They left the brawling prisoners alone and started to regroup. The men who were in on the plan broke for the horses, too, getting in the way and complicating matters.

Frank and McCoy were the only ones who had managed to get their hands on rifles and partially free themselves, though, so they had an advantage. They reached the horses first. A guard sprang in front of them, trying to block their way. McCoy swung his rifle toward the man, but before he could fire, Frank had lunged forward and smashed the stock of his Winchester into the guard's face. The man went down, possibly with a broken jaw, but that was better than being dead, as he would have been if McCoy had shot him.

McCoy grabbed the reins of a spooked mount and swung up into the saddle. Frank was reaching for one of the animals when a heavy hand came down on his shoulder and jerked him around.

"Oh, no, you don't!" Jessup bellowed as he threw his tree-trunk-like arms around Frank in a crushing bear hug. "You ain't gettin' away, Morton!"

Jessup cared more about avenging himself on Frank than he did anything else. That much was obvious. Frank groaned as he tried to pull free, but it was like being caught in a bear trap. He felt his ribs creaking, and knew that in another few seconds they would begin to snap under the awful pressure. He did the only thing he could. Since he had levered another round into the Winchester's firing chamber after using the weapon to blast apart one of McCoy's chains, he pressed the muzzle against Jessup's left foot and pulled the trigger.

Jessup screeched in agony but didn't let go. Frank head-butted him in the face and felt the bald man's nose flatten under the blow. The combined pain was too much for Jessup to withstand. His arms fell away and he collapsed. Blood spouted from his foot where Frank had shot it.

McCoy was already on the move, galloping back and forth, shouting, and firing his rifle in the air to stampede the other horses. Frank made a desperate grab for one of the animals as it lunged past him and managed to get hold of the saddle. He leaped, shoved a foot in a stirrup, and hung on for dear life. Bullets ripped through the air around his head as he finally managed to clamber aboard the horse and get settled in the saddle.

McCoy shouldn't suspect there was anything phony about this escape, Frank thought grimly as he leaned forward over the racing horse's neck. The amount of lead flying around in the air made it seem all too real. Hell, it *was* all too real!

The other horses had scattered. McCoy headed north, banging his heels against his mount's flanks to get as much speed out of the horse as he could. Frank followed. He glanced back over his shoulder to see that the other men who'd been part of the plan were running around aimlessly. They had hoped to grab horses, too, but they hadn't known that Frank and McCoy were going to stampede the other mounts. Even if a few of them managed to escape, they would be rounded up quickly.

Frank might feel a little bad about that, too, one of these days, like he would about Gideon, but that would have to wait. Anyway, those men were all hardened criminals and didn't deserve much sympathy.

He wouldn't forget, though, how Gideon had helped him roll those boulders, even with a bullet hole all the way through him.

Not far north was the spot where the Gila River flowed into the Colorado from the east. When Frank and McCoy reached that confluence of streams, they turned and rode east along the bluff that overlooked the Gila, which ran through a narrow, twisting canyon. They slowed their horses to a walk, knowing that they couldn't afford to run the animals into the ground.

"We did it!" McCoy said with a savage grin of triumph on his face. "We'll never see the inside of those damned walls again, Morton."

"That's right," Frank said, "because I figure on making the bastards kill me before I'll ever let myself be taken prisoner again."

"You won't have to worry about that. If we can stay ahead of them long enough to get to that cache of mine, we'll have enough money to get across into Mexico and spend the rest of our lives there, sipping tequila and patting señoritas on their fat little rumps."

Frank chuckled. "Sounds good to me."

So far McCoy had shown no signs of pulling a double cross. Maybe the outlaw was playing things straight for once in his life. Frank wasn't going to fully believe that until he saw it with his own eyes, though.

"We've got to do something about these chains and prison uniforms," McCoy said after they had ridden along in silence for a while. "Anybody who sees us will know right away that we're escaped convicts."

"I don't know what we can do about the chains," Frank

said. "Since we don't have the keys, it'd take a hacksaw to get them off."

"We'll find a place where we can get a hacksaw," McCoy declared. "And some normal clothes. There are bound to be some ranches out here somewhere. They're probably pretty few and far between, since it takes a whole hell of a lot of ground to support any stock in this godforsaken territory, but if we can find one, we can take what we need."

Frank was careful not to allow the concern he felt at McCoy's words to show on his face. He didn't want to put innocent people in harm's way any more than he had to. And a rancher and his family would definitely be in harm's way if Cicero McCoy paid them a visit. As McCoy had said, he would take what he needed—and probably kill anybody who got in his way.

Frank told himself to cross that bridge when they came to it. Maybe McCoy wouldn't hurt anybody. If he tried to, Frank would stop him, even if that meant abandoning the plan. Conrad might not like it, but the lives of innocent folks meant more to Frank than eighty thousand dollars worth of bank money. As he had told his son, that loot could be replaced. Frank would never miss it. He had gotten involved in this only because of the spirit Conrad had shown and the desire to truly bring McCoy to justice, which included recovering the money.

They pushed the horses to a fast trot again. Frank and McCoy both looked behind them on a regular basis. McCoy was checking their back trail for signs of pursuit. Frank didn't have to do that. He *knew* the pursuit was back there, in the form of Abner Hoyt and the other bounty hunters working for Conrad. What Frank wanted to be sure of was that Hoyt and the others weren't crowding him and McCoy.

"We gave the bastards the slip," McCoy said around the middle of the afternoon. "That plan we hatched worked like a charm, Morton."

"Except that Gideon got killed," Frank said.

"Yeah, well, that's too bad. But we weren't really going to bring him with us, anyway, now were we?"

Frank shook his head. The man he was pretending to be wouldn't show a great deal of concern over Gideon's fate—wouldn't really even give a damn, probably—so he told himself not to say anything else about it.

A few minutes later they were both distracted, anyway, when McCoy suddenly reined his mount to a halt, stood up in the stirrups, and pointed. "Look yonder," he said.

Frank looked and saw black smoke coiling into the air. There was too much of it for the smoke to be coming from a chimney. Yet it had to be coming from somewhere.

"Must be some sort of trouble," Frank said. Out here in this rugged country, so close to the border, that much smoke couldn't mean anything else.

"Let's go find out," McCoy said, and he heeled his horse into a run.

Frank didn't have any choice but to ride after him and hope that they weren't waltzing into something they couldn't get out of.

Chapter 16

They topped a rise a few minutes later and looked down across a shallow valley where a creek meandered into the Gila River from the south. The stream had to be spring-fed because there was water in it even at this dry time of year. A few scrubby cottonwoods grew along its banks, and a sparse carpet of grass covered the valley floor. There was enough graze here to support a small herd of cattle. The animals cropped peacefully at the grass on the far side of the valley.

There was nothing peaceful about the scene on the near side of the valley, though. The roof of the adobe cabin that had been built there in the shade of a cotton-wood was on fire. Flames leaped from the windows of the cabin as well. The adobe walls wouldn't burn, but the roof and the interior would.

Nearby in a corral made of peeled poles, a milk cow lay on its side, arrows bristling from its body. In the yard between the corral and the cabin were the bodies of a couple of dogs, big shaggy curs that reminded Frank of Dog. They had been skewered by arrows, too, and the sight made Frank's jaw tighten with anger.

Likely, there was even worse to be found down there, though.

McCoy kicked his horse into a run. "Come on!" he tossed over his shoulder. "Maybe we can save some of the clothes and find something to get these chains off of us!"

Frank didn't care about that right now. He was more concerned with the possibility that some of the settlers might still be alive down there, remote though that chance might be.

He rode hard down the hill with McCoy. They reined in when they reached the yard. Frank saw a huddled shape lying just inside the cabin's open door. He swung down from the saddle and hurried closer. The heat of the flames beat against his face. The fire was blazing away inside the cabin. Anybody trapped in there had to be dead. But the man in the doorway might still have a chance. Frank crouched, sidled closer, and reached out to grasp the man's shirt. He backed up, hauling the dead-weight out of the cabin.

Unfortunately, deadweight was exactly what it was. The rancher lay facedown, and the back of his shirt was dark and sodden with blood. When Frank had pulled the man about ten yards from the cabin, he stopped and rolled him onto his back. The rancher's eyes stared up sightlessly at the brassy Arizona sky, marred now by the clouds of smoke rising from the cabin.

"You reckon Apaches did this?" McCoy asked from the back of his horse.

Frank nodded. "No doubt about it. I tangled with them a few times, back in my younger days."

"I never was much of an Indian fighter myself. Used to ride with a fella who was half-Apache, half-Mex. He said the Apaches down in Mexico still raid up here across the border sometimes."

"That's right. That's what happened here. They killed everybody, set fire to the cabin, and ran off the horses."

McCoy nodded toward the other side of the valley where the cattle still grazed. "They didn't bother the cows."

"An Apache doesn't have much use for a cow," Frank said with a shake of his head. "You can't ride cattle, and Apaches prefer horse meat to beef."

McCoy turned his horse. "I'm going to see if there's a hacksaw or anything else we can use over there in that shed. I reckon all the extra clothes are probably burned up already in the cabin."

"Look for a shovel, too."

McCoy glanced back. "What for? We're not going to take the time to dig any graves. Check the man's pockets for extra ammo. We're going to run out soon."

Frank nodded, although it made him sick inside to not bury the man. He found a large handful of cartridges for the rifles that he transferred to his pocket.

The adobe shed was separated from the cabin by about forty feet of open ground. McCoy rode over to it and dismounted. A door hung crookedly on leather hinges. He swung it open—

Then jerked back as a shot blasted from inside the shed. Frank saw the crimson bloom of Colt flame in the shadows.

"Son of a bitch!" McCoy yelled as he swung the Winchester up.

"No!" Frank shouted. He lunged toward the outlaw, grabbed the barrel of the rifle, and wrenched it up as McCoy pulled the trigger. The shot blasted harmlessly into the air. Frank shoved McCoy to the side, out of the line of fire, and ducked the other way himself. "Don't shoot!" he called to whoever was inside the shed. "We're friends!"

McCoy glared at him, but didn't fire again. He kept his rifle trained on the open door from his side of the shed, though, as did Frank.

"Come on out of there," Frank urged. "We won't hurt you, whoever you are." Had to be a member of the rancher's family who had taken shelter in the shed when the Apaches attacked, he thought.

There were no more shots, but a weak voice said, "H-help me, mister. . . . I'm hurt awful bad. . . . Sorry I tried to . . . gun you . . . thought you was some o' them . . . redskins come back to . . . to . . ."

The voice trailed away as if the speaker had passed out. Frank thought it belonged to a young man. He took a step toward the doorway, but McCoy snapped, "Careful! I reckon it could be a trick."

"I don't think so," Frank said. "The boy sounded hurt pretty bad to me."

But he kept his rifle ready anyway as he stepped into the doorway.

He saw the pistol lying on the ground where it had fallen from the youngster's hand. The gun was a cap-and-ball revolver that was old enough to have belonged to the boy's grandfather. It still worked, however, as the young man had proven by nearly ventilating McCoy with it.

Frank dropped to a knee next to the bloody shape lying on the ground inside the shed. Enough light came through the open door and gaps in the ceiling for him to see that the unlucky young fella was shot to pieces. He must have been wounded several times as he ran for the shed. It was a little surprising that he was still alive. Frank knew there was nothing he could do for the boy.

But he lifted him anyway and pillowed his head

against his thigh. "Take it easy, son," he said. "You're going to be all right now."

The young man was sixteen or seventeen, with sandy hair and blue eyes that were revealed as his eyelids flickered open. Those eyes were filled with pain, too, but there was nothing Frank could do about that.

"It was . . . 'Paches," he gasped. "They come outta . . . nowhere. Pa! Ma! Are they . . . are they . . ."

"They're fine," Frank told him. The lie was a mercy. The rancher, this boy's pa, was dead, and his mother was probably inside that burning cabin. If she wasn't, then the Apaches had taken her with them, so she was as good as dead. But Frank didn't really think that would turn out to be the case. A small raiding party from south of the border likely wouldn't want to be bothered with taking prisoners. They were just out to kill settlers and steal horses and cause as much terror and destruction as possible.

The boy found the strength somehow to lift a hand and clutch at Frank's arm. "You got to . . . help them!"

"Don't worry, son," Frank told him. "We'll take care of your ma and pa, too." That meant burying them, since it was all that was left that anyone could do for them. McCoy rolled his eyes at the idea, but Frank ignored him for the moment. "Was there anybody else here? You got any brothers or sisters?"

"N-no . . . didn't mean them . . . meant the Sorengaards. . . . Injuns were . . . headed for their place . . . when they rode out."

A chill went through Frank. If there was another ranch in the area, as the youngster's words indicated, it would probably prove too tempting a target for the Apaches to pass up.

"Gotta . . . help Ingrid . . . don't let . . . 'Paches get her," the boy was muttering. His eyes had slipped closed.

Frank leaned closer, and urgency was in his voice as he asked, "Where's the Sorengaard spread? How do we find it?"

"East . . . east o' here . . . 'bout three miles . . . help Ingrid!"

Frank didn't know for sure who Ingrid was, but he could make a pretty good guess. The Sorengaard family probably had a daughter about this boy's age, and he was sweet on her. Now he was scared that the raiding party would hit the Sorengaard ranch next, and he was probably right about that, too.

"We'll head over there right now," Frank told the youngster. "You'll be all right until we get back—"

He stopped short as he realized that the boy was already all right . . . or as all right as he ever would be again. His chest had stopped rising and falling, and the peacefulness of death had smoothed away the lines of pain and terror on his face.

"There's an ax here," McCoy said. "Maybe we can use it to chop these chains off. Can't do anything with it about the shackles themselves, though. That'll have to wait."

"It'll all have to wait," Frank said as he gently lowered the boy's head to the ground. "We've got to head for the Sorengaard ranch and give them a hand, if it's not too late already."

McCoy stared at him, "Are you serious, Morton? That's none of our damn business."

Frank picked up the cap-and-ball pistol and checked the cylinder as he straightened to his feet. The gun had five shots left in it. The boy had managed to reload after he made it into the shed, and he hadn't fired any of the rounds except the one when McCoy opened the door.

The youngster had probably expected to see an Apache standing there, Frank thought.

"I gave that boy my word."

"Well, I didn't. I'm not going to waste my time burying him or his folks, and I'm not riding to the rescue of those Scandahoovians he was talking about, either. Hell, the Indians have probably wiped them out already, anyway."

"Maybe not," Frank said as he stepped out of the shed and started toward the horses. "I gave my word," he said again, "and if we help them, maybe they'll help us. We still need a hacksaw and some clothes."

"Yeah, there's that," McCoy said in a grudging tone. "Oh, hell. Wait up, Morton. I'll ride over there with you. But I'm bringing this ax along."

They mounted up and rode hard across the valley, still following the Gila River. Frank hated to leave those folks behind without giving them a proper burial. By the time he and McCoy could have gotten back, it would be too late. The scavengers would have been at the bodies already. Anyway, the dead were beyond caring. Ceremonies were strictly for the living.

By the time they had ridden up and down a couple of ridges, Frank began to hear gunfire in the distance. The sound of shots could travel a long way out here in this dry air. He and McCoy glanced at each other and kept riding. As long as they could hear the shots, they knew that the Apaches hadn't succeeded in overrunning the Sorengaards.

Frank couldn't help but think about Abner Hoyt and the other bounty hunters who were back there somewhere behind them. The addition of eight battle-hardened fighting men might make all the difference in the world if Hoyt and his companions pitched in to help run off the Apaches. But to do so would reveal their presence to McCoy and ruin the plan. Frank didn't think Hoyt would do that. The man wanted the rest of the reward Conrad had promised too much to risk it.

On the other hand, if McCoy was killed fighting the Indians, that hidden loot would never be found. Frank decided that Hoyt and the others would hang back, close enough to keep an eye on what was going on, but wouldn't take a hand unless circumstances forced them to do so.

No smoke rose against the pale-blue sky, which was another good sign. The Apaches hadn't been able to get close enough to the ranch buildings to set any of them on fire. Maybe somebody at the Sorengaard place had seen the smoke from the other spread and been warned that an attack was imminent.

Frank and McCoy topped another rise, and found themselves looking down into a valley much like the one where the other ranch was located. The creek that ran through this one was about dried up, though, with only a few puddles left in its bed, and the vegetation was sparse. The ranch house, barn, and a long, low building that was probably a bunkhouse were all built of adobe with thatched roofs. Puffs of powder smoke came from the main house and the bunkhouse as defenders fired at the figures in high-topped moccasins, breechcloths, blue shirts, and red headbands who crouched behind every available bit of cover and blazed away at the buildings.

As Frank and McCoy reined in to study the situation for a moment, movement on a sandstone bluff behind the ranch house caught Frank's eye. An Apache crept along the top of the bluff. He held a burning torch in one hand, and when he reached a point directly behind the house, he raised himself up and lifted his arm, poised to throw the torch down onto the roof and set it afire.

If the warrior succeeded in that move, the flames from the roof would spread and eventually force the defenders out of the house. In the instant that Frank had to act, he snapped the rifle he carried to his shoulder, drew a bead, and pressed the trigger. The whipcrack of the Winchester rolled across the valley.

The Apache on the bluff was driven backward by the slug that punched into his broad chest. He dropped the torch and Frank watched anxiously, worried that the burning brand might still fall on the roof. It landed at the edge of the bluff, though, and stayed there. The warrior was sprawled on his back, unmoving in death.

"Hell of a shot, Morton," McCoy said.

"Yeah, and it got some attention down there, too," Frank replied with a nod toward the Apaches who were attacking the ranch. Several of them had twisted around at the sound of the shot, and now they opened fire on the two newcomers at the top of the hill.

Coolly, ignoring the bullets whistling around them, Frank and McCoy reined their horses back over to the far side of the slope where the animals would be safely out of the line of fire. They swung down from the saddles and hurried back up to the crest, dropping flat and thrusting the barrels of their Winchesters over the hill so they could draw a bead on the renegades below.

Frank opened fire. He didn't hurry his shots, and neither did McCoy beside him. They raked the attackers with regularly spaced shots, and their deadly accurate aim knocked two more Apaches off their feet. The rest of the war party broke and ran then, because they were still taking fire from the defenders in the ranch house and bunkhouse, too. Caught between three forces like that, the raiders had no choice but to abandon their attack.

Frank counted seventeen Apaches as the renegades fled, taking their wounded with them. They would have to leave the dead warrior on the bluff, although they might come back and try to recover his body in the dark of night. That meant the war party had totaled twenty, a good-sized band of renegades who had come up from the mountain strongholds below the border. The lure of the old, bloody days had been too much for the Apaches to resist. This bunch was trying to relive those days, when the white settlers who dared to venture into the territory lived in fear of Apache wrath.

Frank and McCoy hurried the renegades on their way with a few more well-placed shots. A couple more Indians were dragging bullet-punctured legs as they fled. They followed the mostly dry creek, disappearing around a bend in the stream. The landscape in that direction was rocky, rugged, and uninviting. The Apaches would be able to lose themselves in that wasteland without any trouble.

"I reckon we're not going after them?" McCoy asked, his voice dry.

"I reckon you're right," Frank replied as he looked over the barrel of his Winchester at the spot where the members of the war party had vanished.

McCoy came to his feet. "Let's get down there and see if those folks are properly grateful for our help."

Frank stood, too, and said, "Better be careful. One good look at these clothes and the chains, and they'll know we escaped from Yuma."

"That doesn't matter," McCoy said. "We saved their hides. That redskinned bastard up on the bluff would've burned them out if not for your shot, Morton. All of them would've died. They'll give us a hand."

Frank wished he could be as confident of that as McCoy was. He hoped, too, that they weren't just trading one set of problems for another.

Standing on top of the hill like that, both of them were visible to the people in the buildings down below. McCoy raised his rifle over his head in one hand and waved it back and forth. "We're coming in!" he shouted. Frank didn't know if the bank robber's voice carried that far, but in all likelihood it did. They turned to retrieve their horses, and a few moments later they were both riding down the ridge toward the Sorengaard ranch.

Several dogs emerged from the barn and ran barking to meet them. That reminded Frank of the murdered dogs at the other spread, and he was glad to see that these big, shaggy fellas were all right. A couple of men came out of the bunkhouse and followed the dogs. They held rifles and watched the two strangers like hawks.

A mostly bald man with a drooping white mustache stepped out of the main house, followed by a couple of blond youngsters and a woman with gray braids. That would be the Sorengaard family, Frank guessed. The pretty blond girl who was about fifteen had to be Ingrid. Frank could see why the unfortunate young fella on the other spread had been smitten with her. Chances were, the two of them would have gotten married sooner or later and started a ranch and a family of their own.

Now that would never happen, because of the bloodlust of those renegades.

"Hello the house!" McCoy called as he and Frank drew closer. "Howdy, folks!"

The white-mustachioed man swung up the rifle he held so that it covered Frank and McCoy and ordered, "Hold it right there, you two jailbirds!"

Chapter 17

"Don't come any closer!" the rancher went on as
Frank and McCoy reined their horses to a stop. The man
had a slight Swedish accent.

"What the hell!" McCoy burst out. "Didn't you see us
up there shooting at those damned Apaches, mister?"

"Yah, and I can see those prison outfits, too, and the
chains on your wrists and ankles. Jailbirds, that's what
you are, the both of you!" The man's hands shook a little
from clutching the rifle so tightly. The other members of
his family were armed, too, the woman with a shotgun,
the boy and girl with pistols.

"Take it easy," Frank said, keeping his voice calm and
level. These folks had already had their nerves stretched
to the breaking point by the Indian attack. He didn't want
them to open fire on him and McCoy. "We don't mean
you any harm," Frank went on. "That's why we pitched
in to help run off those renegades, Mr. Sorengaard."

The rancher's bushy eyebrows shot up in surprise.
"How do you know who I am?"

"A young fella on a spread west of here told us
about you."

The blond girl in her teens spoke up excitedly. "That would be Tim!" she said, adding, "Tim Faraday." Fear shone in her wide blue eyes. "We saw smoke in that direction. Tim and his folks, are they—"

She broke off her question and swallowed hard, unable to go on.

"I'm sorry," Frank said, making his voice as gentle as he could. "The Apaches hit there first. They killed your friend, Miss Sorengaard, and a fella I reckon was his father. I don't know about Mrs. Faraday, but the cabin was burned out and I suspect she was in there."

Both of the females began to cry. The boy looked mighty upset, too. He and young Tim Faraday had probably been friends. The two men who had come from the bunkhouse, who Frank had pegged as ranch hands who rode for the Sorengaards, had stepped up behind him and McCoy to cover them. Now those men began to curse in low, bitter tones.

Sorengaard looked shaken, too, but he just muttered, "*Gott hilfen* those poor people. Did you at least have the decency to bury them?"

"There wasn't time," Frank said with a shake of his head. "The boy was still alive when we found him. He told us about your spread over here and must have known that the Apaches would head here next, because he asked us to come help you. Those were his last words, in fact."

The blond girl sobbed harder. The graying woman clutched at her husband's arm and said, "Lars, we have to go over there and tend to those poor people."

Sorengaard nodded his head. His prominent Adam's apple bobbed up and down in his stringy neck. "Yah, yah," he said. "If the buzzards and the coyotes have left anything to bury."

"Lars!"

Her father's comments just made the girl cry even more. Mrs. Sorengaard turned, put her arm around Ingrid's shoulders, and led her back into the house.

Into the grim silence that followed, McCoy said, "Listen, we're sorry about what happened to your friends, but do you think you could give us a hand? We'd like to get these chains off—"

"Yah, I'll just bet you would!" Sorengaard said.

McCoy's jaw tightened in anger. "We risked our own lives to help you people, and all we're asking is a little help in return."

"You are convicts! You have escaped from the prison at Yuma. We have seen others like you before. The law always comes hunting them."

"What business is that of yours?" McCoy snapped back. "I don't see a badge pinned to your shirt, Sorengaard. All I see is a man who might be dead along with his family by now if we hadn't come along. You know one of those damned Apaches was about to set fire to your roof when Morton here shot him, don't you?"

Sorengaard looked surprised again. He turned his head to gaze up at the roof and the bluff behind the house. The body of the dead Indian couldn't be seen from down here.

"He's tellin' the truth about that, Boss," one of the cowboys put in. "Hank and me seen that redskin up yonder, but we couldn't get a good shot at him from where we were."

"He had a torch," the other puncher added. "Looked like he was about to toss it down on the house."

Sorengaard swallowed again. He had to know that if the renegade had succeeded in firing the house, it would have doomed him and his family. He looked at Frank and said, "You shot that Indian?"

Frank shrugged. "Seemed like the thing to do at the time."

"Yah. Yah . . ." Sorengaard nodded and lowered his rifle to his side. "I owe you a debt I cannot ever repay. But I can at least try, even though it means going against the law. You men can get down from your horses." He turned to the boy. "Sven, go to the barn and find my hacksaw."

The youngster tucked his pistol behind his belt and hurried off to do his father's bidding. Lars Sorengaard looked at Frank and McCoy again and went on. "What else do you want? There is water and grain for your horses, and plenty of food in the house . . ."

"We could use some regular clothes," McCoy said as he dismounted. Frank swung down from the saddle as well and nodded in agreement with McCoy's request.

"We got some extra duds that'll likely fit you," one of the cowhands offered. "I don't much cotton to helpin' escaped convicts, neither, but I reckon after what you hombres done, you deserve it."

"Go out to the bunkhouse," Sorengaard said. "I will tell my wife to prepare a meal, and then I will bring the hacksaw when my boy finds it. Zeke, tend to their horses. Hank, hitch the team to the wagon. As soon as we can, we will go over to the Faraday ranch and see what needs to be done there."

"What about the Injuns?" the cowboy called Hank asked. "Reckon they'll double back and hit us again?"

Sorengaard shook his head. "I do not know, but I doubt it. When renegades like that cross the border, they hit and run and move on to the next place they want to attack."

"You've been here for a while, haven't you, Sorengaard?" Frank asked. The settled look of the place told him that much.

The rancher nodded. "Fifteen years. Many times I have fought the Apaches. Geronimo himself came here once and tried to run me out." Sorengaard squared his shoulders. "But I am still here."

"I reckon you know what you're talking about, then, when you talk about what the Indians will do."

Frank and McCoy walked over to the bunkhouse, carrying their rifles with them. McCoy still had the old cap-and-ball pistol, too. Frank wondered if they might be able to rustle up some newer handguns here to go along with their Winchesters. He knew he would feel better with the weight of a Colt on his hip again.

It took a while for Sorengaard to saw the shackles and leg irons off the wrists and ankles of Frank and McCoy. He had to be careful to keep from cutting their flesh, too. By the time he was done, Mrs. Sorengaard had food ready. Frank and McCoy changed into the well-worn range clothes and battered Stetsons provided by the two ranch hands, Zeke and Hank, and walked to the house with Sorengaard.

"I want you men gone by the time I get back here," the rancher said as they went inside. "Hank and I will go see that the Faradays receive a proper burial. Zeke and my son Sven will still be here, though, and they are both good shots."

"Still worried about the Apaches?" McCoy asked.

"The Apaches . . . and other savages."

McCoy grunted. "Still don't have it through your head that we don't mean you any harm, do you, mister?"

"A man who lives on the frontier must always be cautious, especially with his family."

"Don't worry, Sorengaard," Frank said. "We've got places to go, so we'll be moving on as soon as we've eaten." He broached the other subject that was on his mind. "I was wondering if you might have a couple of extra revolvers around here. . . ."

Sorengaard's mouth hardened under the drooping mustache, but he nodded. "Yah. You should have guns and ammunition, and we have plenty of both. But you must give me your word you will not use them against innocent people."

"Where we're going, we won't be running into any innocent people," McCoy said. "Maybe those Apaches again, though."

"If you do . . . kill some of them for me, yah?"

McCoy laughed. "Sure."

The food was simple but good, and washed down with strong black coffee, it made Frank feel better. That was somewhat canceled out, however, by the grief on the faces of Mrs. Sorengaard and her daughter. Ingrid's eyes were red from crying, but she had gotten it under control and only sniffled a little every now and then.

When they had finished eating, they buckled on the gun belts that Sorengaard had left for them. Frank drew the Colt from the holster, spun the cylinder to check the action, and then thumbed bullets into the chambers.

Sven Sorengaard watched him intently. After a minute, Frank asked, "Got something on your mind, son?"

"Are you going after those damned Apaches?" the boy asked.

"Sven!" his mother snapped. "Such language in your own house! If you must talk like that, go to the bunkhouse . . . or the barn!"

"I'm sorry, Mama." Sven looked at Frank again. "But I still want to know if you're going after them."

McCoy answered instead. "Not likely, kid. Why? You thinking about coming with us?"

"Tim was my friend. His death should be avenged."

"You're right about that, Sven," Frank said, "but we're not in the business of chasing down Apaches. If we happen to run into them again, that's one thing, but unless we do . . ." He shrugged. "Sooner or later, one way or another, they'll get what's coming to them. I know that's not much comfort, but it's the best we can do."

"You're right," Sven said. "It's not much comfort."

The horses had been unsaddled, rubbed down, grained, and watered. As Zeke was putting the saddles back on them in the shade of the barn, he said to Frank and McCoy, "I reckon you fellas stole these horses. Those brands on 'em mean they belong to the territorial government."

"What business is that of yours, mister?" McCoy asked in a hard, dangerous voice.

"Not a bit," Zeke replied without hesitation. "I don't know what you done to get yourselves throwed in Yuma Prison, and I don't want to know. Just as soon not even know your names. But I've had some friends who wound up behind bars, and they weren't such bad fellas. I just hope neither one of you did anything too awful terrible, so I won't feel too bad about us givin' you a hand like this."

"Just think of us as a couple of strangers who pitched in to help fight off the Apaches," Frank advised, thinking that there was no need for anyone on the Sorengaard ranch to know that McCoy was a bank robber and cold-blooded murderer.

"I got to tell you," Zeke went on, "when the lawdogs show up lookin' for you, the boss will tell 'em that you were here. He'll tell 'em which way you went, too. Don't expect any favors along those lines."

McCoy frowned, and Frank suddenly knew what he was thinking. It might be better if they didn't leave any witnesses alive behind them to tell the law anything. Frank hoped that McCoy wouldn't try to act on that thought. If he did, Frank would just have to stop him, no matter what the cost.

There wasn't any posse on their trail . . . but McCoy wouldn't know that. The only ones following them were Abner Hoyt and the other bounty hunters, and they already knew where Frank and McCoy were headed. The manhunters might not even stop at this ranch.

"Let's just get moving," Frank said. "We've stayed here long enough."

"Yeah," McCoy agreed. Frank was relieved when the bank robber swung up into the saddle and turned his horse toward the east. Over his shoulder, McCoy said to Zeke, "Maybe if you went back in the barn, you wouldn't see which direction we rode off in."

"That's right," Zeke said. "I surely wouldn't." He retreated into the cavernous adobe structure as Frank mounted up as well.

Then the two riders put the Sorengaard ranch behind them and continued east along the Gila River.

They didn't travel in that direction for very many miles, though, before McCoy veered to the south, paralleling a range of small but rugged mountains.

"Is this the way to Ambush Valley?" Frank asked.

The question caused McCoy to shoot a sharp, suspicious glance toward him. "What do you know about Ambush Valley?" the bank robber asked.

"I told you, I heard about that loot you're supposed to have hidden somewhere. The newspaper stories all said that you'd been captured in a little wide place in the road called Hinkley, near Ambush Valley. Speculation is that you cached the money somewhere in there."

McCoy didn't say anything for a long moment, then finally replied, "Well, since we're riding together now, I reckon it won't do any harm to tell you. The money's in Ambush Valley, all right. I had planned to leave it there for six months, maybe a year, and hide out in Mexico until things had cooled down enough for me to come back and get it. But I hadn't figured on getting caught before I ever got across the border. I'm not taking a chance on anything like that happening again. I want to get my hands on that money, light a shuck for Mexico, and never come back." He grinned. "I reckon eighty grand will keep me in fine fashion down in Mañana-land for the rest of my life."

"Fifty-six thousand," Frank corrected. "Remember that thirty percent of the loot is mine."

"Yeah, sure," McCoy said with a casual wave of his hand. "I just forgot."

I'll just bet you did, Frank thought. McCoy's slip told him that the outlaw had no intention of honoring their deal. McCoy would ride with Frank and pretend to be partners with him until they reached the money, just in case he needed Frank's help in getting out of some other jam, but once McCoy had his hands on the loot again . . .

Well, Frank would be expendable then. As in bullet-in-the-back expendable.

Frank didn't intend to let that double cross take place. But he would have to be mighty careful. McCoy was tough as nails and good with a gun. McCoy probably thought that *Frank* intended to double-cross *him* and take

all the money, too. Crooks always believed that everybody was just as crooked as they were.

So even though they might fight side by side against
shared dangers, in McCoy's mind they were just waiting
for the right moment to try to kill each other. That meant
Frank would be on hair-trigger alert once they reached
Ambush Valley and recovered the loot.

A few hours after turning south, they came to a set of
railroad tracks. The shining double line of steel ran east
and west, shimmering into the distance as far as the eye
could see in both directions.

"This is the Southern Pacific track," McCoy said as he
reined in beside the rails. He nodded toward the east.
"There's a water stop over yonder, just this side of the
mountains. We'll ride over and refill our canteens, because it'll be a long, thirsty trek from there to where
we're headed."

"What if a train comes along?" Frank asked.

"What about it? We don't have to worry. We're not
convicts anymore, Morton. We're just a couple of saddle
tramps. Nothing the least bit unusual about us."

They turned their mounts and started riding along
beside the tracks. "You ever hold up a train?" Frank
asked after a few minutes.

"Why do you want to know?"

"Just curious, that's all. I know you pulled a lot of
bank jobs, but I'm not sure about the other."

McCoy laughed. "Yeah, I've held up trains. Not very
many, though. Never liked it. Sometimes the express car
is almost empty, and when there is money there, you
have to dig through a bunch of mail and other worthless
junk to find it. Then there's the business of cleaning out
the passengers. That's usually a penny-ante haul, and you
run the risk of some pilgrim deciding to be a hero and

going for a gun. Too much risk and not enough reward, unless you happen to get a tip that a particular train is hauling a lot of money. I'd rather hit a bank because you *know* there'll be cash there. And the sort of hombre who works in a bank isn't as tough as a trainman, either." McCoy looked over at Frank. "How about you?"

Frank shook his head. "Never robbed a bank or a train, either. Or a stagecoach, for that matter. Until I shot that sheriff and his deputies, my lawbreaking was confined to dabbing a loop on other men's cows and slapping a new brand on them."

"You're plenty tough, though," McCoy pointed out. "Maybe instead of splitting up, we ought to ride together for a while after we get that money. I might want to put together a new gang."

"I thought you were going to Mexico and retiring from being an outlaw."

"Oh, I am, I am." McCoy grinned. "But a fella likes to keep his hand in. And there are banks in Mexico, too."

"That there are," Frank agreed with a chuckle. He grew more serious as he went on. "Mighty tough, getting all your partners killed like they were."

McCoy frowned over at him again. "How do you mean?"

"Wiped out by that posse the way they were. From what I read, they must've all been wounded before you got to Ambush Valley and died while you were in there."

"That's what happened, all right," McCoy nodded. "Damn shame, too. They were good men."

But not good enough to keep you from double-crossing them. Frank was more sure than ever now that McCoy had murdered at least some of the members of his gang. Some might have died from wounds received at the hands of the posse, as Frank had said, but not all of them. Frank was certain of it.

The elevated water tank that sat beside the railroad tracks appeared in the distance ahead of them. It took a long time to get there, since distances were deceptive out here, and night had fallen by the time they did.

"We'll camp here," McCoy decided. "Not right beside the tracks, but there's probably an arroyo not far off. Let the horses drink their fill and rest for the night, then fill the canteens in the morning."

"Sounds like a good idea. How long will it take to reach Ambush Valley?"

"Couple of days, I reckon."

They pulled down the sluice attached to the water tank and filled their hats, then let the horses drink from them. McCoy stuck his head under the stream of water and let it soak and cool him. Frank did likewise. It had been a hell of a long day. When they woke up that morning, they were still behind the walls of Yuma Territorial Prison. Now they were a good twenty-five miles away—and they had fought Apaches since then, to boot!

They found a gully—it wasn't even worthy of being called an arroyo—about a quarter of a mile south of the tracks. They didn't have bedrolls or even any blankets, so they would just have to shiver through the chilly desert night. Frank had put up with much worse in his life. Anyway, it beat being stuck in prison, didn't it?

They hobbled the horses and made a cold supper on some biscuits and jerky that Mrs. Sorengaard had put in a sack for them. Then they took turns standing watch, and when it came time for Frank to sleep, he dozed off without worrying about what McCoy might do. He was confident that the bank robber wanted to keep him alive . . . for now.

Exhaustion caused Frank to fall into a deeper sleep than

he might have otherwise, so it was nearly dawn when he awoke. And he might not have roused then had it not been for the rumble of a locomotive and the clanking clatter of a train coming to a stop nearby. He opened his eyes and lifted his head to see Cicero McCoy crouched just below the lip of the gully, peering off to the north in the gray light.

"Train stopping for water?" Frank asked.

"Yeah," McCoy replied without looking around. A cold laugh came from him. "Bastards don't have any idea that somebody's around. If you threw down on the engineer and fireman, I could hit the express car. . . ." He laughed again. "No, that's crazy. Just the two of us couldn't pull it off. Anyway, like I said, I don't like to rob trains. I reckon old habits are just hard to break."

Old habits like robbing and killing? Frank supposed so. That was all that a man like Cicero McCoy really knew.

The train crew filled the boiler on the locomotive from the water tank, and then the brakeman, who had climbed onto the scaffolding around the tank, pulled the sluice back up and swung it into place. He was ready to climb down when a shot suddenly rang out, loud in the early morning stillness. The brakeman staggered, clutched his belly, doubled over, and fell off the scaffolding, plunging to a hard landing on the ground under the tank.

Frank glanced at McCoy, thinking for an instant that McCoy had killed the brakeman, even though he knew logically that the shot hadn't come from the gully. Then, a second later, he knew what had happened.

Because with shrill yips and cries and a flurry of gunshots, renegade Apaches on horseback suddenly plunged out of the concealment of some nearby brush and attacked the train.

Chapter 18

"Oh, hell!" McCoy burst out. "Them again!"

As Frank leaped up, grabbed his Winchester, and joined McCoy in crouching at the lip of the gully, he looked at the Apaches and supposed that the outlaw was right. It was possible, of course, that two separate war parties of renegades had slipped over the border from Mexico, but not very likely. And the number of attackers looked to be right, the same as the band Frank and McCoy had encountered at the Sorengaard ranch the day before.

The train crew scrambled for safety as the Indians charged. Such a small number of Apaches couldn't hope to take over the train, but they could kill some of the crew and passengers and terrorize the others before fleeing. Glass flew from some of the windows in the passenger cars as the renegades shot them out.

Puffs of powder smoke came from those same cars as the passengers fought back. More shots came from the engine and the express car. Even though none of the Indians were hit, at least not badly enough to make them fall from their horses, they peeled back, curving away from the train.

In the gully, McCoy asked, "Are we going to take a hand in this?"

"I don't see any real reason to," Frank said. "It looks like those renegades are already starting to be a mite sorry that they decided to attack a train."

"Yeah, they didn't do much damage, did they? Killed that brakie up on the water tank and broke a few windows, but that's about it."

Still whooping as if they had just experienced the biggest triumph for the red man's cause since the Little Big Horn, the Apaches dashed away from the railroad tracks, raising a cloud of dust that moved off to the south. While Frank and McCoy watched unseen from the gully, the engineer and fireman climbed out, retrieved the body of the brakeman who had been shot off the water tank, and placed it in the caboose. Then they returned to the engine and a few minutes later, the locomotive's drivers engaged, smoke boiled from its diamond-shaped stack, and the train lurched into motion. It rumbled and rattled off to the west.

"I'm glad we didn't have to get mixed up in that fracas," McCoy said as he stood up, once the train was out of sight. "I don't want anything else slowing us down."

Frank got to his feet, too, and commented, "There's one thing we might have to worry about."

"What's that?"

Frank nodded toward the south. "Those Apaches took off in the same direction that we're going. We're liable to run into them again if we keep going toward Ambush Valley."

"We're going on, all right," McCoy said with a determined scowl on his face. "And if those redskins get in our way, it's their own damned lookout."

One thing McCoy wasn't lacking for, Frank thought, was confidence.

If the renegades got between McCoy and that loot . . . well, he'd just kill 'em. That was all there was to it.

Frank was glad they had made a cold camp the night before. Those Apaches had been hiding in the brush only a couple of hundred yards from where he and McCoy had spent the night. They were fortunate that the war party hadn't stumbled over them in the darkness. If that had happened, the two white men probably would have been wiped out.

They finished the last of the biscuits and jerky for breakfast, let the horses drink at the water tank again, topped off their canteens, and headed south, keeping the mountains to their left.

"Ambush Valley is down at the tail end of this range," McCoy explained. "We have enough water to get there if we're careful, but we're liable to get a mite hungry."

Frank nodded toward the mountains. "We might be able to find a deer or some other game in the foothills."

"I don't know if we want to be shooting, though. Not with those Apaches around."

That was a good point. Well, it wasn't like Frank had never gone hungry before.

The heat increased as the sun rose higher and the men continued their trek. When the blazing orb was directly overhead, the blistering heat forced them to veer over into the foothills and find some shade, so that they could wait out the worst of the inferno. They took shelter between a couple of massive slabs of sandstone that looked like they had been leaned together by a giant hand. The shadow under the rocks was blessedly cool after the blast furnace they'd experienced out in the open.

Frank and McCoy sat down on the sand to rest. "Wish I had a smoke," McCoy mused.

"You can buy all the tobacco you want after we get our hands on that money," Frank pointed out.

"Yeah." McCoy chuckled. "I wish I could've been there when that pasty-faced runt found out that I'd escaped from Yuma, too."

"Pasty-faced runt?"

"Yeah. The Eastern dude who owns that bank I robbed in Tucson."

Conrad, in other words. Frank kept his face carefully neutral as he asked, "What do you know about him?"

"Not much, except he was there in Tucson when we hit the bank. If he hadn't been, if he hadn't posted that reward on my head, those bounty hunters wouldn't have come after me and I'd be in Mexico now. So all this is his fault."

"You wouldn't have the eighty grand," Frank said. "You cached it before you got caught."

"I took enough money with me to live comfortably for a while, like I told you I planned to do. It would have worked out, if it hadn't been for that bastard Browning."

Conrad wasn't a bastard, Frank thought, but of course he couldn't say that. As far as McCoy was aware, Frank had no connection at all with Conrad Browning.

"Only thing better than seeing the look on his face when he found out I'd escaped would be putting a bullet right between his beady little eyes," McCoy went on. "Don't reckon I'll ever get a chance to do that, though."

Damn right you won't, Frank vowed. I'll kill you myself before that happens.

As the sun began to lower in the west and the worst of the heat was over, the two men left the shelter of the rocks and rode south again. Hunger gnawed at Frank's belly, but there was no food. They stopped for a little while at dusk to let the horses rest, then pushed on as night settled down. With the mountains looming on their left to guide them, they didn't have to worry about losing their way in the darkness.

They didn't make camp until about midnight. Frank slept fitfully when it was his turn, haunted by cold and hunger. He was just as glad to hit the trail again early the next morning, when the sky was barely gray enough for them to see where they were going.

There had been no further sign of the Apaches. Frank hoped the war party had headed back to the border and wouldn't complicate things any further for him.

McCoy noticed Frank looking back over his shoulder at one point and said, "Don't worry. Nobody's behind us. We would've seen them by now if they were."

That was where McCoy was wrong. Abner Hoyt and the other bounty hunters were back there, staying far enough behind so that they wouldn't be spotted by the two fugitives.

But what if they weren't? Frank suddenly wondered. What if something had happened to Hoyt's party? Those Apaches could have doubled back, circled around, and attacked them. Hoyt and his men were tough, but they would have been outnumbered by more than two to one and the Apaches were fine fighting men, too. Or some other accident could have befallen them. Frank thought it was unlikely, but he had to admit that it was possible he was out here on his own with McCoy, deep in these Arizona badlands that were about to get even worse when they reached Ambush Valley.

If that proved to be the case, he would deal with it when the time came, he told himself. He wasn't afraid of McCoy. It had been a good many years since he had wasted time being afraid of any man.

Around midmorning, McCoy reined in abruptly and dismounted, drawing his gun as he stalked toward some small rocks. Frank started to ask him what the hell he was doing, but McCoy motioned him to silence. McCoy crouched next to the rocks, reversed his gun, and waited. After several minutes, he struck with blinding speed at something, bringing the butt of the revolver down on some target Frank couldn't see.

When McCoy straightened, he had a large lizard dangling from his left hand as he held the creature's tail. The lizard's head was smashed. That was what he'd walloped with the gun butt.

"Not much meat on one of these scaly little bastards, but it's better than nothing, I reckon."

Frank's stomach clenched in revulsion. "Some of those critters are poisonous, you know," he pointed out.

"Yeah, but not this one. Fella I used to ride with named Cortez grew up in this country. He taught me what you can eat and what you can't."

Frank wondered briefly what had happened to the outlaw called Cortez, but he didn't ask McCoy. Chances were, Cortez had either been killed by the bounty hunters . . . or by McCoy himself.

McCoy scrounged around, gathered some sparse grass and twigs, and built a small, almost smokeless fire. He skinned the lizard and roasted it over the tiny flames, and Frank had to admit that the smell of cooking meat, even lizard meat, made him even hungrier.

"Want some?" McCoy asked.

"Yeah, I guess," Frank said. He took the small hunk of

meat that McCoy tore off the roasted carcass and chewed it. The lizard was tough and stringy, with a rank taste to it, and there wasn't much of it. But what little Frank ate helped to alleviate his hunger, at least for a while.

After that grisly meal they pushed on, and McCoy set a hard, demanding pace. "We can't afford to waste any time," the bank robber explained. "The lawdogs might figure out that I'm heading for Ambush Valley and try to get there ahead of me. They'd like nothing better than to be there waiting when I rode up."

Frank knew that wouldn't happen, because Conrad and Warden Townsend wouldn't allow it to. The trail to Ambush Valley was clear of any interference, at least from the authorities.

But that didn't mean there was no danger. No one involved in formulating the plan had known that an Apache war party was going to be prowling around the area. It was those unexpected things, impossible to account for, that often wound up costing a man his life.

Frank saw concrete evidence of that a few moments later when a lone mounted figure appeared on a rise several hundred yards away. In the clear desert air, the rider's blue shirt and red headband were visible.

McCoy saw the man, too, and let out a bitter curse. "That's one of those damned renegades!" he said. "They're still around. I was hoping they'd gone back to Mexico!"

Frank had shared that hope, but obviously both he and McCoy were going to be disappointed. The distant Indian suddenly wheeled his pony and disappeared.

"He's gone to tell the rest of the war party about the two foolish white men who are riding out here alone," Frank said.

"Yeah. That means we'll have company as soon as

they can get here." McCoy yanked his horse toward the foothills. "We'd better find a place to fort up."

Frank galloped after him. Before they reached the hills, he looked back and saw the line of riders that had come into sight. The Apaches were pounding hard after him and McCoy. The two white men were closer to the foothills and would reach them before the renegades could catch up; Frank had no doubt about that.

But once they made it to the hills, they would have to find a place they could defend against long odds, or else the Apaches would overrun them. That meant, at best, a quick death in battle. At worst . . . a slow, lingering death by torture, a pastime that the Apaches loved so much.

Frank couldn't hear anything except the thunder of hoofbeats as he and McCoy raced for cover. But as they entered the hills and reined in to look around for a suitable spot to defend, the sound of gunshots came to Frank's ears, accompanied by whoops and yells. The Apaches were nothing if not enthusiastic in their savagery.

"Over there!" McCoy called as he pointed to a knoll that was dotted with medium-sized boulders. He and Frank reined their mounts behind the little rise, then leaped from the saddles and hurried behind the rocks, carrying their Winchesters.

Frank dropped to a knee and steadied the barrel of his rifle against the rock. He and McCoy had kicked up a lot of dust with their mad dash toward the hills and some of it still hung in the air, obscuring his view of the charging Apaches. As the renegades emerged from the dust, Frank settled the rifle's sights on one of the warriors who was in the lead. He had already levered a round into the chamber, so all he had to do was press the trigger.

The Winchester cracked and bucked against his shoulder. The Apache Frank had drawn a bead on jerked backward, but grabbed his horse's mane and managed not to fall. Still, Frank could tell that the man was badly hurt from the way he slumped over the animal's neck. The horse slowed to a stop as the charge continued around it.

McCoy fired as Frank worked the lever of his Winchester. "Let's whittle 'em down!" the bank robber called from his position behind another rock about twenty feet from the spot Frank had picked to defend.

Frank selected another target. The Apaches were only a couple of hundred yards away now and closing fast. He and McCoy wouldn't have time to kill all of them before they reached the rocks, no matter how fast and accurate their shots were.

But like McCoy had said, all they could do was try to cut down a little on the odds against them. Frank fired again, and this time the renegade he drilled left his horse, spun in the air, and landed facedown on the ground.

The bloodcurdling yelps were loud now, and calculated to strike terror into the hearts of the Apaches' enemies.

Frank Morgan didn't feel terror.

He felt anger that he had endured so much and come so far, only to have the success of his mission threatened by the random savagery of these renegades.

"Come on, you sons of bitches!" he growled as he jacked the Winchester's lever again. "Come on and eat lead!"

Abner Hoyt heard the faint, distant popping of gunshots for several seconds before he realized what it was. When he did realize the truth, he reined in and uttered a disgusted curse.

"What now?" Deke Mantee asked as he and the other men brought their horses to a halt.

"Shooting," Bob Bardwell said. "I hear it, too."

"And it's coming from the direction Morgan and McCoy went," Hoyt said with a curt nod. "What the hell have they gotten themselves into now?"

Joaquin Escobar leaned forward in the saddle and thumbed his sombrero back on his head. "Sounds like quite a fight," he commented. "Maybe they ran into those 'Paches again. *Quién sabe?*"

For the past couple of days, Escobar and Bardwell had been riding ahead of the main group several times a day, pushing their horses and getting close enough to the men they were trailing to make sure that Morgan and McCoy were still up there ahead of the bounty hunters, without approaching close enough to be easily spotted. The scouts had returned to the group a short time earlier and reported that they were still on the trail to Ambush Valley, just as they were supposed to be.

Now several of the men cast worried glances toward Hoyt, and Bartholomew Leaf asked, "What are we going to do, old boy? If McCoy is killed, we'll never find that bank money."

"And never get the rest of the reward," Ben Coleman added in an angry growl.

"You're not telling me anything I don't already know," Hoyt snapped. "But what can we do? If we ride in and rescue Morgan and McCoy from whatever trouble they're in, McCoy will figure out what's going on. We'll be left trying to torture the loot's hiding place out of him—and that didn't work before, now did it?"

The bounty hunters had to admit that it hadn't.

Hoyt grimaced as he stared off into the distance in the direction of the shots. "I don't like it, but we're gonna have to just hope that those two bastards can get themselves out of whatever fracas they've gotten in, so that McCoy can finish leading us to that money."

"And if they can't?" Mantee asked.

"Then I hope that McCoy dies slow and hard, at least," Hoyt said.

Frank and McCoy shot three more Apaches off their horses during the renegades' charge toward the rocks. That still left about a dozen of them, and they evidently decided that they didn't want to continue their attack right into the face of those deadly guns. The riders whirled their horses around and dashed away. The two men holed up in the rocks sent more rounds whistling after them, but the dust made it impossible to see whether or not they hit anything.

"What the hell!" McCoy exclaimed when he finally lowered his Winchester. "They had us! Why'd they turn tail and run?"

"Don't know," Frank answered as he took advantage of the opportunity to shove fresh cartridges into his rifle. "Maybe the ones who are left decided we aren't worth dying over."

"Think again." McCoy nodded toward the flat desert landscape in front of them. "They're regrouping out there."

It was true. The remaining Apaches had ridden hard until they were out of effective rifle range, then stopped and milled around. Frank saw several of them gesturing angrily with their rifles. They probably wanted to attack again, but wiser, cooler heads prevailed. The group split up into twos and threes, spreading out over the flats and circling toward the foothills, except for one group that parked themselves right in front of the spot where the two white men had taken cover.

"Son of a bitch!" McCoy said. "They're trying to keep us pinned down here while the others spread out and come at us from different directions!"

It was a plan that might well work, too . . . if the intended quarry stayed right where they were.

"Let's pull back through the hills," Frank suggested. "We can slip out of this trap before it closes around us."

"No, damn it! If we do that, it'll slow us down too much. We'll never make it to Ambush Valley before the law wises up and gets there ahead of us. And I'm not gonna get this close to that loot and then lose it!"

They could have taken a week to get there, Frank thought, and they still wouldn't find a posse waiting for them. But McCoy didn't know that and there was no way Frank could explain it to him without giving away the game. All he could do was appeal to McCoy's sense of self-preservation.

"If they keep us bottled up here until dark, they'll close in and get us," Frank warned. "Apaches don't mind fighting at night. We won't see them coming."

"I know, blast it." McCoy snatched his hat off, ran his fingers through his thick, snowy hair, and sighed in disgust. As he clapped his hat back on, he said, "There's only one thing to do."

"What's that?" Frank started to ask, but the words were hardly out of his mouth before McCoy was standing up and running for his horse.

"We're busting out!" McCoy called over his shoulder.

Frank leaped up and ran after the bank robber. McCoy was acting on impulse, but his reckless plan actually stood a chance of working. Most of the Apaches were scattered, and a head-on attack against the warriors who had been left to keep them pinned down was a desperate but possibly successful move. Frank and McCoy would have to strike hard and fast, though.

McCoy jammed a foot in the stirrup and hauled himself onto his horse. He wheeled the animal and banged his heels against its flank. Frank was right behind him. He wished he had Stormy or Goldy underneath him. He would have trusted either of those powerful mounts to carry him to safety. He would have to make do with this horse stolen from a prison guard, though.

The riders burst out of the rocks. The horses bounded down the knoll in long, ground-eating strides. Puffs of smoke came from the rifles of the three Apaches who were now hunkered down out on the flats. The range was still a little long. Frank saw dirt kick up from the ground in front of him as the renegades' bullets fell short.

That wouldn't be the case for very long, however. Frank and McCoy were closing the gap with every passing second. They weaved their mounts back and forth to make themselves slightly more difficult targets.

Frank shoved his Winchester back in the saddle boot since there was no way he could draw an accurate bead from the hurricane deck of the galloping horse. When they got closer, though, he might try a shot or two with his six-gun.

The Apaches had to think that the white men had lost their minds. Well, maybe they had, Frank reflected grimly. That hidden loot meant more to Cicero McCoy than anything else in the world. And right now, helping his son by recovering that money meant more than anything else to Frank. He drew his Colt as a bullet from one of the Apache rifles sizzled past his ear.

From the corner of his eye he saw that some of the other renegades had realized what was going on and had turned back to try to cut him and McCoy off. But they were going to be too late. The three Indians blocking their path leaped up and kept firing. The revolver bucked in Frank's hand as he loosed a shot at them. One of the Apaches went down, and a second later so did another one, courtesy of a bullet from McCoy. The third renegade turned and tried to run for his horse.

McCoy rode him down.

The Apache fell forward as McCoy's galloping horse slammed into him from behind. His body jerked under the impact of steel-shod hooves. Frank grimaced as he saw the Apache's head explode like a melon as the horse stepped on it.

It was just one gruesome glance, though, and then the two men flashed on past. They had broken out of the trap, and now it was up to their horses to keep them ahead of the remaining renegades. Frank leaned forward over his mount's neck and urged the horse on to greater speed. He didn't look back until he had galloped for several hundred yards. When he did, he saw that the renegades had regrouped and were coming after him and McCoy, a dust cloud boiling up behind them.

Now it was a race, with Frank and McCoy against the Apaches.

A race where the stakes were life and death.

Chapter 19

What saved them, eventually, was the fact that the Apaches were such poor horsemen. An Apache could run all day without his lean, muscular body tiring, but he would rather eat a horse than ride one, and he wasn't the best judge of horseflesh in the world, either. The animals Frank and McCoy had stolen from the prison guards were big and strong, not the fastest mounts but with plenty of stamina. One by one, the Apaches dropped out of the chase until, finally, all of them had turned back.

McCoy let out a triumphant laugh when he looked back and saw that all the pursuers had vanished. "How about that?" he said. "We outran them!"

"We were lucky," Frank said as he slowed his exhausted mount. "As strong as these horses are, they're wearing out. We couldn't have pushed them much longer at that pace."

"Yeah, but those redskins didn't know that." McCoy frowned. "We sort of got off course. We're too far west. That'll slow us down some."

"Well, we can't try to make up the time. We'll ride these horses right into the ground if we do."

"You're right," McCoy agreed with a reluctant nod. "I reckon we'll just have to hope that the law doesn't beat us to Ambush Valley."

That wasn't going to happen, Frank thought. Unless those blasted Apaches showed up again, nothing was going to prevent him and McCoy from reaching Ambush Valley.

Dusk was beginning to shroud the landscape when Frank spotted some lights winking into existence in the distance, south and west of where he and McCoy rode.

The bank robber saw the lights, too, and pointed them out. "That's Hinkley, where those damned bounty hunters caught up to me," McCoy explained. "Actually, they had gotten ahead of me and were waiting for me, the bastards. I didn't think it was possible that any pursuit could get around the mountains that fast. They had some sort of Mex tracker with them and he must've known about some passes that I didn't." McCoy sighed and shook his head. "Another hour and I'd've been across the border in Mexico, where the law couldn't touch me."

"No offense, McCoy, but I can't feel too sorry for you," Frank said with a grin. "If you hadn't been sent to prison, I never would have met you . . . and I wouldn't be on my way to a twenty-four-thousand-dollar payoff."

"Yeah, you're going to come out ahead on this deal, Morton."

Frank didn't believe that for a second. McCoy wasn't planning to pay him anything for his help except a few ounces of lead, in the form of a bullet, preferably in the back. But as they rode through the gathering shadows, Frank indulged his curiosity by asking, "How did you come to be a bank robber, anyway?"

"What business is that of yours?" McCoy snapped.

"None at all. I was just curious. Just making conversation."

McCoy seemed a little mollified. "I reckon it's simple enough. I never cared for working for wages. My father was a professor and figured I would be, too, but I wasn't having any of it."

"A professor, eh?"

McCoy laughed. "Wouldn't have thought it, would you? That's how I came by my name. The old man taught history and philosophy, and he named me for some ancient Roman. I was raised on a college campus in Pennsylvania."

Frank had thought before that McCoy talked as if he had more education than most people out here on the frontier, but he wouldn't have guessed that the outlaw came from such a background. He had read some of the orations of Cicero himself, although as a rule he preferred a mite less weighty fare.

"When I got old enough, my father was determined that I'd go to college and follow in his footsteps," McCoy went on, "but I convinced him I wanted to get my schooling at Stanford."

Frank had heard of that university in California. It had been founded by the railroad baron Leland Stanford about a decade earlier and was supposed to be a good college.

McCoy chuckled. "He put me on the train and I headed west, but I got off in Kansas City and never looked back. Made my own way in the world, like I wanted, and drifted farther west. It didn't take me long to figure out that I had talents of my own that didn't have anything to do with book learning."

Like robbery and murder, Frank thought grimly.

"That's my story," McCoy concluded. "What's yours, Morton?"

"Just a cowhand who went bad, I reckon you could say," Frank replied with a shrug.

"Well, you're a good man with a gun, and you've got plenty of sand. Stick with me. We'll have us a fine time down in Mexico."

McCoy sounded almost like he meant the offer. Frank didn't believe it, though. And, of course, he wouldn't have taken the outlaw up on it, even if McCoy was sincere.

He hoped things were all right back up in Buckskin. During the long, hard weeks that had passed since he left Nevada, he had thought often about old Catamount Jack and Tip Woodford and Diana and all the other citizens of Buckskin. He had come to care about them more than he ever thought he would.

At the same time, he had to admit that in a way it felt mighty good to be out here on the trail again, even riding on the edge of danger as he was. Sometimes, a good horse and open sky and a hill to beckon him on with its unknown other side were all a man really needed. An hombre who had spent years on the drift might finally stop somewhere, but could he ever truly settle down? Or would he always feel that restlessness, deep down in his soul?

He'd have to ponder on that later, Frank told himself. After the stolen money had been recovered and Cicero McCoy had been brought back to face justice once again. Once the job was done . . .

Assuming he lived through it.

Most of the light had faded from the sky when McCoy finally said, "There it is. There's the entrance to Ambush Valley."

To Frank it just looked like a couple of rocky ridges thrusting themselves out into the desert, with a dark mouth in between them. McCoy rode straight toward it, pushing his horse into a trot again. Frank followed.

"Keep your eyes peeled," McCoy warned. "We could be riding into a trap."

That was unlikely, but Frank was alert anyway. He hadn't forgotten about those Apache renegades. As long as any of them were still alive and on this side of the border, they represented a threat.

"I've heard that the place is mighty rugged and easy to get lost in. How are we going to find our way around in the dark?"

"We're not," McCoy replied. "We'll just go a little ways in and then make camp for the night. We won't try to find the loot until morning."

"You *can* find it, can't you?" Frank figured a man in the role he was playing would be worried about such a thing.

"Don't worry about that," McCoy snapped. "I can find it. Just keep your eyes and ears open for trouble."

A feeling of foreboding came over Frank as they entered the gloomy canyon. From what he could see of it in the fading light, it looked like the sort of place that would be haunted by doomed souls, and he remembered those cavalrymen who had been wiped out here by the Apache ambush ten years earlier. Although he wasn't by nature a superstitious man, a shiver ran through him as he thought about that.

That feeling wasn't helped by the eerie wail of the wind around towering rock formations deeper in the valley. Frank had heard such sounds before and recognized them for what they were, but still, a part of him wondered if they might be the cries of those doomed souls he'd been thinking about. Logically, he knew better . . . but logic didn't always come into play at a time like this.

The canyonlike mouth of the valley widened out into the valley itself. Frank couldn't see much. Some of those rock spires loomed against the night sky, blotting out the stars in places. When he and McCoy had penetrated half a mile or so into the valley, the bank robber drew rein and said, "This is far enough. We'll wait here for morning. Any farther and I run the risk of getting turned around in the dark."

"I don't reckon we want that," Frank said as he stretched in the saddle to ease weary muscles.

"No, we sure as hell don't. Get lost in here and you might never find your way out. It's a hellhole, that's for sure."

The men unsaddled their horses. There was no graze here, nothing to eat for man or beast. Frank's belly growled from hunger. He sipped a little water from one of the canteens and told himself to ignore the pangs. Then he took a picket stake from his saddlebags, drove it into a crack in the rocks, and tied his horse's reins to it to keep the animal from wandering off in search of grass. McCoy did likewise. Everybody would just have to go hungry tonight. They could put up with that, in exchange for the payoff that was waiting when the sun came up and McCoy located the stolen bank money.

They took turns standing guard again. "Indians sometimes avoid places that they think might be haunted, but the Apaches aren't bothered by Ambush Valley," said McCoy. "At least that's what Cortez told me. They're the ones who wiped out the soldiers who were lured in here. Anyway, they don't really think that white men have spirits that can be left behind to wander the earth after they're dead. Only their own people do."

Frank knew that McCoy was right about that. Those renegades wouldn't think twice about venturing in here, unless they were worried about getting lost. That meant a cold camp again—but he and McCoy didn't have any food to cook, anyway. A fire would have been nice for warding off the chill, but they could get along just fine without one.

McCoy took the first watch. Frank dozed off without worrying too much about what the outlaw might do. If McCoy wanted to murder him in his sleep, there had been plenty of chances before now to do just that. McCoy still wanted him around, just in case, until he actually had his hands on that loot again.

But after that . . . all bets were off.

"Are we goin' in there?" Ben Coleman asked nervously as he stared at the mouth of Ambush Valley. Full night had fallen, but the dark gap that marked the western end of the valley was still visible in the starlight.

Abner Hoyt shook his head and said, "No, I don't reckon there's any need to. Bob and Joaquin saw Morgan and McCoy ride in there at dusk, and they didn't come out. We know the loot is in there somewhere. So we'll just wait right here for them to come out with it."

"Then we grab it, eh?" Deke Mantee asked with a grim chuckle.

"That's right. We grab McCoy, too, so he can go back to Yuma Prison where he belongs."

Mantee looked over in the darkness at the Coleman brothers, who looked back at him. Even though the men couldn't see each other's faces very well, each of them knew what the others were thinking. They had talked about it enough whenever they could catch a moment out of earshot of the others. There was a nine-thousand-dollar reward riding on this job.

But there were eighty thousand dollars in bank notes and gold double eagles hidden somewhere in that valley. Nine grand versus eighty . . .

It wasn't a very difficult choice, at least not for some men.

"You reckon those Apaches are still around somewhere?" Bardwell asked.

Earlier in the day, they had heard the shots in the distance and closed in to see what was going on. It wouldn't do any good for them to hang back if McCoy got himself killed before he could recover the money. Until that loot was found, McCoy's life was the most important of all.

The bounty hunters had arrived on the scene in time to see Frank Morgan and McCoy make their daring escape as the Indians tried to surround them. They had followed as the Apaches gave chase to the two fugitives, still ready to step in if their help was needed.

But Morgan and McCoy outran the war party, and the Apaches veered off to the west after giving up the pursuit. The bounty hunters watched them disappear into the distance, and Hoyt hoped they kept going until they were back over the border in Mexico. The bloodthirsty renegades were an unneeded, unwanted complication.

"I think those Apaches took off for the tall and uncut," Hoyt said in answer to Bardwell's question. "There were only ten or twelve of them left. We can handle a bunch that size if we have to."

Leaf said, "If need be, I can probably pick most of them off before they ever come in range of those rifles they've captured in their raids over the years."

Hoyt nodded. "Kill 'em before they kill you," he said. "Words to live by."

The night passed quietly, except for the eldritch howling of the wind among the rocks. By dawn, the air was so cold that Frank's breath fogged in front of his face as he moved around the makeshift camp. He was tired. With no blankets and only his saddle for a pillow, his sleep had been restless. Today might see the end of this quest, and he was looking forward to that.

The chill in the air vanished almost as soon as the sun crept above the horizon. Heat began to build immediately. Frank knew that by the middle of the afternoon, Ambush Valley would be like a frying pan. He hoped that he and McCoy would be out of there by then.

"Have you decided what you're going to do once we've got our hands on the loot?" McCoy asked as he saddled his weary-looking horse. The animals seemed to be as tired and worn out from the long, dangerous ride as the humans were. "Coming to Mexico with me?"

"I sure might," Frank said, hedging a little.

"That would be best. That way we wouldn't have to divvy up the money right now. We could make the split after we're safely across the border."

"Yeah," Frank said. "That makes sense."

He wondered—was McCoy really playing square with him? Was it possible that the bank robber didn't plan to double-cross him? Frank felt certain that McCoy had betrayed the men who'd been riding with him when he held up the bank in Tucson. But maybe a bond of sorts had formed between him and Frank because of the dangers they had faced together, the times they had fought side by side. Such things happened sometimes. Frank didn't believe that McCoy had an ounce of true human compassion in him. The man was a brutal, cold-blooded killer who cared more about money than anything else.

But he was tough as hell and didn't have any back up in him, either, and while Frank could never respect McCoy as a man, he acknowledged the outlaw's ability as a fighter.

That wouldn't stop him from taking McCoy back to prison, once they had recovered the bank money. McCoy needed to be locked up where he could never hurt anyone else.

Once the horses were saddled, they let the animals drink a little and then mounted up. Frank's empty stomach let out a rumble, causing McCoy to grin over at him. "We'll be stuffing our bellies with enchiladas before the sun goes down tonight, compadre."

With McCoy leading the way, they pushed on deeper into Ambush Valley. The place lived up to everything Frank had heard about it. Stark, desolate, and unforgiving, it was an alien landscape, so harsh that it didn't look like it even belonged on earth. During his travels, Frank had seen places just as bad, but thankfully they were few and far between.

He had a frontiersman's instinct for direction and knowing where he was, and he tried to keep track of the twists and turns in the trail that McCoy followed. But even so, after a while, Frank had to admit that he would be hard put to find his way out of here. He was confident that he could sooner or later . . . but in this hellish wasteland with no food or water, later might be *too* late.

By midmorning, McCoy wore a frown on his rawboned face. "Something wrong?" Frank asked.

"I haven't found the landmarks I've been looking for," McCoy replied in a worried tone. "It hasn't even been two months since I was here. The landscape shouldn't have changed in that amount of time."

"Maybe you've just forgotten," Frank said.

"Forget how to find eighty grand? Not hardly!" A stubborn tone came into McCoy's voice. "I know where I'm going."

Frank bit back the ironic laugh that tried to come from his throat. What if McCoy *couldn't* find the money? Then all the time, all the dangers Frank had faced, would have been for nothing. The loot would go unrecovered. If that was how things turned out, all Frank could do would be to take McCoy back to prison. Conrad would just have to be satisfied with that.

However, a few minutes later, McCoy let out a triumphant laugh. "There," he said, pointing. "We follow that ravine."

So far they had avoided the razor-edged slashes in the earth, but now McCoy sent his horse half-sliding down a slope into one of the forbidding passages. Frank followed. The walls of the narrow cut pressed closely on both sides of the riders. In places they had to proceed single file.

After a while, the ravine became wider as it snaked along through the valley. The two men followed it for a good long while, although it was impossible to say how much ground they were actually covering since the ravine turned back on itself so sharply. Eventually, though, McCoy held up a hand to signal a halt and grinned as he said, "Listen."

Frank listened. A frown appeared on his face. "Is that water I hear?" he asked.

"Yeah, and that means we're close. Come on."

McCoy got his horse moving again. Frank was close behind him as they rounded yet another bend and found themselves entering a clearing of sorts where the ravine widened out to an area about forty feet across. The trickle of water Frank had heard came from the rocky face and dripped down to keep a small pool filled. The thirsty sand of the ravine floor soaked up some of the liquid, but the spring was strong enough to keep the pool from drying up. With its scrubby trees and sparse grass, the area was a veritable oasis in this arid wasteland known as Ambush Valley.

McCoy let out a whoop. He and Frank both had to hold their horses back to keep the animals from lunging at the water and the grass. Frank knew from the look of jubilation on McCoy's rugged face that the bank robber was excited about more than finding the spring.

This had to be where the loot was hidden as well.

He was more convinced of that than ever when he saw the corpses of two men lying on the ground, well away from the pool. Insects had been at them. Bone gleamed white in the sun. The clothes they wore were faded and hung loosely on bodies that had dried out and shrunk as the days passed.

"Who are those hombres?" Frank asked. His face was taut and grim as he looked at the dead men.

"Names were Cortez and Beck," McCoy replied. "They rode with me for a while. They were both wounded when that posse was chasing us, and they made it this far before they cashed in their chips."

Frank didn't really believe what McCoy was saying. His doubts grew even stronger when he noticed the ugly hole in the back of one man's skull. Anyone shot like that would die immediately. He wouldn't have been able to ride all the way in here before succumbing to such an injury.

But that was exactly the sort of wound a man would

have who'd been taken by surprise and gunned down from behind by someone he considered a partner.

Frank looked away from the dried-out bodies and muttered, "Damn shame. I'm sure they were good men."

"Yeah, they were," McCoy said, "but they're dead and gone now, so there's no point in worrying about them. What say we let these horses drink a little before they go loco?"

They watered the horses and then let them loose to graze on the grass. The horses wouldn't wander off, not with something to eat here. Frank and McCoy drank some of the cool, clear spring water, too, and then hunkered on their heels next to the pool.

"So," Frank said, "where is it?"

"Where's what?"

Frank laughed, and after a second McCoy joined in the laughter.

"Yeah, I guess that was sort of dumb, wasn't it?" the bank robber said. "What else would you be talking about but the thing we came all this way to find?" He nodded toward several large rocks on the far side of the pool. "All we have to do is move one of those boulders."

"The money's underneath it," Frank guessed.

"That's right." McCoy straightened and came to his feet. "Give me a hand. I'm eager to see what eighty thousand dollars looks like again."

"I never even saw a tenth that much loot," Frank said, which wasn't strictly true. Eighty grand was a lot of money, to be sure, but he had much more than that in his accounts in Denver and San Francisco. He'd never felt any desire to go and *look* at it, though. To his way of thinking, money was only as good as what you spent it for.

The two men went around the pool. McCoy pointed

out which rock needed to be moved, and they bent to put their shoulders against it. With grunts of effort, they started it rolling. When the boulder was clear, McCoy dropped to his knees and began using his hands to dig in the slight depression that the rock left behind where it had been resting. Frank joined him, and sand began to fly as they scooped it out and a hole started to form.

After several minutes of digging, Frank saw something yellow. He brushed dirt aside and felt the fibers of a rope.

"That's it," McCoy said. "The money is in several canvas bags, and I wrapped them up in my slicker and tied it up tight. Let's get more of this dirt out. . . ."

In less than a minute, then, they had enough dirt cleared away so that they could grasp the rope and pull the bundle out of the ground. It was heavy, which made Frank chuckle to himself. He had never really given much thought—or any thought, to be truthful—to how much eighty thousand dollars would weigh.

The yellow rain slicker hadn't been harmed by being buried for several weeks. It would have held up all right if McCoy had been able to stick to his original plan and leave the loot here for six months or a year. Frank sat back on his heels and glanced around the ravine. The plan Conrad had hatched, and he, Frank, had carried out, really had been the only chance of recovering the money. If McCoy hadn't led him to this spot, a hundred men could have searched Ambush Valley for a year without ever finding this cache. It would have been a fluke, pure luck, if they had.

"Want to take a look at it?" McCoy asked with a grin.

Frank shook his head. "No, that's all right. I reckon it's all there. Where would any of it have gone in the past two months?"

"Yeah, I can tell nobody's disturbed the place." McCoy stood up and turned toward the horses. "I'll fix a place on one of the saddles where we can carry it."

Warning bells went off in Frank's head. There was nothing unusual in what McCoy had just said, nothing unusual in his actions.

But that was just when a man like him would strike, when an unsuspecting companion had been lulled into complacency by the mundane. Frank's muscles reacted instantly, powering him instantly to his feet, and his hand flashed toward the gun on his hip as McCoy whirled, already drawing. . . .

They froze that way, Colts leveled, facing each other over the loot that had brought them to this blistering corner of hell.

Chapter 20

After a tense moment, McCoy chuckled and broke into a grin. "Well, what do you know?" he said. "You were about to double-cross me and take that whole eighty grand for yourself, weren't you, Morton?"

"Looked to me like it was the other way around," Frank replied. "You made the first move, McCoy."

The bank robber shook his head. "We could argue about that all day long and never get anywhere. The question now is, what are we going to do about this?"

"I guess we'll make the split now." Frank had to find some way to get the drop on McCoy, disarm him, and tie him up.

"How are we going to manage that? We'd have to holster our irons to do it, and somehow I just don't trust you anymore, Morton. So much for teaming up and going to Mexico together. That's a damned shame, too. We would have made good saddle pards."

Not in a million years, Frank thought.

"Back away from the money," he said. "You can still cover me, but I want you to go around on the other side of that pool. I'll keep my gun on you while I open the bundle and split up the money."

"How are you going to count out your share and watch me at the same time?" McCoy asked, his face still wearing that wolfish grin.

"How many bags are there?"

"Four."

"My share is now two of them. I'll take them and leave the other two for you."

McCoy lost his grin. "The hell you will!" he snapped. "I never agreed to go halves with you. Anyway, there probably aren't equal amounts of money in each bag."

"Probably not," Frank agreed. "But you get what you get and so do I. Otherwise . . . well, I guess we can shoot, and neither of us will get anything except some lead."

He could see the wheels of McCoy's brain turning as the outlaw considered the suggestion. Finally, McCoy nodded grudgingly and said, "I reckon it'll have to do."

Again, Frank didn't believe him. Despite their agreement, McCoy would be just watching and waiting for a chance to kill him. That was fair in a way, Frank supposed, because while he didn't plan on killing McCoy, he was biding his time, too. He wasn't really going to divvy up the money, now or any other time. All of it would be going back to the bank in Tucson where it belonged.

McCoy backed away, and began working his way around to the other side of the spring-fed pool. The gun in his hand remained rock-steady as he moved, and his eyes never wavered from Frank's eyes.

Slowly, Frank lowered his body until he crouched next to the slicker-wrapped bundle. His Colt was just as steady as McCoy's was, his gaze equally intent. He reached down with his free hand and brushed his fingers over the rope that held the bundle closed.

McCoy smiled again. "How are you going to cut that rope, Morton?"

Frank knew what the outlaw meant. He had no knife, and if he took his eyes off McCoy in order to untie the knots in the rope, McCoy would kill him. It was a dilemma, all right. But when McCoy had tied up the bundle, he had left a few inches of rope trailing from one of the knots. Frank grasped that now and said, "I'm not going to untie it."

He uncoiled from his crouch, driving hard and fast with his legs as he threw himself to the side. At the same time, he whipped up the heavy bundle of loot and slung it toward McCoy as hard as he could.

McCoy jerked the trigger of his gun, but Frank's hastily formed plan worked. The bank robber's bullet thudded harmlessly into the bundle, stopped by the layers of slicker, canvas, greenbacks, and coins. Frank rolled across the sand and fired, trying to knock McCoy's legs out from under him.

His slug only grazed McCoy's thigh, staggering the outlaw for a second but not knocking him down. McCoy swung his pistol toward Frank and triggered two more shots. The reports echoed back from the walls of the ravine. One bullet plowed into the sand; the other whined off a rock.

The deafening shots spooked the horses. They began to plunge back and forth, interfering with the aim of the two men. Frank crouched behind one of the boulders and tried to draw a bead on McCoy.

"Damn it!" McCoy cried, and through the legs of the skittish horses, Frank saw what had the bank robber upset. The bundle of stolen money had fallen in the pool when McCoy's shot hit it. That bullet had put a hole in the slicker and probably in at least one of the canvas bags inside the package. Some of those greenbacks might be getting soaked.

McCoy slammed a couple of shots at Frank, but again the bullets just glanced off the rocks. They came close enough to make Frank duck, though, and in that brief second, McCoy reached into the water, snagged the bundle, and jerked it out of the pool. He lunged for the closest horse and grabbed the saddle horn. Frank sent a bullet whistling past McCoy's head as the outlaw jammed a boot in one of the stirrups and yelled at the horse. The animal broke into a run as McCoy threw a leg over its back and hung on for dear life.

He clung to that bag of loot with equal determination.

With his face set in grim lines, Frank leaped for the other horse. He caught the frightened animal's reins, dragged its head down, and swung up into the saddle. In a heartbeat he was racing after McCoy, who was heading east through the ravine in a hard gallop.

Frank held his gun ready to try another shot, but the way the ravine ran such a jagged course through Ambush Valley, it was hard to catch more than a glimpse of his quarry before another bend in the trail hid McCoy from view again. When they did reach a relatively straight stretch, McCoy hipped around in the saddle and fired, forcing Frank to bend low over his mount's neck in order to make himself a smaller target. He wasn't hit and his horse didn't break stride, so he assumed that McCoy's shot had missed entirely.

More than that, it had also emptied McCoy's gun. Frank saw him jerk the trigger a couple more times, but no shots sounded. Frank lifted his Colt and squeezed off a shot. McCoy kept going without slowing down, and a second later was out of sight again as his horse pounded around a bend in the ravine.

Frank didn't think McCoy would be able to reload, hang on to the loot, and control the horse all at the same time. McCoy would have to outrun him now, as they had outrun the Apaches together. Frank leathered his iron and concentrated on getting all the speed he could out of the horse, which happened to be the one that McCoy had been riding before the fight at the water hole. They had inadvertently swapped mounts. Not that it mattered much, since both men were about the same size and weight.

It was a wild ride through the ravine with the sheer stone walls flashing past, sometimes close enough that Frank could have reached out and touched them. The pounding hoofbeats of his quarry's horse echoed back at him, and he was sure McCoy could hear the pursuit coming up behind him, too.

Frank swept around a bend and saw McCoy up ahead, maybe fifty yards in the lead. That encouraged Frank, and he urged the horse he was riding on to greater speed. Once again, he wished he had one of his own mounts. Stormy and Goldy were both swift and sure-footed. Unfortunately, they were also hundreds of miles away in Buckskin.

McCoy popped in and out of sight, depending on the turns that the ravine took. Each time Frank spotted him, he was a little closer. Frank wondered just how long this slash in the earth was. As long as they were in it, McCoy couldn't do anything but keep moving forward with Frank behind him. The walls were too steep and high to let them out. But if McCoy reached a place where he could leave the ravine and make it out into the wilds of Ambush Valley, he might be able to give Frank the slip. Frank had to catch up to him before that happened.

He saw McCoy up ahead again. The bank robber jerked his horse around a turn, and the animal's hooves suddenly skidded on the sandy floor of the ravine. The horse tried to recover its balance, but it was already too far gone. The horse went down, taking a heavy fall.

McCoy was thrown out of the saddle. He sailed clear of the falling horse, crashed to the ground, and rolled over a couple of times. Amazingly, he still held on to the bundle of stolen money. Lashing his horse with the reins, Frank pounded closer as McCoy struggled to his feet. The outlaw turned to run, but it was too late. Frank was practically on top of him already.

Frank left the saddle in a diving tackle. He crashed into McCoy from behind and wrapped his arms around him. Both men went down, but Frank landed on top with his weight driving McCoy into the ground.

McCoy was a long way from beaten, though. He twisted and brought his elbow back in a sharp blow that caught Frank on the jaw and rocked his head to the side. Frank grunted and smashed a clubbed fist into the side of McCoy's skull. They grappled and rolled over, each seeking even a momentary advantage. McCoy got one hand on Frank's throat and clamped down hard, but at the same time Frank got his knee in McCoy's belly and heaved him to the side. McCoy's choke hold came loose.

Frank sprang after him and landed another punch, this time on McCoy's mouth. Blood spurted from pulped lips. McCoy tried to knee Frank in the groin, but Frank was able to twist aside. McCoy shoved him away and came up on his knees just as Frank did, too. They hammered punches at each other, slugging it out in sheer desperation. Both men were bloody and weakened. Frank knew the fight couldn't go on much longer.

He supposed that he could have drawn his gun and ended it. He still had bullets in his Colt. But he was caught up in the heat of battle and not as clearheaded as he might have been otherwise. Like an old warhorse answering the bugle, he swung again and again, pounding blows to McCoy's face and body, absorbing the punishment that the bank robber dealt out to him in turn.

It was inevitable that a missed punch would end the fracas. McCoy's fist grazed past Frank's ear, throwing the bank robber off balance for a heartbeat. That was long enough. Frank's left shot forward in a short but powerful punch that stunned McCoy and left the outlaw unable to defend himself from the looping right that exploded on his jaw. McCoy landed on his back, his eyes glazing as they rolled up in their sockets. He tried to lift his arms, but they fell back weakly. After that, he didn't move except for the ragged rising and falling of his chest.

Frank was almost as bad off. One of the horses was close enough so that he could reach out, grab hold of the stirrup, and use it for support as he pulled himself to his feet. Breathing as heavily as McCoy was, he leaned against the horse and tried to recover. He palmed the Colt from its holster and covered McCoy as awareness began to seep back into the bank robber's eyes.

"I know you can hear me, McCoy," Frank rasped. "It's over." He leaned down, ripped the gun from McCoy's holster, and tossed it aside. The revolver was empty, but Frank didn't believe in taking chances.

McCoy rolled onto his side and groaned. "You . . . you bastard . . . Morton," he gasped. "I reckon you'll . . . kill me now . . . and take all the money."

A grim chuckle came from Frank. "It's worse than that, McCoy. Worse for you, anyway. I'm taking you back to Yuma Prison . . . and returning the money to its rightful owners." He drew in a deep breath. "And the name's not Morton. It's Morgan. Frank Morgan."

McCoy stared up at him, pale blue eyes widening in

shock. "Frank . . . Morgan?" he managed to say. "The gunfighter?"

"Used to be," Frank said.

McCoy shook his head, clearly unable to comprehend what he was hearing. "But . . . you were in prison. You rustled those cattle, killed that sheriff and his deputies. . . ."

"That's what we wanted you to believe, so that you and I could break out together and you'd lead me to that money."

"We?"

Frank said, "Conrad Browning is my son."

McCoy stared at Frank in uncomprehending disbelief for a long moment, as if Frank had spoken in some language that the outlaw had never heard before. Then McCoy let his head fall back on the sandy floor of the ravine and began to laugh. It was a bitter sound that rolled out of him as he lay there, beaten.

Frank let it go on for a minute or so and then said, "Get up."

McCoy rolled onto his side and slowly, painfully pushed himself to his feet. He swayed there unsteadily for a few seconds. The grin he directed at Frank was ugly as sin.

"You know you'll never get me back to Yuma alive, don't you, Morton . . . I mean, Morgan?"

"Oh, you'll get there, all right," Frank said.

McCoy shook his head. "No, the ride back is too long. Somewhere along the way you'll let down your guard. Then I'll kill you . . . or make you kill me."

"Well, that might be true," Frank said, "if the two of us were traveling alone."

McCoy blinked in surprise as his grin disappeared. "What the hell are you talking about?" he demanded.

Frank inclined his head toward the western end of the ravine. "There'll be somebody waiting for us right outside Ambush Valley. You remember Abner Hoyt and the rest of the bounty hunters who captured you in Hinkley?"

A red flush crept over McCoy's face as he glared murderously at Frank. "You bastard!" he hissed. "They've been following us all along?"

Frank nodded. "Ever since we escaped." He hoped the bounty hunters were actually where he expected them to be and that nothing had happened to them. For now, that was what he wanted McCoy to believe, anyway. He gestured with his gun and went on, "Now mount up. We're going back to that water hole."

McCoy climbed onto his horse, his slow, awkward movements showing how much pain he was in from the pounding he had taken. Frank wasn't in much better shape himself, but he tried not to show it as he picked up the slicker-wrapped bundle, hung it from his saddle horn, and pulled himself up into the saddle.

As the two men started back along the ravine, with McCoy leading and Frank following, McCoy said, "I still don't understand. Those fights you had with Jessup, the time you spent in the Dark Cell, all those bullets the guards shot at us. . . It all seemed real to me."

"It *was* real," Frank explained. "We didn't want anything to tip you off that I wasn't an actual convict. Warden Townsend was the only one at Yuma who knew who I really am."

"But you could've gotten killed a dozen times over!"

"Yep," Frank admitted. "I reckon that's true."

"You did all that just to get back some stolen money? Your boy means that much to you?"

"Conrad didn't want to let you get away with it," Frank explained. "He thought there was a good chance you'd escape from prison sooner or later, grab that loot, and make it across the border where nobody could ever touch you."

"I would have, too," McCoy grumbled.

"So we decided to just speed the process up a mite and send me with you. I wanted to be sure you got what's coming to you, too, McCoy."

The bank robber looked back at Frank and sneered. "You're talking about justice, aren't you?"

"It means something to some of us," Frank said.

"Then you're fools. There is no justice in the world, only strength. People don't get what they want just handed to them. They have to be strong enough to *take* it."

"Some folks would rather *work* for what they want out of life."

McCoy shook his head. "Fools," he muttered again.

They reached the spring and the pool a short time later. Frank glanced at the bodies of the two men who had died here weeks earlier and wished that they could be given a proper burial. If he'd had a shovel, he would have put McCoy to work digging graves at gunpoint. But he didn't have a shovel, and he wasn't going to take the time to have the graves dug by hand. He wanted to get out of here and rendezvous with Hoyt's group. So he just had McCoy refill the canteens from the spring instead.

"Mount up and get moving," he told McCoy when that chore was finished.

McCoy started his horse walking along the ravine again. As he did so, he looked back and said, "You know there's eighty thousand dollars in that bundle, Morgan."

"I know it," Frank said.

"You could turn around and head east with it. There's nothing I could do to stop you."

"And all I have to do is let you go, eh?"

"Eighty thousand dollars," McCoy repeated. "That's a hell of a lot of money. Enough to keep a man living in high cotton for the rest of his life."

"A dishonest man, maybe."

"Hell, you're a gunfighter!" McCoy burst out. "Don't go getting all high-and-mighty and moral on me! How many men have you killed in your life?"

The total was higher than Frank liked to think about, way higher. But he was able to say honestly, "None who didn't force me to it, in one way or another." The truth of that answer was the reason he was still able to sleep peacefully at night.

McCoy gave a bark of contemptuous laughter. "You've hired out your gun plenty of times. I've heard about you, Morgan. You're nothing but a low-down killer. And now you're doing Browning's dirty work. You're just a hired gun for your own son."

Frank told himself not to honor that statement with a response. But he couldn't stop himself from saying, "You've got that wrong."

"The hell I do. So take the payoff, Morgan. Take the eighty grand. It's all yours. Just ride away, and you won't ever have to see me again."

A weary sigh came from Frank. "Give it up, McCoy," he said. "What you're talking about isn't going to happen. You're going back to prison where you belong."

"Well, you can't say I didn't give you a chance."

They reached the end of the ravine and rode up the slope leading out of it. Frank looked at the arid, rocky wasteland that surrounded them and realized that he wasn't sure which direction they needed to go. McCoy had been here in Ambush Valley before and knew the way out a lot better than Frank did.

McCoy realized that, too, and laughed. "What are you going to do now, Morgan?" he asked. "Maybe you can find the way out and maybe you can't. Could be we'll wander around in here until we starve or die of thirst. Just don't expect *me* to help you."

Frank thought he had a pretty good idea where to find the trail. Anyway, as long as they were moving in a generally westward direction, sooner or later they would come to the end of the valley. It might take longer if he had to hunt around for the way out, but they would get there.

"That way," he said as he pointed with his gun. "Get moving, McCoy."

"Sure," McCoy replied with that ugly grin of his. "If you're certain that's the right direction."

Frank wasn't certain, but he was willing to risk it. He and McCoy rode between a couple of towering spires of rock and through a field of scattered boulders that were nearly as big as houses. The landmarks looked familiar to Frank, and his feeling that they were going in the right direction grew stronger as they rode up a slope and then down from the ridge into another boulder-dotted flat. The green of vegetation was nowhere to be seen in this part of the valley, but there were plenty of other colors— the red, brown, and tan of sandstone, the gray of granite, even stretches of volcanic rock that were a deep black. Arching over all of it was a pale blue cloudless sky dominated by the brassy orb of the sun, which beat down with increasing heat and strength.

McCoy was starting to look a mite nervous as he glanced back at his captor. The bank robber knew that they were on the right trail, Frank thought. McCoy's final chances to escape were slipping away.

"Eighty thousand damned dollars!" McCoy suddenly cried in ragged tones. "That's almost a hundred grand, you stiff-necked son of a bitch! Take it! Just let me loose. I won't go back to Yuma."

"Yes, you will," Frank said, his voice calm. Sweat

darkened his shirt, as well was McCoy's. Some of the salty beads were about to drip into his eyes, so he sleeved them away from his forehead.

McCoy reined in, turning his horse so that he faced Frank. The gun in The Drifter's hand came up, and his eyes narrowed. "Whatever you're thinking, forget about it, McCoy," he grated.

McCoy shook his head. "I told you I wouldn't go. You're going to have to kill me, Morgan . . . because if you don't, I'm going to kill you with my bare hands. I'm coming for you, you bastard."

Frank wondered if he could just wound McCoy. In the bank robber's weakened condition, and in this murderous heat, even the shock of a bullet might be fatal, even if the wound wouldn't be a mortal one under normal conditions. But if Frank had to, he would shoot, and to make sure McCoy understood that, he warned, "Stay back, mister. Don't make me pull this trigger."

McCoy laughed. "You've known all along you'd have to do it. After all . . . you're a hired killer, remember?"

McCoy stiffened and lifted his reins. He was about to send his horse plunging at Frank's mount, and Frank was going to have to shoot him out of the saddle.

It might have happened that way, too . . . if at that moment a furious volley of gunshots hadn't blasted through the scorching air of Ambush Valley as if a war had just broken out.

Chapter 21

Abner Hoyt and the rest of the bounty hunters had made camp within sight of the entrance to Ambush Valley the night before. As usual, Hoyt made sure that a couple of men were standing guard all night. The fastest way to get killed out here on the frontier was to be taken by surprise. Hoyt didn't like surprises.

That was why he was glad when the night passed quietly. The next morning, as he hunkered next to a small fire and sipped scalding hot coffee from a tin cup, he peered toward the place where the mountains petered out and Ambush Valley began.

"Are we going in there, Abner?" Leaf asked from the other side of the fire. The Englishman had tea instead of coffee. He carried his own supply of the stuff wherever he went, along with a special pot for "brewing up," as he called it.

"Not unless there's some need for us to go in," Hoyt replied, "and I don't reckon that's very likely."

"What if Morgan needs help?" Bob Bardwell asked.

Hoyt shook his head. "Morgan didn't strike me as the sort of hombre who'd need help with one man, even if

that man is an ornery son of a bitch like Cicero McCoy."
He took another sip of Arbuckle's and added, "But if
we hear any shooting in there, I reckon we'll have to go
take a look. If we ride into the valley, can you find our
way back out again, Joaquin?"

Escobar nodded. "*Sí,* don't worry about that, Abner.
We won't get lost."

Hoyt grunted and said, "Never figured we would."

Time passed slowly that morning. Hoyt had never
liked waiting for anything. He was an impatient man by
nature, even though his perilous profession had taught
him to be less so. Sometimes, being able to just wait
without making a move or a sound was what it took to
save a man's life.

Especially a manhunter's life. There was no more dangerous quarry in the world than a human being.

Jack and Ben Coleman spread a blanket on the ground
and played cards. Deke Mantee joined them. Deke had
been spending a lot of time with the brothers lately, Hoyt
thought with a slight frown when he noticed the game
going on. Mantee was a good hombre and had been with
Hoyt longer than any of the others except Bardwell. Hoyt
didn't particularly like the Colemans, although he re-
spected their abilities. They were good men to have on
your side in a fight. But something about them rubbed
him the wrong way.

Bartholomew Leaf found himself a shady spot in the
lee of a rock and sat with his back against the boulder
while he read a book that he took from his saddlebags.
Leaf was a great one for reading.

Bardwell and Escobar kept their eyes on the mouth
of Ambush Valley. When and if Frank Morgan and
Cicero McCoy emerged from the valley, they wanted to
know it as soon as possible.

Somebody should have been watching the other direction, Hoyt realized late in the morning when he glanced to the west and stiffened as he saw a dust cloud boiling up from the desert. "Somebody's coming," he snapped as he came to his feet and took a quick step toward the horses. As he took a pair of field glasses from his saddlebags, he added, "Looks like it might be a lot of somebodies."

Everyone in camp was instantly alert. The Coleman brothers and Mantee put away the cards and forgot about their poker game. Leaf marked his place in his book and picked up his rifle instead. Bardwell and Escobar turned away from the mouth of Ambush Valley and looked out at the desert instead.

Hoyt brought the glasses to his eyes and peered through them. It took him a moment to locate the group of riders at the base of the dust cloud. As he focused on them, a chill tingled along his backbone despite the stifling heat.

"Those Apaches are back," he said. There was no mistaking the colorful shirts and headbands, which were visible through the field glasses.

"That's a lot of dust for a dozen riders to be kicking up," Bardwell said, his voice taut.

Hoyt drew in a deep breath and then let it out in a sigh. "That's because there are thirty or forty of the sons of bitches."

"The ones who ran off yesterday must've gone back to fetch some friends," Mantee drawled. "We've got a fight on our hands now, boys."

Hoyt lowered the glasses and snapped, "Yes, and we can't take them on out here in the open. Throw your saddles on your horses. We're heading for Ambush Valley."

There was no time to waste. The Indians would be on top of them in five minutes or less.

As Leaf saddled his horse, he asked, "Would you like me to stay here and pick some of them off while the rest of you skedaddle, Abner?"

Hoyt knew that the Englishman was offering to sacrifice his own life to give the rest of them a better chance. "No need for that," he said. "We'll find us a place to fort up in there, and then you can potshot those redskins to your heart's content, Bart."

Leaf nodded as he tightened the cinch on his saddle. "Very well."

There was no sense of panic about the bounty hunters, although Jack and Ben Coleman sent several glances toward the charging Apaches as they saddled up. The rest of the men just concentrated on the task at hand, their movements smooth and efficient. Within two minutes of Hoyt giving the order, camp was broken, the horses were saddled, and the men were ready to ride. "Let's go!" Hoyt called as they galloped toward the mouth of Ambush Valley.

Hoyt figured the Apaches were still at least a quarter of a mile away. He and his companions would have time to reach the valley. Once they got there, they would have a tough fight facing them, no doubt about that. The odds against them were steep.

But not overwhelming. If they could find some good cover, they had plenty of food, water, and ammunition. They could stand off the renegades for a long time, and Hoyt was confident that with each attack he and his friends would do more damage to the Apaches. Even with a big war party like this, the Indians might decide the price they'd have to pay to kill these white men was too high.

The bounty hunters had good horses, big, strong animals that possessed both speed and stamina. They were well cared for, too, although the long ride from Yuma had taken something out of them, as it had the men who rode them. Still, they reached the mouth of the valley well ahead of the pursuers. As they galloped between the rugged mountains toward the scorching wasteland of the valley, Hoyt began looking around for a good place to take cover.

They didn't have the luxury of a long search, though, because guns began barking from the heights to the right and left of them. Hoyt didn't hear the shots at first over the pounding hoofbeats, but he saw the spouts of dirt kicked up by the bullets as they plowed into the ground, and when he glanced up toward the rocky slopes, he saw puffs of gunsmoke scattered across them. A curse ripped from his mouth. He knew instinctively what had happened. While he and his men slept the night before, Apache warriors had crept past them and into the valley to take up positions on the heights. Then the rest of the reinforced war party had attacked this morning, right out in the open where they were plainly visible, and because of that Hoyt and the rest of the bounty hunters had waltzed right into the trap set by the renegades.

Ambush Valley was living up to its name once again, Hoyt thought as he heard the wind-rip of a bullet past his ear.

And just like ten years earlier, unless some sort of miracle occurred, there was going to be a slaughter here.

The sound of shots from not too far away took both Frank and McCoy by surprise, but that didn't last very long. McCoy yelled as he lunged his horse toward Frank.

Frank held off on the trigger and wheeled his mount aside just as McCoy leaped from the saddle at him. He lashed out with the gun and felt the barrel thud against the outlaw's skull. McCoy's momentum carried him on into Frank, anyway. The collision knocked Frank out of the saddle. Both men fell to the ground, landing hard.

McCoy was stunned from the blow to his head. Frank rolled away, came up on a knee, and pointed the gun at the bank robber. All the fight had been knocked out of McCoy, he saw. In fact, McCoy was unconscious.

Frank knew that wouldn't last long. He leaped up and hurried to McCoy's side. Holstering his gun, he bent down and tore McCoy's belt from the loops on his denim trousers. Then Frank jerked McCoy's hands behind his back and quickly lashed his wrists together with the belt.

He could come back for McCoy later, he thought, after he had found out what all the shooting was about. But just in case something happened to him and he wasn't able to return, he bound the outlaw loosely enough so that McCoy would be able to work his hands free sooner or later. Frank wouldn't condemn even a man like McCoy to a slow, lingering death in this hellhole by tying him so tightly that he couldn't get loose.

Once that was done, Frank caught his horse and swung up into the saddle. He had his Colt and McCoy's revolver and his Winchester. He made sure that all of the weapons were fully loaded before he set off toward the battle, following the sound of the shots.

His route led him past several other landmarks that were familiar from the journey into the wasteland. Frank was confident that he was headed toward the end of the valley. The shots became louder and he saw a haze of powder smoke floating in the air ahead of him. He was getting close to the battlefield.

He rounded a bend in the trail and saw the long straight stretch that led between half-mile-long, finger-like ridges to the desert. This was the mouth of Ambush Valley.

And the slopes overlooking it were dotted with gunmen hidden behind rocks and scrubby clumps of brush. As Frank reined in, he caught glimpses of bright red and blue here and there and knew that the men on the ridges were Apache. More renegades, these on horseback, were milling around at the end of the valley.

Trapped between the ridges, pinned down by gunfire and bottled up by the Apaches at the mouth of the valley, were Abner Hoyt and the other bounty hunters. Frank saw several of them crouched behind rocks as they tried to return the fire of the bushwhackers above them. Some of their horses were down, obviously shot out from under them, but Frank didn't see any human bodies.

It was only a matter of time, though. Hoyt and his men were in a bad spot.

None of them—white, Mexican, or Apache—had spotted Frank yet. He wheeled his horse around and rode back out of sight. He looked down at the bundle of loot tied to the saddle horn by the excess rope wrapped around it. McCoy was his prisoner—all he had to do was ride back and pick him up—and he had recovered the money stolen from Conrad's bank. The Apaches probably didn't know that he and McCoy were even in Ambush Valley. If he stayed out of sight and waited, the renegades would wipe out Hoyt and the others and then ride away, more than likely, satisfied with the massacre they had carried out. Then Frank and McCoy could make a run for Hinkley, and Frank could find a place there to lock up the bank robber until he could get word to the authorities about what had happened.

It took perhaps a heartbeat for those thoughts to run through Frank Morgan's mind—and less time than that for him to discard the idea of abandoning Hoyt and the other bounty hunters to their fate.

He dismounted and left his horse tied to a jutting rock. Then, carrying both rifles, he began working his way toward the top of the ridge on the north side of the valley mouth.

The sun beat down powerfully. The heat from the rocks came through the soles of his boots until it felt like his feet were blistering. Every time he had to put a hand down to catch his balance during the arduous climb, the rocks were almost too hot to touch. The sweat dried on his shirt, leaving great white rings on the cloth. After a few minutes, Frank stopped sweating, and he knew that was bad. One of the canteens was looped over his shoulder. He stopped and took a short drink from it. If he passed out from the heat, he couldn't do the bounty hunters any good.

The firing continued as Frank made his way through the rocks and up steep slopes. From the sound of it, Hoyt and the others were putting up a good fight, and that was encouraging. Most of them were still alive. If he could help even the odds a little, they might have a chance to get out of this trap.

He finally reached the top of the ridge and moved along it until he could see most of the Apaches who were hidden up here, pouring fire down at Hoyt and his men. Frank paused long enough to study the situation and pick out the order of his targets. Chances were, the Indians wouldn't notice the extra shots, and if he took them from highest to lowest, they wouldn't see their fellow warriors falling. He knelt, set one of the Winchesters beside him, and rested the barrel of the other one on a rock as he drew a bead. A moment later he squeezed the trigger, and the crack of the rifle was followed by the sight of the renegade highest up on the slope jerking under the impact of the bullet in his back and then folding up in death.

Some people would call what he was doing murder, Frank thought as he worked the rifle's lever and shifted his aim. He didn't hate Indians, never had. But he couldn't stand by and let them slaughter Hoyt and the other bounty hunters, either. Came a time when a man had to pick his side and do what was necessary to win. Frank Morgan had made his decision, and he knew that like most of the others he'd made over the years, he wouldn't have much trouble living with it.

Assuming, of course, that he survived this ruckus, he reminded himself as he drilled the next Apache in line.

The killing was swift and merciless. Frank needed only one shot for each of the renegades he downed. He ventilated all the ones he could see, then started in on the ones whose position was marked only by puffs of powder smoke. He knocked down a couple who were hidden in some brush, then sent some slugs bouncing into a nest of rocks where another Apache was concealed. The ricochets caused the man to leap to his feet, and when he did, that put him in clear sight of the men trapped below. The bounty hunters were good shots, too, and the renegade's head exploded as at least two slugs smashed through it. He dropped like a puppet with its strings cut.

Frank wondered if the Indians hidden on the south slope had noticed what was going on. He got his answer as bullets began to whistle around him. The first Winchester was empty, so he tossed it aside and snatched up the second one. Hunkering down in better cover, he opened fire on the warriors across the valley mouth. The air around him was filled with sparks and flying chips of stone and the whine of slugs as they ricocheted from the rocks.

This wasn't murder. Far from it, in fact. This was a showdown battle with an enemy who outnumbered him more than a dozen to one.

But Frank wasn't fighting alone. As he saw several of the Apaches suddenly stand up, double over, and slide headlong down the ridge because his bullets had found them, the bounty hunters kept up their deadly accurate fire and took a toll of their own. Every time Frank's shots forced a renegade out of cover, Hoyt or one of the other men drilled him. After five minutes of intense firing, Frank estimated that there were only three or four of the Apaches on the south slope who were still alive.

The warriors on horseback realized that, too. They had been content for a while to sit back and let the riflemen hidden on the slopes kill the whites. But it hadn't worked out that way. The trap had been sprung, but somehow its intended victims were still alive.

Seeing that, the infuriated Apaches charged toward the scattering of boulders where Abner Hoyt and his men had taken cover.

Frank saw them coming and shifted his aim in that direction, emptying the rest of the Winchester's bullets into the howling, yipping mob of renegades. The bounty hunters blasted slugs at them, as well. So much powder had been burned over the past quarter of an hour that the air was thick with smoke everywhere. The dust kicked up by galloping hooves added to the obscuring clouds.

Some of the horses in the forefront of the attack went down, causing other horses to trip over them. Shrill animal screams tore through the midday heat. Renegades disappeared into a welter of flailing, shattering limbs.

The grisly collisions failed to break the back of the charge, though. At least two dozen Apaches still thundered toward the bounty hunters, and the surviving renegades on the south slope were still a threat, too.

Frank knew there was no time to reload the rifles. He dropped the Winchester he had just emptied, drew his Colt from its holster, and jerked the gun he had taken from McCoy from where he had tucked it behind his belt. With his hands full of six-gun, he stood up and started down the slope, bounding from rock to rock, sliding on his heels in places, and doing his best not to start tumbling out of control.

Twice he felt bullets pluck at his shirt, and countless times they whispered to him as they went past his ears. But somehow he reached the bottom of the ridge unscathed. The Apaches were almost on top of the bounty hunters by now. Frank saw Abner Hoyt desperately emptying a revolver at the renegades. The other men were fighting just as doggedly. Frank's revolvers began to boom and buck in his hands as he opened fire with them, squeezing off shots, right, left, right, left, with deadly, cool-headed accuracy. Apaches flew off their horses as The Drifter's bullets ripped through them.

Then the renegades overran the defenders, and the fighting was hand-to-hand, mano a mano.

One of the Apaches dove off his horse and tackled Frank. They slammed to the ground and rolled over and over. Frank lost one of his guns, but both Colts were empty anyway. He used the one he still held to block the downward sweep of a knife as his enemy tried to gut him. Driving a fist into the Apache's face, Frank knocked the warrior backward. He crashed the barrel of the pistol against the Indian's head and felt the man's skull crunch and shatter under the blow. The Apache spasmed and lay still.

Frank scrambled up in time to see three of the mounted renegades closing in on him. They were no more than forty feet away, and the only weapon he had was an empty gun.

Then, suddenly, a figure flashed between Frank and the Apaches. The man held a rifle, and it spouted flame as he opened fire on the renegades. The Apaches returned that fire, and the man who had intervened to save Frank's life, at least for the moment, jerked as bullets slammed into his body. He kept shooting, though, emptying the rifle, and two of the Indians toppled off their horses, blood gushing from mortal wounds.

That respite gave Frank time to grab the knife that had been dropped by the Apache whose skull he had crushed. He wasn't an expert with a blade, but the same uncanny coordination between hand and eye and muscles that made him one of the deadliest gunfighters to ever roam the West guided his throw as his arm went back and then whipped forward. The knife was a silver streak as it flew through the air and then embedded itself with a thud in the chest of the last Indian who was charging at Frank. The Indian cried out, dropped his rifle, clutched at the knife that had penetrated all the way to his heart, and then pitched off the horse, dead before he hit the ground.

Frank ran to the man who had saved him. He had seen the thick white hair and recognized it and the clothes, but he could hardly believe his eyes. He had left Cicero McCoy tied up, well out of harm's way. How in blazes had the bank robber gotten here, in the thick of the fighting?

And why had he saved Frank's life?

Frank dropped to a knee beside McCoy and rolled the

man onto his back. The front of McCoy's shirt was sodden with blood. He had been hit at least four times. But he was still breathing, and as the gunfire began to die out around them, Frank said, "McCoy! Damn it! McCoy!"

The outlaw's eyelids flickered, and then rose to reveal the pale blue, pain-wracked eyes. "M-Morgan!" he gasped. "I . . . I'm shot to hell!"

"Yeah, you are," Frank agreed. He didn't see any point in trying to give McCoy any false hope.

To his surprise, McCoy chuckled. "Told you . . . I wouldn't go back . . . to Yuma."

"That's why you did it? That's why you saved me?"

McCoy frowned. "Saved . . . you? I didn't even . . . see you . . . too much . . . gun smoke and dust . . . I just wanted to . . . get in some licks . . . on those damn redskins."

Frank couldn't help but laugh. "Well, I'd likely be dead now if it wasn't for you, McCoy. I'm much obliged."

"You're not welcome, you . . . son of a bitch . . . you stole my . . . money . . . I got loose . . . came here to find you . . . and kill you." McCoy grimaced as a fresh wave of agony rippled through him. "Now you tell me . . . I saved your life. . . . Things just . . . never work out . . . do . . ."

He didn't finish the question. Instead, he shuddered and blood welled from his mouth, and the glassy sheen of death slid over his eyes. He was gone.

But, like he'd said before, at least he hadn't gone back to Yuma.

Frank used a couple of fingers to press McCoy's eyes closed again, then lifted his head and looked around. He was aware that the shooting had stopped now, and he wasn't surprised to see Abner Hoyt and several more of the bounty hunters standing there watching him. All of them had bloodstains on their clothes, and some of them were leaning on their rifles, using them as makeshift crutches. But as more of the men limped up, Frank counted them and got seven. Hoyt's whole group had made it through the fight. Not without injury, of course, but at least they were alive.

"McCoy's dead?" Hoyt asked in a harsh voice.

Frank nodded. "That's right. Reckon he won't serve out his sentence after all."

"What about the money?"

"I've got it," Frank said.

"That's what we need for the reward," Hoyt said. "More than McCoy himself." He grunted. "Can't help but think that the bastard got off easy, though. He should've spent the next twenty years behind bars in that prison."

Frank pushed himself to his feet and said, "Justice has a way of working itself out. We may not always like the way it happens, but sometimes it's out of our hands." He looked around. "What about the Apaches?"

The ground in the valley mouth was littered with bodies. Hoyt said, "Weren't but three or four of them left alive. They lit a shuck out of here." He joined Frank in gazing around at the corpses and then shook his head. "There was a heap of killing here today."

"Enough to last a long time," Frank agreed. He turned and started limping toward the place he had left the horse with that slicker-wrapped bundle of loot tied to the saddle. . . .

The reason they had all come here to Ambush Valley, which today had certainly lived up to its name.

Chapter 22

Over the years, Frank had seen dozens of border towns like Hinkley, Arizona Territory. Maybe more. It was an ugly, squalid little place.

But today, in some ways, Hinkley looked a mite like heaven.

Old Cyrus Hinkley, the owner of the general store and the founder of the town, also had some medical training in his background. He patched up all the bullet holes and creases the bounty hunters had suffered during the battle with the Apaches. Hoyt and his men could have tended to that themselves, having some experience with such things, but Hinkley had whiskey on hand to douse the wounds before he bandaged them up—and for the bounty hunters to take a drink or two of, as well.

While Hinkley was busy with the injuries, the settlement's citizens crowded into the store. They had heard all the shooting in the distance and were full of questions, wanting to know what was going on. Several of them guessed that another Indian fight had taken place over at Ambush Valley, which was correct, of course. The outcome had been different, however. The Apaches had lost this time.

There was nothing anybody could do for Cicero McCoy except bury him. And in this heat, his body certainly couldn't be taken back to Yuma just to be put in the ground. So the Mexican undertaker and his sons got busy digging a grave in the small cemetery behind the church.

Frank was content to sit in the shade on the porch of the general store . . . once he had locked the bundle of stolen loot securely in Cyrus Hinkley's big iron safe, which was the only one of its kind for a hundred miles or more.

Abner Hoyt came out of the store and sank down in the cane-bottomed chair next to the one in which Frank was sitting. "You're the one who actually recovered the money," he said without preamble. "I reckon when you come right down to it, Morgan, you're the one who's got the reward coming."

Frank shook his head. "I'd be paying it to myself. Conrad Browning is my son, remember? I own a share in that bank and most of his other business holdings."

"And here I always thought you were just a drifting gunhand."

Frank thought about his job as marshal in Buckskin and all the folks who lived there, and he said, "There was a time that's all I was. But no more."

"Well, if you ever want to get into the bounty hunting business . . ."

Frank shook his head without the least bit of hesitation. "No offense, Hoyt," he said, "but I've been on the other side of that fence too many times to ever cross it on a permanent basis."

Hoyt grunted and fished a black cigarillo out of the pocket of his buckskin shirt. He put it in his mouth and left it unlit, chewing it for a moment before he said, "I hope nobody ever puts a big price on your head again, Morgan. I'd hate to have to go hunting you."

Frank smiled and asked, "But you'd do it, wouldn't you?"

"If the reward was high enough?" Hoyt's teeth clenched on the cigarillo. "Damn right."

Other than the undertaker and his sons, and the priest from the church, Frank was the only one on hand late that afternoon for McCoy's burial. Hoyt and the other bounty hunters were at the cantina, celebrating in advance the reward they would collect when they got back to Tucson.

The plain pine coffin had already been lowered into the grave with ropes as Frank stood there beside the hole in the ground, his hat in his hand. The priest said a few words commending McCoy's spirit to the Lord, then intoned a prayer in Latin. He looked up at Frank with a solemn expression on his kindly, nut-brown face, and asked, "Would you like to say anything, Señor?"

Frank started to shake his head no, then reconsidered. "I don't reckon anybody could call you a good man, McCoy," he said. "But you had courage, and you fought well. I hope that's worth something on the other side. And you saved my life, whether you meant to or not. For that I thank you, and I ask that El Señor Dios have mercy on your soul. But I reckon that'll be up to Him." Frank nodded, stepped back, and put his hat on.

"Amen," the priest muttered. He motioned to the undertaker's sons, who started forward with shovels.

Frank turned and started around the big adobe church with its bell tower that dominated this end of town. Dusk had begun to settle down, and it was quiet in Hinkley, so quiet that Frank had no trouble hearing the guitar music and the laughter that drifted from the cantina at the other end of the settlement.

The priest fell in step beside him. "You are a religious man, my son?"

"Not really, Padre," Frank replied. "I don't make it to services too often, and haven't for a long time. But I've seen the mountains and the desert, and right now I see those beautiful colors in the sky from the sunset."

"Ah. You see the hand of God in His creations, and that is your way of worshiping."

Frank shrugged. "Call it that if you will. I've seen men kill each other, too. I've seen all the cruelties, big and small, they indulge in."

"But that . . . that is the hand of the Devil at work, not Our Lord."

"Can't be one without the other, can there?"

The priest obviously didn't know how to respond to that, so he just stopped in front of the church and said, "I will pray for you, my son."

"I appreciate that, Padre," Frank said as he lifted a hand in farewell. "I reckon I can use all the help I can get." As he walked away, he added under his breath, "We all can."

Abner Hoyt leaned back in his chair and rubbed the hip of the pretty señorita sitting on his lap. She giggled and turned so that the valley of her ample breasts was visible in the low-cut neckline of the blouse she wore. Now there was a valley where a man could pure-dee enjoy being ambushed, he thought.

He'd had enough tequila to feel it, but he wasn't drunk.

He knew his capacity quite well, and he hadn't reached it yet. He intended to, though. The job was over, and since McCoy was dead, they didn't even have a prisoner to worry about. They had spent the evening in the cantina, enjoying the tequila and the young women, filling their bellies with beans and tortillas and *cabrito*. On the other side of the room, Bartholomew Leaf was trying to learn how to play the guitar from the old man who usually strummed on the strings of the instrument. At a nearby table, Bob Bardwell was flirting with a señorita of his own. Joaquin Escobar had already vanished with one of the girls who worked here in tow. The Coleman brothers and Deke Mantee were gone, too. Hoyt hadn't noticed them leave, but they'd either slipped out with some women or gone in search of a poker game, he thought.

Hoyt didn't know where Frank Morgan was, either. He assumed that when they rode out for Tucson in the morning, Morgan would be riding with them. Hoyt didn't figure that Morgan would want to let that bank money out of his sight for very long, especially not after all the trouble he had gone to and suffering he had endured to recover it.

A sudden frown made Hoyt's bushy eyebrows draw down. That loot was locked up in old man Hinkley's safe, but just how secure *was* that safe? Hoyt had to admit that he didn't know. The iron box had looked pretty sturdy, but there might be somebody in Hinkley who could bust the lock. Hell, a stick of dynamite could blow the door right off the safe, Hoyt thought. And it wasn't so big the whole thing couldn't be picked up by several men and put in the back of a wagon, so that it could be hauled off and opened at leisure.

Maybe it would be a good idea to post guards in the store overnight, he told himself. He realized he should have thought of that earlier.

"What is wrong, Señor?" the girl on his lap asked as she traced the creases on his forehead with a fingertip. "You no like Juanita?"

Hoyt pushed her hand away, causing her to pout. "I like you just fine, honey," he said, "but all of a sudden I've got other things on my mind."

She turned even more so that she could press the soft mounds of her breasts against him. "Juanita will make you forget everything but her," she promised.

Hoyt shook his head and snapped, "Not now." He stood up, causing Juanita to leap to her feet so that she wouldn't get dumped in the floor of the cantina. Her dark eyes flashed with anger.

Hoyt didn't care whether she was mad or not. He was about to motion to Bardwell and Leaf and tell them to follow him over to Hinkley's store, when he saw Deke Mantee stride swiftly into the room. Hoyt could tell from the expression on Mantee's dark, lean face that something was wrong

Shit! he thought. There was a problem with that loot. Had to be.

Mantee spotted him and hurried over to him. In a low, urgent voice, Mantee said, "There's something going on over at that store where the money's locked up, Abner."

"I knew it! What's wrong?"

"Maybe nothing," Mantee replied with a shake of his head, "but Jack and Ben and I were on our way back down here when we spotted some hombres skulkin' around the back of the building. Looked like they were taking a wagon back there or something."

"They're gonna steal the whole safe!"

Mantee jerked his head in a nod. "That's what we got worried about. I left Jack and Ben there to keep an eye on the place. Figured I'd better round up you and the rest of the fellas, so we could get over there and put a stop to whatever's about to happen."

"I don't know where Joaquin is, but I reckon six of us can handle any trouble we run into." Hoyt got Bardwell's attention and jerked his head toward the door. Bardwell, as stolid as ever, maneuvered the señorita off his lap and motioned to Leaf, who gave the guitar back to its elderly owner and picked up his rifle instead. Quickly, the four men left the cantina and started down the street toward the store. In clipped tones, Hoyt filled Bardwell and Leaf in on what was happening.

As they reached a shadowy doorway across the street from Cyrus Hinkley's business, Mantee said, "Blast it, I left Jack and Ben right here to watch the place. Where'd they get off to?"

"Maybe they were afraid the men who are after the safe were going to get away with it before we got here," Bardwell suggested. "They could have slipped around to the back of the store to try to get the drop on them."

Mantee nodded. "Yeah, that must be what happened." The whisper of steel against leather sounded in the darkness as he drew his gun. "We'd better get over there and see what's going on."

"Be careful," Hoyt cautioned as they drew their guns and started across the street. "We want to be sure what we're walking into."

He motioned for Leaf and Bardwell to go one way around the store while he and Mantee went the other. With militarylike precision, the men followed Hoyt's orders.

The building was dark; Hinkley had already closed for the night. He probably didn't lock the doors when he left for the day. Most folks, even merchants, seldom locked their doors. That way, if somebody found themselves in need of supplies in the middle of the night, they could go in and take what they wanted and leave the money to pay for it. For a system that depended on people being honest and honorable, it worked remarkably well . . . although back East any storekeeper who did business that way would be cleaned out in a single night, more than likely.

So the would-be thieves wouldn't have any trouble getting in, Hoyt thought. The only difficulty they would encounter would be in lifting the heavy safe and loading it into the wagon. Then they could drive away with it—and the eighty thousand dollars inside it.

As he and Mantee catfooted along the alley beside the building, staying close to the wall, Hoyt listened for the sound of voices. He didn't hear anything. He stopped at the corner and pressed his back to the wall. Not far away, a horse blew through its nostrils and stamped a foot. Somebody was back there behind the store all right. Hoyt risked a look.

A wagon with an open bed sat there, parked near the rear door. A team of four horses was hitched to the vehicle. Hoyt could see them clearly enough in the light from the moon and stars. No humans were in sight, though, and the door into the store appeared to be closed.

Where were the thieves? Already inside? Hoyt supposed it was possible, but he wasn't sure why they would have closed the door behind them. It made more sense to leave it open if they were going to haul out that safe.

Hoyt put his mouth close to Mantee's ear and said, "The wagon's there, but I don't see anybody."

"What about Jack and Ben?"

"No sign of them, either." Hoyt motioned with his gun. "Come on. We'll take a closer look."

They approached the wagon slowly and carefully. Part of the way there, Hoyt spotted movement on the far side of the vehicle and stiffened. Then he heard a low whistle, indistinguishable from that of a night bird, and knew it came from Bardwell. That meant he and the Englishman were closing in on the wagon from the other side.

With Mantee a few feet behind him, Hoyt reached the wagon. It was empty except for some blankets thrown in the back. Hoyt frowned in puzzlement. He didn't like mysteries, and he couldn't figure this one out. Where were the men Mantee and the Coleman brothers had seen? For that matter, where were the Coleman brothers?

"Go see if that safe's still in the store," he told Bardwell, who nodded and disappeared silently into the building. The rest of them waited for a long, tense moment until Bardwell stepped out into the alley again.

"It's there," he reported. "Right where we left it."

"No sign that it's been disturbed?" Hoyt asked.

"Nope."

"And there's nobody around?"

"I didn't see anybody," Bardwell said, and Hoyt knew that if there was anything important to be seen, Bardwell would have noticed it.

Hoyt muttered a curse and jammed his Colt back in its holster. Bardwell and Leaf leathered their irons as well, and Leaf tucked the rifle under his arm.

"Some of us should stay here and guard the safe while the others search for Jack and Ben," Leaf suggested.

"That won't be necessary," Mantee said. "I know right where they are."

Hoyt started to turn toward him, saying, "I thought you said—" He stopped short when he realized that Mantee's gun was pointed at him.

At that moment, the blankets in the back of the wagon were thrown aside and the Coleman brothers sat up with revolvers already clutched in their fists. They had Bardwell and Leaf covered before either of the bounty hunters could make a move. Even Bardwell's usually impassive face looked startled in the moonlight.

"Oh, hell, Deke," Hoyt said.

"Don't try for your gun, Abner," Mantee said. "I know you're fast, but there's no way you can outdraw a gun that's already lined up on you."

"You three are the ones stealing the money, aren't you? You brought the wagon back here to carry off the safe. There was never anybody else skulking around."

Ben Coleman said, "You're a smart hombre, Hoyt. But not so smart that you can see there's eighty grand here for the takin'."

"That's not our money," Bardwell said.

"And we'll be getting a reward, old boy," Leaf added.

Mantee snorted in contempt. "A reward!" he repeated. "A measly nine thousand dollars. There's nine times that much in the safe!"

"It's not right," Hoyt said. "That money doesn't belong to us. We work for rewards, remember?"

"You mean we risk our hides for a piddling fraction of what we recover." Mantee shook his head. "Anyway, don't go gettin' high-and-mighty on me, Abner. I've ridden with you long enough to know that you'll run roughshod over anybody who gets in your way when you're after a bounty. You've bent the law more'n once."

"Bent it, maybe," Hoyt allowed. "But I never broke it. Not like this. I never out-and-out stole."

"Oh, it gets worse than stealin'," Jack Coleman said. "We're gonna kill the three of you, too."

"We talked about it," his brother put in. "We decided we didn't want you boys trailin' *us*. Only one way to make sure you can't."

"That's not sporting," Leaf said. "Not sporting at all. You're not giving us a fair chance."

Jack laughed. "I thought even a damn Englishman would know enough not to expect life to be fair."

If they were going to kill him and Bardwell and Leaf, Hoyt thought, they should have done it right away. Just gone ahead and pulled the triggers as soon as they had the drop on their intended victims. But since they hadn't, Hoyt thought it might be a good idea to try to keep them talking a little longer.

"You know, Deke," he said, "just last night I started to wonder a little about you and these two, since you'd been spending so much time together lately. I never really trusted Jack and Ben."

"Yeah, well, we don't like you either, you son of a bitch," Ben said.

Hoyt went on as if he hadn't heard the interruption. "But I put it out of my head and decided not to worry about it. You know why, Deke? Because I trusted *you*. I figured we'd been riding together long enough that you'd never try to double-cross me, even if you were tempted."

"You figured wrong," Mantee said, but the raw edge in his voice told Hoyt that he was under a strain. "It takes a lot to make me turn on a friend, but hell, Abner, eighty grand *is* a lot. More than twenty-five thousand apiece."

"Yeah, if those snake-blooded Colemans don't decide to turn on *you*, too, as soon as they've got the money. They might plan on keeping your share as well as theirs."

"That won't work, Hoyt," Jack snapped. "Deke knows we wouldn't do that. Hell, takin' the money and killin' you three was *his* idea!"

Hoyt didn't want to believe that, but Mantee didn't deny it. Instead, the lean gunman just raised his revolver a little more. The slightest pressure on the trigger would send a bullet through Hoyt's brain.

"Joaquin will hunt you all down!" Hoyt said quickly. "He won't let you get away with this!"

Both of the Coleman brothers laughed. "We're not worried about Escobar," Ben said. "He's dead. I put a knife in his gut fifteen minutes ago, before Deke ever came to the cantina to fetch you over here."

Hoyt felt despair well up inside him. It was an unfamiliar emotion, and it tasted bitter and sour under his tongue, the way defeat must taste.

"Morgan will come after you," he grated. "He's already gone through hell to get that money back. He won't sit back and let some no-accounts like you have it."

"That old man don't scare us, neither," Jack said. "He's just a washed-up gunslinger. We can handle him. Shoot, Deke could take him."

Hoyt looked at Mantee. "Is that what you think, Deke? You reckon you can outdraw Frank Morgan?"

"What I reckon is that we've all flapped our jaws more than enough," Mantee grated. "So long, Abner."

That was it, then. All that was left was for Hoyt to make a desperate grab at his gun and try to get it out and squeeze off a shot before he went down. Dying might not be so bad if he could get some lead in that traitor Mantee first. . . .

Like a burst of thunder, gunshots exploded in the alley behind Hinkley's store.

Even in his younger days, Frank hadn't been much of one for carousing. He'd drink a beer or even a shot of whiskey every now and then, but for the most part he much preferred a good cup of coffee. That was what he had steaming by his plate as he finished up the meal he had ordered in the settlement's only café, down by the church.

The ordeal in Ambush Valley had left him famished, and it felt mighty good now to have a full belly. He sipped the strong black brew from the cup as he reflected on his plans, which for the immediate future included strolling back down to his room in the small adobe hotel, stretching out on the bed, and sleeping the sleep of the just for, oh, the next ten or twelve hours. Then, after a good breakfast, he would be ready to start back to Tucson with Abner Hoyt and the other bounty hunters—and that bundle of loot that was now locked up in Cyrus Hinkley's safe.

Frank frowned a little as he thought about the money. Eighty thousand dollars made a mighty tempting target, and nearly everyone in town knew about it, knew it was being kept in the store for the night. Hoyt must have told some of his men to stand guard over it, Frank thought . . . but as he cast his memory back over the events of the evening, he couldn't recall hearing Hoyt say anything about that.

After emptying the cup, Frank laid a coin on the table to pay for his meal and stood up. It wouldn't hurt anything to take a walk down to Hinkley's store and check on the money before he turned in for the night. That way he could be sure that nothing was going to happen to it.

And if Hoyt *hadn't* posted any guards, then Frank would find him and see that it was done right away. Frank had seen Hoyt going into the cantina earlier, and figured he was probably still there.

Millions of stars glittered overhead in the clear air. The moon had risen over the mountains to the east, and now cast its silvery illumination over the landscape. Frank was tired and sore, but he was satisfied with the way things had gone, other than Cicero McCoy's death. And Gideon's, he thought, remembering the man who had befriended him inside Yuma Prison. He never had known for sure what

Gideon's crimes were, and it was possible the man had deserved to spend the rest of his life behind bars. But still, Frank wished that Gideon's life hadn't been cut so short.

He was musing on that when a dark shape suddenly loomed up out of the shadows and staggered toward him.

Frank's instincts had the Colt out of its holster in less than a shaved whisker of time. He held off on the trigger, though, as a pain-wracked voice came from the figure in a weak whisper. "*Por favor, señor . . . por favor . . .*"

The fella was asking for help. Still wary of a trap, Frank stepped forward and asked, "What's wrong, son?"

He could see now that the man had an arm pressed across his belly. The hombre stumbled again and almost fell as he gasped, "Señor . . . Morgan?"

Frank used his free hand to grasp the injured man's arm and steady him. "Escobar?" he said, recognizing the bounty hunter now. "What happened to you?" Warning bells went off in Frank's mind as he asked himself if this could have anything to do with the loot in Hinkley's safe.

Joaquin Escobar clutched at Frank's arm. "Señor Morgan . . . I have been stabbed!"

"Who did it?"

"B-Ben . . . Ben Coleman."

A shock went through Frank. Ben Coleman was one of the bounty hunters. Had he attacked Escobar in some sort of personal quarrel, or—

"They . . . they are after the money!" Escobar said, as if he'd read Frank's mind. "The Coleman brothers . . . and Deke Mantee."

Mantee was the lean, dark-faced gunman. Frank had seen Mantee watching him intently several times and recognized the look. Mantee had been wondering if he was faster on the draw than the notorious Drifter. Frank hadn't intended to find out the answer to that question.

Now it sounded like he might not have any choice in the matter.

"You must . . . stop them, Señor," Escobar went on.

"I intend to," Frank assured him, "but first we've got to get you some help." He saw dark tendrils of blood snaking over Escobar's hand from the wound in his belly. Escobar was probably doomed no matter what Frank did, but he wasn't going to give up on the man.

Yellow light showed through the windows of one of the nearby houses. Frank led Escobar over to the dwelling and pounded on the door. A man with a white spade beard jerked it open a moment later, with an ancient horse pistol in his hand. "What the hell's goin' on out here?" he demanded in an irritated voice. "Who're you?"

"This man's hurt," Frank said, steering Escobar toward the old-timer. "Take care of him. Make him comfortable and then go fetch Cyrus Hinkley for him."

"What . . . who . . ." the man sputtered. "Why, he's a greaser!"

"He's a friend of mine," Frank said, his voice hard as flint. "Now do as I told you, mister."

Nobody in his right mind was going to argue with Frank Morgan when he got that tone in his voice. The old-timer set his pistol aside and reached out to help Escobar. Frank turned and ran into the night.

He had to get to Hinkley's store before Mantee and the Coleman brothers could steal that money. It had been stolen once already, and Frank wasn't going to let that happen again.

Not after everything he had gone through to bring it back.

Chapter 23

Nothing was going on in front of the store. The place looked quiet and dark and peaceful. But Frank knew that looks could be deceptive, so he slowed his run to a gliding walk and moved silently along the wall of the building toward the rear. He heard voices, and detected the undertone of anger and menace in them. As he swung around the corner, his experienced eyes took in the scene instantly: Deke Mantee had his gun pointed at Hoyt, while the Coleman brothers stood in a wagon parked nearby, covering Bob Bardwell and Bartholomew Leaf.

Colt flame bloomed in the shadows as Mantee fired.

Hoyt was moving even as Mantee squeezed the trigger. He wasn't fast enough to avoid the bullet entirely; probably no one alive would have been. The slug hit him in the shoulder and slewed him halfway around. He fell to one knee as he continued trying to claw his gun from its holster.

In the instant after Mantee fired, Frank shifted his aim to the two men in the wagon. The Coleman brothers hadn't triggered their guns yet, but they had Bardwell and Leaf dead to rights. Frank's Colt bucked twice as he smoothly squeezed off the shots. Even in this relatively poor light, Frank's accuracy was astonishing. Jack and Ben Coleman went over backward as the bullets punched into them, toppling them from the wagon bed to the ground. Jack was dead before he landed, with a bullet in his heart. Ben took a few seconds to die, drowning in his own blood from the slug that had ripped through his lungs.

Mantee whirled when he heard the pair of shots behind him. His reactions were fast, Frank had to give him that. Mantee's gun blasted and sent a bullet whistling past Frank's ear. Frank fired back at him, but Mantee was already moving. He lunged to one side, looped an arm around the neck of the wounded Abner Hoyt, and hauled Hoyt to his feet. Frank had to hold his fire, as did Bardwell and Leaf, as Mantee backed away. Frank couldn't risk a shot as long as Mantee was using Hoyt as a shield.

The barrel of Mantee's gun cracked across Hoyt's wrist and forced him to drop the gun he had finally succeeded in drawing. Hoyt cursed bitterly. He fell silent as Mantee ground the barrel of the gun against his head.

"Drop it, Morgan!" Mantee shouted. He snapped at Bardwell and Leaf, "You, too!"

"Don't pay any attention to him," Hoyt said. The pain of his wound could be heard in his voice. "Shoot the son of a bitch. Shoot through me if you have to, but kill the backstabbing bastard!"

Mantee laughed harshly. "They won't do that, Abner, and you know it. Bardwell and Leaf are your friends, and Morgan's not the type to shoot an innocent man."

"You might as well give up," Frank said. "None of us are going to drop our guns, and you know you can't just walk away from here, Mantee."

"Mr. Morgan is right, Deke," Leaf said. "We'll hunt you down. All of us."

"You killed Joaquin," Bardwell accused.

Mantee shook his head. "I didn't kill anybody. Ben's the one who knifed Joaquin."

Frank said, "Escobar's not dead. He's the one who told me what was going on over here."

Mantee's breath hissed between his teeth. "Not dead? Damn it, those Colemans couldn't do anything right! I should've had better partners."

"You should've *been* a better partner," Hoyt grated. "You never should've double-crossed us, Deke."

"Eighty grand," Mantee reminded him. "You didn't give me any choice." He glared at the others. "Are you gonna let me go, or do I blow his brains out?"

"You pull that trigger and you'll be dead a second later," Frank told him.

"No doubt about it," Bardwell said.

Mantee's head moved with a jerky desperation as he looked at Frank, Bardwell, and Leaf. He had to know that things had gone too far south to salvage now. His allies were dead, and he was faced with three utterly deadly enemies.

But he wasn't willing to surrender. Even in the moonlight, Frank could see that. So he wasn't surprised when Mantee said, "I'll holster my gun . . . if you'll holster yours, Morgan."

"You want to draw against me?"

"Damn right. I've been hearing for years about how fast you are. Reckon I'm gonna have to see that for myself."

Hoyt said, "Morgan, don't."

Accepting Mantee's challenge would get Hoyt out of harm's way, Frank thought. And either way, no matter what happened in a showdown, Mantee wouldn't escape. The surviving bounty hunters would see to that.

"All right," Frank said. He lowered his iron, slipped it back into leather. "Now it's your turn, Mantee."

For a second, Frank thought the gunman was just going to turn the pistol away from Hoyt's head and try to shoot him while his Colt was holstered. But then Mantee dropped his arm and pouched his gun, just as he'd said he would. He gave the wounded Hoyt a shove that sent him stumbling toward Leaf and Bardwell, then turned so that he faced Frank head on. His hand hovered over the butt of his gun, ready to hook and draw. "All right, Morgan," he said. "Whenever you're ready."

Frank gave a slight shake of his head. "You've got it to do, Mantee," he said.

Mantee's lean face contorted in a snarl, and his hand flashed toward his gun in a stabbing draw.

Even without that giveaway, Frank would have had him beaten. Mantee was fast, the fastest of all the group of bounty hunters he had betrayed.

But Frank Morgan was The Drifter.

Frank's Colt boomed while Mantee's gun was still coming up. Mantee took a fast step backward as the bullet hit him. He stayed on his feet and tried again to lift his gun, breathing curses as he struggled against the suddenly heavy weight.

Frank fired again, and this time the slug took Mantee in the forehead and exploded on through his brain, bringing oblivion crashing down on him for good. Mantee landed on his back with blood and brains leaking from his head into the dust of the alley.

Calmly, Frank lowered his gun and began to reload it. The threat was over, but a wise man kept one chamber empty for the hammer to rest on—and the others full of steel-jacketed death.

The three bounty hunters looked at Mantee's body for a second, then came toward Frank. Leaf helped the wounded Hoyt. Bardwell asked, "You said Joaquin is still alive?"

"He was a few minutes ago," Frank answered, "but he was hurt pretty bad. I hope Cyrus Hinkley is tending to him by now." He nodded toward Hoyt. "That shoulder could use some looking after, too."

"Yeah," Hoyt said. "It hurts like a son of a bitch. We'll go find Hinkley. But somebody needs to stay here at the store and keep an eye on that loot."

"I'll do that," Frank said. "I don't think anyone else will try to bother it."

Hoyt grunted. "No," he said with a shake of his head as he watched Frank slide that deadly Colt back into its holster. "I don't reckon they will."

A week later, Frank lowered the slicker-wrapped bundle onto the desk in the office of the manager of the First Territorial Bank in Tucson and said, "Here you go. It's all there."

Conrad looked up at him from behind the desk and said, "I never doubted that it would be."

"You'll see to it that Hoyt and those other fellas get the rest of the reward they've got coming to them?"

"Of course. But I'd say that you deserve it as much as they do."

"I don't need it," Frank said. "And that'd be a mite silly, don't you think, paying myself a reward that way?"

"I suppose so." Conrad hesitated, then asked with what sounded like genuine concern, "What about you,

Frank? I know the time you spent in Yuma had to be terrible, and there was all that trouble after you and McCoy escaped. Are you all right?"

Frank considered the question. He was well rested. He had taken his time making the ride back from the border settlement of Hinkley, delaying his departure for several days until he was sure that Abner Hoyt was going to be all right. Mantee's bullet hadn't broken any bones, but Hoyt had lost quite a bit of blood. He'd been bouncing back nicely, though, by the time Frank left town.

Surprisingly, Joaquin Escobar had pulled through, too, and although it would be a good while before he fully recovered from the knife wound Ben Coleman had given him, at least he had a strong, fighting chance to do so. Hoyt and the others planned to bring him to Tucson when he was strong enough to travel in a wagon.

Frank would have brought the money back to Conrad by himself if he'd had to, but a couple of days after the shootout a patrol of United States cavalry from Fort Grant had shown up in Hinkley looking for him. Conrad's status as a financier and highly successful businessman meant that he had numerous influential friends in Washington, so he had pulled some strings and gotten the War Department to order out that patrol. The troopers had accompanied Frank to Tucson, ostensibly because of the continuing threat of Apache excursions across the border. Frank knew the soldiers were really there to protect the money. After the last war party to cross the border had gotten whipped so thoroughly, he thought it might be a while before any more renegades ventured north from their mountain strongholds.

But you never could tell about things like that. He didn't mind having the company on his ride.

Now, freshly bathed, shaved, and wearing his own

clothes and carrying his own gun, Frank had completed his mission. He smiled at Conrad and said, "I'm fine. I reckon I'll be moving on."

"Back to Buckskin?"

"That's right." Back home, Frank thought, then felt surprise go through him as he realized that he truly did consider Buckskin his home now. "And you'll be heading for Boston? You've been away for quite a while."

"Yes, but I don't believe that Rebel has missed it very much." Conrad laughed. "My wife isn't that fond of life in a big Eastern city."

"I don't figure she would be, growing up out here on the frontier like she did."

"It's not really the frontier much anymore, though, is it? What with the progress civilization has made and all."

Frank thought about the way he had spent the past few weeks, the danger from outlaws and Indians, the wasteland that was Ambush Valley, and he said, "For some of us, it'll always be the frontier."

"I suppose so. At any rate, I don't think Rebel is ready to return to Boston just yet. And as it happens, there's a troublesome situation regarding the Browning mining interests in the area around Buckskin, so . . ." Conrad stood up. "What I'm trying to ask, Frank, is how you'd feel about having some company on your journey back to Nevada?"

Frank didn't even have to think about it. He smiled as he reached across the desk to shake hands with his son and said, "I reckon that'd be just fine."